DEATH ACTUALLY

DEATH ACTUALLY

DEATH. LOVE. AND IN BETWEEN.

ROSY FENWICKE

Published by Wonderful World

Author website: rosyfenwickeauthor.com

This is a work of fiction. Names, characters, places, and incidents either are the product of the author's imagination or are used fictitiously, and any resemblance to actual persons, living or dead, events, or locales is entirely coincidental.

A catalogue record for this book is available from the National Library of New Zealand.

Cover design by Estella Vukovic.
Permission for the use of *High Country Weather* is granted by the James K Baxter Trust.

To the friendship of women

High Country Weather

Alone we are born
    And die alone;
Yet see the red-gold cirrus
    Over snow-mountain shine.

Upon the upland road
    Ride easy, stranger:
Surrender to the sky
    Your heart of anger.

– James K Baxter
4 October 1945 1948

CHAPTER ONE

———

Peeping around the door, Maggie smiled to see tendrils of dark hair draped across the pillow and to hear the slow breathing of her daughter's exhausted sleep. This bedroom had been empty for two years, a tidy testament to a daughter full grown and travelling the world. In just five hours, Kate had managed to recreate the chaos of her youth. The contents of two backpacks were sprayed across the room, socks and underwear dangling from open drawers, bottles jumbled amongst magazines, and T-shirts dumped in dirty piles, mingling with unmatched shoes and boots.

Maggie pulled the door shut and tiptoed downstairs. She was late. Letting herself out into the half-light of early morning, she walked carefully over the icy cobblestones to her car, where Elka stood waiting.

"You're late!" said Elka accusingly, in the soft German accent that hadn't faded in the twenty years she'd lived in New Zealand.

"I know. I'm sorry," said Maggie, unlocking the car. "Kate's plane was diverted and it was almost one o'clock in the morning when she finally arrived. I slept in."

"You could have called – texted even," replied Elka, getting in and reaching for her seatbelt. "I've been waiting outside for over five minutes. But I am pleased she's back."

There were times when Maggie could cheerfully have throttled her friend for her German ways, but this wasn't one of them. She was too happy and the morning was too perfect.

"I think we should do the loop, today," said Maggie, changing the subject.

Without waiting for a reply, she drove out of Queenstown and into the surrounding countryside just as the sun crested the mountains.

After the night's snowfall, a duck egg blush on the horizon heralded the start of a stunning day.

The council's grader and grit machine had tilled the new snow onto the roadsides in gravelly mounds, de-icing and clearing the way for the bumper-to-bumper traffic for which Queenstown was now famous. The ski season had started early, and with two huge dumps of snow in the past month, the town was packed with eager skiers from around New Zealand and Australia.

Travelling away from town, Maggie made good time and parked her car beside a fence under an ancient macrocarpa tree. Fifteen or so sheep were taking shelter from the snow on the other side of the fence on the only patch of bare earth for miles. Lichen-tufted fence posts glistened with frost, and icicles dripped on the wires.

"It's a perfect morning for a walk," said Maggie as she clicked the key to lock the car.

Elka grunted.

They had been friends for more than twenty years, meeting soon after Maggie's return from Australia and just after Elka had opened her restaurant in town. They were the same age, both single and both busy in their work. Neither woman could bear the false cheeriness in the town's gyms, so they walked together most mornings, around the lake or in the surrounding countryside, traffic permitting, enjoying the seasons and the silence, not feeling the need to talk unless there was something important to discuss. On this basis a friendship had been built, sustaining them through good times and bad.

Maggie shivered and huddled deeper into the upturned collar of her black down vest, before clamping her beanie firmly over her blonde ponytail. They set off, their breath mingling in their wake, their feet crunching frozen gravel, one woman in black and the other in every bright colour ever invented.

"How is she?"

"Hard to tell," said Maggie. "From London to Doha then another seventeen hours to Auckland without a break is pretty gruelling. The plane was diverted to Invercargill, so a four-hour bus ride on top of all that didn't help. I guess I could say she's tired, worn out and just a little emotional to be home after two years. Or maybe she's tired and emotional about having to leave London because her work visa ran out. You know what Kate's like."

"I do, and I'm looking forward to seeing her, but you know – can't today," said Elka. She stopped but Maggie didn't notice, and Elka had to run a few steps to catch up. "It's been very quiet without her."

"Understatement," said Maggie. "So quiet. Thank goodness Nick was here or I might have had to get a dog." She stopped and grabbed Elka's arm. "I'm so stupid. I forgot. You're going to Dunedin."

"At one."

"And?"

"Ben said they'd tell me the results of last week's tests. And the surgeon, Sally, will examine me, do a scan and tell me what it all means. After everything he's said, I'm pretty sure I'll need surgery but I'll have to wait to find out. If I'm lucky, it could all be over and done with this afternoon, so here's hoping. What do you say? Fingers crossed."

"Yes, fingers crossed, and toes and legs – everything crossed," said Maggie.

They started walking again.

"So far Ben seems very good and thorough. He's like the doctors back in Germany, which is a relief. He listened to me and didn't tell me I was feeling tired because I was stressed, like the first doctor I saw."

"Betty agrees with you," said Maggie, referring to their friend. "She told me he knew what he was doing, which is high praise coming from her. Do you want me to come to Dunedin with you this afternoon? I will if you need me."

Before Elka could answer, Maggie's phone rang deep in her pocket and she stopped to retrieve it.

Elka walked a few steps ahead and stretched her arms above her head.

"It's Betty," said Maggie softly as she put the phone back in her pocket. "She died half an hour ago. I'm sorry, but I can't come now. Betty made me promise that I'd be the one to look after her. She didn't want any of the other funeral directors in town seeing her bits and pieces. Just me. I promise I'll come with you if you have to go back – which you won't of course, but if you do."

They drove back to town in silence, both thinking of the day ahead, paying little attention to the traffic. Carloads of excited young people were whizzing past in the opposite direction, chains rattling on the road as their occupants' eyes strained to get their first look at the new snow on the fields above them.

When they reached Elka's house, Elka gave Maggie a quick hug.

"It will be OK, I know it will," Maggie whispered, hugging her back.

"Tell Kate I'll see her soon," said Elka, "and please tell Jim I'm thinking of him and will call first thing tomorrow. I don't know how he'll cope without Betty."

"You'll be fine, but text me when you know."

Elka waved her off and Maggie drove home. Turning into the stable yard, she saw the empty patch in last night's snow where Nick's scooter had been parked. It never ceased to amaze her how many people wanted fast food delivered so early in the morning, but if home deliveries kept her son in work and saving money for his education, who was she to judge?

The signs of his hurried breakfast were littered all over the kitchen bench, but dear boy that he was, he'd put the coffee on and it was just coming to the boil as she walked in.

Cradling her cup in both hands, Maggie leaned back against the bench and listened to the silence. For so many years when Kate and Nick had been younger she'd longed for such a moment, when she could take her time and drink her coffee in peace. Now, though, the atmosphere was oppressive with the prospect of the looming emptiness.

Kate was home, but for how long? Next year Nick would be gone. And then what?

Maggie had been younger than most mothers when she'd had her children. Bursting with the misguided determination of youth to escape her home, and more importantly her father's expectations, she'd been eighteen when she'd run off with the first good-looking silver-tongued Australian who had paid her more than a passing attention on her nightly jaunts to the bars in town

Whether he really was attractive, or she was just burnt out by her lifestyle, it took very little persuading for her to agree to accompany him back to his home-town of Melbourne at the end of the ski season. Their relationship was already starting to wear thin when Maggie became pregnant with Kate. But Andy was a good bloke brought up by his family to do the decent thing, and they'd married in a registry office before their daughter was born.

Times were hard for the young couple. His paid work as a personal trainer was sporadic and didn't bring in enough money for them to have a place of their own, but it did mean Andy was able to represent his beach volleyball club in the interminable summer tournaments that were his true love. They moved in with his mother, who reassured Maggie she was happy with the arrangements and was looking forward to being a grandmother.

Maggie had had little contact with her family since leaving. She was too ashamed to call often, and angry that her father had been right about what would become of her if she left home. Every now and then she'd talk to her mother, to let her know she was safe and to hear the familiar voice. Most of all she missed Simon, her older brother, who was now firmly ensconced in the family business. But he seemed different when she called – quieter and more subdued, and not the fun-loving mad skier she'd grown up with.

When Kate was seven months old and things were starting to improve, Maggie became pregnant for the second time. She was hurt and surprised when her mother-in-law suggested an abortion, which she refused. From then on this woman, who had been so good to Maggie when she'd first moved in, started to distance herself not only from Maggie but also, inexplicably, from her baby granddaughter.

"You can't keep living here with two children," she overheard her say to Andy one day. "It's not fair to me or to you."

Andy had said nothing, walking out and slamming the door behind him on his way to the beach.

Seeing Maggie standing in the kitchen, tears running down her face, beside Kate in her highchair covered in mashed banana, his mother had explained clearly but not unkindly, "Well you can't stay, dear. You know that. It's time your family helped out. Andy doesn't earn much and he's so young. He needs a life away from work, away from being a father with so many responsibilities. It breaks my heart to see him like this. Couldn't you have been more careful?"

Maggie wiped Kate's face and put the mushy bib in the washing machine. She picked her daughter up and hugged her close. A chubby hand reached up and patted her hair, smearing it with banana.

"Maybe you should put Kate in day care for the next few months, get a job and then you could afford your own place. Andy's worn out. He'll do what's right, of course, but you could do more, you know."

Maggie knew her family back home would help, but was determined not to ask, being too proud to admit all was not as she pretended. She organised day-care for Kate, and found work with a local cleaning firm.

Andy was away playing interclub when Maggie moved into their new home. She had walked the streets to find an affordable one-bedroom apartment in a suburb close to the beach. The other side of the city would have been cheaper, but Andy and his mother made it clear they had to live near the beach so he could follow his dream and play volleyball. He couldn't let his team down, he explained.

Maggie was at work when she went into labour. One of the other cleaners took her to the hospital, and by the time Andy finally arrived, covered in sand, with Kate still grubby and tired from day care in his arms, her son was three hours old. They named him Nick, after Maggie's grandfather.

Andy was not as entranced with Nick as he had been with Kate. The novelty of reproduction was seemingly inversely proportional to the work involved in the children's care. He moaned to Maggie about having to miss club night to look after his daughter, and asked when she would be home to take over. Cuddling her daughter and son on the narrow hospital bed, Maggie had sighed and promised to leave first thing in the morning.

The next day when Andy collected them in his mother's car, she saw his packed bags in the back. On the drive home he told Maggie he couldn't cope anymore. His mum had suggested he take a break and move back in with her while they sorted everything out. Grudgingly he helped Maggie with her bag and the babies in their cumbersome car seats, before pecking Kate on the cheek and galloping down the stairs to his car. He drove off without a backward glance.

A short while later, sore and exhausted from the birth, Maggie was standing in the kitchen looking blankly at her children, wondering what on earth she was going to do, when the phone rang. It was Andy telling her not to worry – he'd paid the rent till the end of the month, stocked the fridge, and there was money on the bench by the cooker.

Maggie said nothing and hung up. Speechless with disbelief she'd tucked Nick into the middle of her bed and wrestled her laughing, wriggling baby daughter to the ground to change her smelly nappy. The three of them slept wrapped in each other's arms for a few hours.

She was lucky to have plenty of milk, because the money for food didn't last long and Andy's mother was running interference for her son whenever Maggie called.

A week later, just before the next rent payment was due, Maggie called her mother-in-law's number and was greeted with disconnected pips.

Still in her post-partum fug, it took Maggie a little while longer to realise this was it. She was the twenty-one-year-old mother of two beautiful babies in a foreign country with no friends, no family, and worse – no means of support. Her babies were depending on her to look after them, not just today, but tomorrow, next week, next month and next year. There was no one else.

It was sheer terror that pushed her into to calling home.

Simon answered. "My God, Maggie," he said. "Where've you been? I was just about to ring the police in Melbourne to ask them to find you." Cutting off her response he continued, "Maggie, are you sitting down? I have terrible news. Mum and Dad died two days ago in that helicopter crash in Milford Sound."

"What helicopter crash?"

"It's in all the papers and it's been on TV."

"Sorry, Simon, I've been busy." The exhaustion in her voice must have been obvious.

He paused for a moment. "I've been trying to find you but the number you gave me is disconnected. Maggie, you have to come home, I can't do this by myself. I just can't." Maggie heard her big brother sobbing on the end of the phone.

"I don't have any money. That's why I was calling." She heard her practical voice talking a long way off in another place and another time, anywhere but here and now and about this.

"I'll buy your tickets for chrissakes, Maggie. Just go to the airport and pick them up from the counter. Please come home, I need you. There's a flight at six tonight – you can get it, if you hurry."

"Simon, I can't leave until I get the kids their own passports. I don't have any money to pay for them. I don't have any money for anything."

Simon calmed down at that, and asked for her bank account number so he could transfer some money. The woman at the passport office could not have been more helpful when, in tears, Maggie explained what had happened. Three days later she was back in Queenstown in time to attend the double funeral of her parents – holding two babies, with no husband in sight. Amidst the crying and the whispers of those who had watched her grow up, she was home again and wearing black.

The next day, Simon left town.

CHAPTER TWO

Nick unhooked the box, filled to the brim with extra-large double-crust pizzas, from the back of his scooter. He hadn't been to this address before, but the stories of its occupant's fury if there was a mistake in the order were legendary. And her temper was apparently matched by her size.

Balancing the pizzas under one arm, with a satchel containing six large bottles of coke on the other, he went up the stairs to Unit 3B. The steps were old and rickety, just like the rest of the building, which was situated on the edge of the shopping centre. Judging by the overwritten tags and designs sprayed across it, street artists used the side wall as their private message board. Together with the green slime on the steps, this contributed to the overall ambience of decay on one side of the forgotten cul de sac in the otherwise high-end tourist town. On the other side, buildings were being converted into cafés and shops in keeping with the rest of the town. Nick reckoned it would only take a day to have the graffiti painted out, if the landlord or the council cared. The culprits could probably be found too, if they chose. Queenstown catered to tens of thousands of tourists every year, but the local resident population was quite small. The good citizens of the town kept tabs on everything that happened, making it hard for anyone get away with even the most minor acts of vandalism.

Reaching the landing at the top, Nick noticed the door to the flat was ajar. Getting no response when he knocked, he pushed it open and stepped into a gloomy room.

"Pizza delivery," he called again, hoping this was the right place and the legendary Lizzie would be here to sign his slip. He looked around at the open plan kitchen and living area, partly shaded by torn orange curtains hanging limply at two small windows set into concrete block walls. A heat pump was operating at full blast, pointlessly battling the morning cold, the warmth escaping out the open door. The only piece of furniture was a sofa in the middle of the room, facing a giant TV sitting against the far wall. He recognised the game on the screen. It was one of his favourites, and he'd thought he was good at it – until now. He watched transfixed, until the weight of his bags reminded him why he was there.

Dragging his eyes from the screen he noticed fast-food boxes of every brand squashed into rubbish bags beside the door. Empty plastic drink bottles overflowed a bin beside them. Hefting his bags onto the empty kitchen counter, he called out more loudly this time.

The game continued, the numbers in the top corner clicking over rapidly.

As he approached the sofa, the smell of unwashed flesh grew stronger. He saw the rolls of fat in the back of her neck covered by a grey ponytail draped down her back. Her hands – pudgy fingers gripping the handset, thumbs clicking buttons furiously – were the only part of her that moved. She was largest person he had ever seen, her bulk taking up most of the sofa, mounds of fat rolling down to her knees. She was playing *World of Warcraft*, and playing it bloody well.

"Ms Martin," he said loudly, "I have your order, if you could sign for it ...?" His voice faded to nothing when she still didn't react. The other guys had warned him how nasty she could get if the pizzas were too cold. On the other hand he appreciated she was at a crucial point in her game and would be upset if he interrupted her now.

But he didn't have all day. He had more orders waiting, more customers to placate if he didn't get a move on. Lizzie was damned good, though. It was a pleasure to watch her, and now he was closer he saw why she hadn't heard him. Earbuds. Of course, the neighbours in the next flat were the thickness of one concrete block wall away, and would hear everything if she didn't use buds.

He leant forward to tap her, and nearly gagged at the smell. Suddenly it was more important than ever to get his delivery done and signed for, so he could get outside into clean air. Damn the game. He touched her on the shoulder, his hand meeting soft flesh. The giant woman heaved around in fright and yelled, "What the fuck are you doing in my bloody house?"

Nick took a step back out of range. "Your order, I have your order," he said waving to the boxes on the bench.

Lizzie's gaze swung past him to the bag of pizza boxes and she visibly relaxed. Turning back to the screen, she paused and saved her game.

"Sorry about the language," she said. "Always found attack is the best form of defence, especially now I can't move." She waved an arm over her legs, and for a moment Nick assumed she was referring to her bulk, but when he looked past the food-spattered material of her dress he could see that her right foot was twisted and scarred. Uncut nails curled over and around the ends of her toes, which were dark with built-up grime.

"Buggered," she said lifting her foot off the footstool so he could see it better – Exhibit A by way of explanation.

The woman, the rubbish, the smell, her filthy clothes, and now this proffered excuse for it all, her filthy twisted foot ... everything about this place disgusted him and he could feel his morning muesli rising in the back of his throat. He was desperate to leave, to breathe clean air, but he still needed her to sign for the order.

"Give me the bloody chit then."

He handed it to her and she signed it, keeping her eyes fixed on his face.

"You're new, aren't you? What's your name?"

Nick had to back away, closer to the door, to get air, before he could reply. He unpacked the bag, piling the boxes on the bench.

"Nick Potter. Started at the beginning of the month."

"You aren't Maggie Potter's son, are you?" She tapped the pen against the chit. "Of course you are. You've got the Potter blue eyes. You look more like Simon, her brother – your uncle. Same height, same colouring, but you're better looking than he was and that's saying something." She held out the pen and chit and he had no choice but to go and get it. She waited, her eyes narrowed and glinting in the half-light.

"Don't leave them over there," she barked, just as he was about to leave.

The broad side of one huge arm swiped the empty boxes from the table in front of her. An empty coke bottle bounced as it hit the floor. Taking a deep breath of fresh air, Nick quickly relayed everything from the counter to the table.

Lizzie was already chewing by the time he reached the door again. He could just make out her final command as she spoke through a mouth full of food. "Leave the door open. The nurse and home help are coming later."

Nick felt sorry for whoever had to clean the flat. It would be a thankless task, and as for the nurse, what on earth was she supposed to do? He couldn't escape fast enough, and clattered down the stairs in his boots, gulping great breaths of clean air, filling his lungs, trying to rid himself of the smell of unwashed human that clung to the roof of his mouth.

Nick always tried to give others the benefit of the doubt, and considered himself the least judgmental of his friends, but he was struggling to find one good thing to say about this woman apart from the fact that she spoke nicely – but only when she wasn't swearing and didn't have her mouth full.

The promise of a clear day had been broken. It was snowing lightly, making travel by scooter especially treacherous. He made another couple of deliveries, to tourists who had drunk too much the night before and were in urgent need of fat and sugar to feed hangovers before facing the day. Hung-over tourists were always good tippers, and by mid-morning his mood had improved.

Hunched forward over the handlebars of his scooter, trying to see past the snowflakes gathering on his visor, he didn't notice the black Porsche Cayenne until it appeared from nowhere in front of him. He braked. His back tyre slid out behind, throwing him sideways into a drift of dirty snow piled next to the stop sign that the Cayenne driver had just ignored.

Protected by the snow he was unhurt, and only a little shaken. His jeans were quickly soaked by the slush, and his pride had been knocked, but hey, he rode a scooter on icy streets for a living – what could he expect? Picking himself and his scooter up he watched the Cayenne power off down the street, oblivious to his plight and the road rules.

His phone rang and he was relieved to see *Home* and not *Work* come up on the screen. His mum asked him if he was free in about twenty minutes, and if so could he meet her at Betty's place and help?

Nick couldn't find the words.

She asked if he was all right, and he said of course, and he'd be there, but he needed to change into dry clothes first. He'd explain later.

It wasn't such a good day after all.

The driver of the Cayenne, warm in the comfort of his car, was blissfully absorbed in the company of the woman sitting next to him.

"Which field?" he asked. "Coronet, Cardrona or the Remarkables? You choose."

"Coronet," Lucy said without hesitation, and reaching over she caressed the light growth of soft hair on the back of Mark's neck. A single large ruby buried in a band of beaten gold adorned her right middle finger, an anniversary gift he'd surprised her with at breakfast.

Mark turned at the next corner, taking the river road to the ski field behind the town. They were happy in the car. Being together as a couple was enough.

CHAPTER THREE

When Maggie made an effort she could be quite beautiful. Betty had told her so in one of the many "Count your blessings" talks she was so good at, and which she'd delivered to Maggie on regular occasions over the years.

In Betty's honour, and because her friend would expect nothing less, Maggie had changed out of her running clothes into a black cashmere jumper under a black down vest, with black ski leggings and boots. On a shopping trip last winter, Betty had said the boots made her legs look longer and thinner. She had tied her thick blonde hair into a high ponytail, and had taken the time to put on tinted moisturiser, and mascara – Betty had said this made the blue in her eyes "pop" – they'd hooted with laughter at the word, gleaned from one of the women's magazines strewn across Betty's sickbed during one of Maggie's visits.

Standing on Betty's front step, Maggie remembered the times she'd stumbled to this same door in deep pain, hoping for some relief from the loneliness and desperation she'd felt in the years immediately after her parents' deaths. Betty had always listened, then given her the hug she needed before taking her firmly by both shoulders and administering just the correct dose of advice as to where exactly she could find her backbone. Then she'd turned her round and sent her out into the world again with enough pride to get through whatever had to be borne. And not once did Betty tell Maggie the whole goddamned mess she had found herself in was her own fault.

Betty and Jim Turner lived in a house high on the hill overlooking Queenstown and the lake below. There weren't many houses like theirs left. Developers had snapped up the modest sixties-built homes, set on large grassy sections, knocking them down and replacing them with the more compact modern homes favoured by busy families. High-density apartments and easily maintained homes on small sections, with panoramic views over the lake below, had taken over the street. Walls made from the local schist featured strongly internally and out, displacing the more highly coloured purple and green Queenstown stone that had been a desirable feature in previous decades.

The couple had lived in their home in Suburb Street on Queenstown Hill for more than fifty years. Jim had built the house himself as soon as they became engaged, and they had moved in on their wedding night and never left, layering the house and garden with memories and reminders of their lives together.

Betty had given birth to all three children there, because in the early years road access to the cottage hospital at Frankton was limited, especially in the cold winters, which seemed so much more ferocious then. Because Betty's labours weren't difficult, she could see no point in driving all the way to "the home" as it was called, when she could manage just as well in her own bed with the local midwife to help – but only if needed. Betty was one of those rare women who could manage most things, and did.

While Betty laboured, Jim dug the vegetable garden, not wanting to be far from his best friend should she need him. Knowing he was just outside her window, Betty gave birth without complaining, delivering two healthy boys and a girl. Jim's vasectomy, the first in the district, was the talk of the town for all of six months.

Jim was a plumber, and his business went from strength to strength as the town and surrounding area grew. He took on more staff as new housing developments and hotels were built. Betty did the accounts, initially by hand at the kitchen table, after the children had gone to bed.

When all three were finally at school, Betty took herself off to Dunedin and did a course in computing. She lugged home a "PC", one of the first in the district, and set it up in their new office in town. DOS and spreadsheets took over her life, but only after she had taught the rest of the staff how to master the mysterious programmes and cope with the frequent software malfunctions. The couple's children were growing up and Betty liked going down to the office where she could keep an eye on the comings and goings in town.

The Turners were always amongst the first customers in each new café and restaurant, as these became increasingly sophisticated, catering for overseas tourists with high expectations. Shops selling skis and souvenirs, clothes and food gradually replaced the draperies and newsagents of 1970s New Zealand. Streets designed for cars came to be seen as a waste of prime real estate, and were turned into pedestrian malls where tourists wandered, looked, sampled, and spent their holiday money.

Younger visitors wanted more than scenery and lakeside walks, and in the eighties adventure tourism arrived in force. Betty drew the line at bungy-jumping, but Jim, happy to give anything a go and having updated his will (at Betty's insistence) the day before, plunged headfirst off the bridge over the gorge, declaring it the tenth-best thing he'd ever done. The rest of the local Rotary Club followed him a month later, raising $2,500 towards the upgrade of the children's playground on the lake foreshore, beside the 1920s band rotunda. This had also recently been transformed, from a rundown building into a café with history. And the food was good. Betty and Jim said so.

Betty stood for the local council and was elected with the highest number of votes every three years for fifteen years. She devoted time and common sense to guiding the future development of what was to become one of the country's most important tourist areas. Shoulder tapped to stand for parliament, Betty didn't see the point, doubting her ability to be any more effective for her district than she was already. And more importantly, she didn't want to be away from Jim, just when the last of their children had moved out and they finally had time together.

Maggie knew and appreciated that both as a couple and individually, the Turners added to the life and energy of the growing town by the lake, their natural enthusiasm setting them apart from most of the other permanent residents who, born of dour Scottish stock, were innately suspicious of others' achievements. Betty, though, held a special place in Maggie's heart. It was Betty who had taken her under her wing after her parents died and Simon had left, helping her with the babies and providing a shoulder to cry on – not that Betty let her do much crying. Betty was a "shoulders back and get on with it" type of woman, and she'd expected nothing less from Maggie.

Elka often spoke about how she owed the success of her restaurant to Jim and Betty. They had been the only people in town willing to back the young German woman, who was determined to make a go of her new life. The Turners always gave timely advice freely and without prejudice, helping young entrepreneurs whenever they were asked.

Maggie was the first person Betty told about the cancer, after Jim, of course. She'd never been a smoker, so a diagnosis of lung cancer was a bitter irony. The doctors at the medical school and hospital in Dunedin did their best, and with the support and sympathy of the town, Betty had valiantly battled through the agonies of nausea and exhaustion from her chemotherapy.

But the disease had spread, and Maggie watched Betty become a desiccated shell of her former self. Her spirit was intact but worn down, surfacing less and less as the disease sucked the life force from her. The chemotherapy wasn't enough to stem the malignancy invading her vital organs. On hearing this, Betty had made the decision to stop all treatment and return to the home on the hill overlooking her beloved lake and mountains.

Such was the demand for time with Betty that Jim set up an appointment system for visitors. Their children came home and stood guard, ensuring their mother wasn't taxed beyond her ability to cope. Maggie had been one of the few allowed to visit at any time, which she did, often sitting with Betty while she slept. Sometimes, when the drugs let Betty talk, one of them would remember something funny from their years as friends. Only a few words were needed to bring forth memories that sent them both into chuckles of shared happiness. Betty would struggle to breathe through the resulting coughs, but her eyes sparkled.

After six weeks Maggie could see that Betty's body had stopped functioning. It took another week before her soul was ready to leave. Jim and the children took turns, with Elka and Maggie occasionally helping out, nursing, cleaning, tending. And Betty loved them all in return, right up until the bitter end.

The doctor visited most days, but he was new to the district and hadn't known the old Betty, or her friends. For all her comings and goings to the house on the hill, Maggie never met him – but she heard about him. The only important thing he could do as far as Maggie was concerned was to ensure Betty had no pain. Before the longer sleeps took over, Betty told Maggie the new doctor was very good looking, around her age, and *single*! The woman was on her death bed and was matchmaking. She even went so far as to offer to fake an attack while Maggie was there, so the doctor would come and she could introduce them. Maggie politely declined.

Betty spent her last conscious days with Jim, turning her head to the wall and slipping into the darkness only after he and she knew they had said all two people could say to each other.

Now it was time for Maggie to perform one last service for Betty.

Jim answered the door. Hollowed out by grief and fatigue, he looked his age for the first time since she had known him. Maggie put down her satchel and hugged him tight, trying to give him her strength, but the void was too great.

His daughter Susan came to the door, and between them they supported Jim on the short walk back to the kitchen where the family had lived through their important times together. Betty was still all around them.

The Turner sons and their wives were seated at the long scrubbed pine table, drinking tea in silence. One of them offered Maggie a cup, which she accepted willingly.

"This is the difficult part," said Maggie, nursing the hot tea in both hands. "I need to ask you what you all want for Betty. The two of us talked about it before she died and she made her wishes quite clear, but she also told me I was to ask you and to do what you wanted."

"I say we do what she said," said Susan. "Mum always had to organise everything and she usually got it right."

Maggie looked across at Jim, who was staring out the window. The boys nodded and Maggie thought it best to keep moving through the formalities.

"Has the doctor been and left anything for me?" she asked.

Susan handed her an envelope, and inside was the necessary certificate stating time and cause of death. Even though Maggie was used to dealing with these documents, seeing Betty's name written in black and white on the death certificate was a shock. She refolded it quickly into three and put it back in the envelope.

"Would you like her to come with me now, or later? It's completely up to you."

As close as she was to the family, today Maggie felt like an intruder, here to take away the person most precious to them all. She watched them exchange family glances and then nod, the code for a decision made.

"Mum can go with you. We're ready," said Susan, and the others murmured their agreement.

Jim got up quickly and blurted, "I can't watch. Call me when it's over." He left the kitchen to go outside to his snow-covered vegetable patch.

The ensuing silence was interrupted by a knock at the front door.

"Nick," Maggie explained. "He's come to help."

When Susan and the boys had left, Maggie and Nick gently wrapped Betty securely in a blanket, making sure her head was covered and supported. Nick picked her up in his arms and carried her carefully out to Maggie's waiting hearse. Jim was nowhere to be seen, but Betty's children and their partners watched their mother's last slow ride from home, down the steep street towards the lake.

CHAPTER FOUR

Maggie had realised she was resigned to the inevitable when she decided to upgrade her father's hearse. It had been his father's before and so it was a momentous decision. Two-year-old Nick and three-year-old Kate had nodded seriously when she told them her plans for modernisation. She chose a long wheel base 4WD, which she imported from the States, the advantage being that it would cope with the snow and ice blanketing the district's steep roads in winter. She had the almost-new vehicle repainted with twenty coats of black high-gloss paint, giving it a deep luxurious finish. Taking everything out from the back, she had installed two slim wheel-lined rails that could be locked in transit, thus making sure there were no undignified slippages. The rear windows were refitted with darkened glass, and thickly ruched black velvet side curtains ensured privacy. Painted on the driver's door was the name of the family firm, established in the district over one hundred years earlier:

The Stables
Maggie Potter: Funeral Director

Betty was transported in a temporary casket from Suburb Street to the funeral home, situated in an old stable block on the far side of the botanical gardens. Maggie's great-grandfather had converted the stables in the late 1890s, when he saw the unmet demand for burial services in the area. Her father renovated the facilities in the sixties, and then in the nineties Maggie updated everything again, using the latest technology from the States to accommodate changing fashions and people's expectations. So far her small business had been able to resist takeover offers from the big Australian firms that were starting to dominate the New Zealand market, imposing their chain-store approach to the care of the dead. She continued to offer a personalised boutique service in the face of intense competition from the other local firms who had taken the Australian dollar, and who now offered a standard burial product for cut-price fees. The atmosphere between the different companies had become strained, but they still managed to cover each other when illness or holiday required it.

Growing up, Maggie would never have believed she'd take over the business. She was teased about her father's work at school, known as 'school-ghoul' by the cool crowd in her class. She had vowed never, ever to join the firm. Simon, her older brother, was completely disinterested and her mother wanted nothing to do with what happened inside The Stables, even though it was next door to the house. From very early in the marriage, she had used her children as a reason to excuse herself from anything to do with her husband's work. She'd known what he did when she'd accepted his proposal, but when it came to the mechanics of managing the dead and the grief-stricken, Maggie's mother preferred wilful ignorance and kept her distance.

Maggie's father had insisted there was no extra money to pay a stranger to assist him – and if there had been, he wouldn't have paid for one because he had a daughter perfectly able to help him at no cost. So as she grew up, Maggie was left with little choice. She learned the business when she was young – too young, she thought. Initially she took on very small tasks, until gradually her father came to rely on her more and more. If she complained, her father would point out to her that this was how he paid the bills, and she should respect the work and the comfortable lifestyle it gave the family. He also tried to tell her about the privilege of being able to help people when they were at their most vulnerable, but teenage Maggie, with her thoughts on boys, skiing and school (in that order) had no interest in what he meant. Meanwhile Simon, the blue-eyed boy, was under his mother's protection and spent his weekends skiing or working in one of the cafés in town.

Maggie was a lonely child and teenager. She had no friends at school, other than Lizzie Martin, who became too preoccupied with skiing to spend much time with her. Then at the age of fourteen, Lizzie was sent to a training camp in Europe, leaving Maggie at the mercy of the bitches at school.

Maggie decided her best option was to go along with the childish expectations of her peers. Ahead of her time, she became the town's only Goth. Her father thought she was making fun of him and all he stood for, but hoping she would grow out of her need to hurt him, said nothing. Her mother just shrugged, while Simon would pretend he didn't know her when he was with his friends.

When she was sixteen, Maggie started sleeping with men passing through town either as workers or as tourists. She couldn't explain it and she didn't enjoy it. Despite his later abandonment of her and their children, Maggie would always be thankful she'd met Andy when she did. The young Australian had seen through the tough facade she had cultivated, and to him she was more than a one-night stand. When he asked her to go to Melbourne at the end of the season, she hadn't needed a second invitation. Emptying her savings account, she left town without saying a word to her parents. Looking back, Maggie realised how hurtful this must have been, but at eighteen, escape to a new life, and freedom from death, was all that mattered. She phoned her mother a week later to let her know she was alive, and told her not to worry.

In Melbourne, Maggie heard from Betty, a family friend, that Simon had had no choice other than to take on the workload she had abandoned. Naturally irresponsible and fun loving, he started drinking too much and the reputation of the business sagged under the disapproval of the local population, who preferred their loved ones to be buried with dignity by someone who didn't look and smell as though he'd been out on the town the night before.

Simon happily and quickly relinquished his role as son and heir immediately after their parents' funerals, when Maggie found a lawyer's letter turning the property and business over to her. In her absence the life insurance policies for both parents had been changed to make Simon the sole beneficiary, and he left town with enough capital to go anywhere in the world for as long as he chose.

Maggie now had a home where she could bring up the children, but no income, and so she had no choice (according to Betty) but to settle down and make a go of it and (again according to Betty) should realise just how lucky she was. Simon's emails and phone calls from far-flung exotic locations became less frequent, and it was now five years since Maggie had last heard from him, when he'd been working as a bartender in Buenos Aires.

It was just before lunch when Maggie backed the hearse into the courtyard beside what her father had called his "funeral parlour". She'd hated the term, with its connotations of black drapes, dusty ostrich feathers, dour-faced men in morning suits and The Addams Family. Irritated by the nonsensical term "funeral home", she referred to her premises as The Stables.

The building dated back to the late 1860s, and once housed the coach horses taking gold from the central Otago fields to Dunedin. It was a handsome building made with local schist in tones of mellow gold. The roof had been replaced with corrugated iron, and Maggie had put in skylights to open it up to the light and fresh air in summer. She'd had four refrigerated cabinets installed, and in front of these stood her work table. An antique French wardrobe sitting against the back wall contained her equipment. Due to popular demand and her own queasiness, she'd been pleased to stop embalming her clients, and getting rid of the bottles and tubing had freed up a lot of space. Instead, just outside the back door there was now a large freezer where she stored the long ice packs which, when changed regularly under a corpse, slowed decomposition.

The double doors leading from her workroom had been made from timber recycled from an old hotel near the Arrow river, abandoned when the gold ran out. These opened into an area which could be used for burial and remembrance services, and where Maggie welcomed the relatives and friends of those who wanted to spend time with their loved ones before the funeral. Her desk was placed discreetly behind a screen. Larger timber doors opened directly onto the courtyard, across which was the house where Potters had lived for more than a hundred years. It too was made of schist and recycled wood. It was just large enough for Maggie and the children, cosy in winter and able to be opened up to breezes from the lake in summer.

Nick arrived just after her. Standing to one side she watched as he easily lifted Betty's body from the back of the hearse and carried her into the workroom, where he pulled a metal stretcher out of a cabinet and laid her gently down. Maggie was grateful for his help. Knowing she'd have to manage without him next year, she'd devised a system she could use alone. No need to tell him just yet, she thought.

Typically, Betty had wanted to know everything that happened to bodies after death. She'd listened carefully to all the options and asked to have a few days to think about them. When Maggie had returned, Betty had had a list of detailed instructions ready.

"Promise me I won't look like a dead person," she'd said. "I don't want my family to remember me as a corpse. Make me beautiful, one last time, Maggie." She'd handed over the list and a bag of make-up. That had been a month ago, and now the time had come for Maggie to keep her word.

She took a scented face cream from the bag and massaged it gently into Betty's cold, kind face. Then she smeared a generous dollop of lip gloss onto her lips. Lastly, she slipped eye-caps under her eyelids to hold them firmly closed, and to stop the eyes from drying out.

"Dehydration is the enemy of skin tone, even in death, Betty," she whispered. "That's all for today. I'll get you gussied up according to instructions tomorrow, when you've had a chance to work through a few changes."

Maggie pushed the stretcher back into the cabinet and shut the door. The refrigerator hummed into life. Wearily she took off her apron and put it with the bag into the wardrobe.

Nick was waiting for her in the office. He held out his arms and she walked straight into a hug. Arm in arm they walked across the cobblestones to the house and a hot cup of very strong coffee.

"Nearly lunchtime and no sign of Kate," said Nick, putting a cheese sandwich in the toaster. "Not like her. We know how much she likes her food."

CHAPTER FIVE

A film crew had taken over a motel complex on the outskirts of the town. Three large trucks spiked with antennae and draped with coils of thick cables occupied the forecourt. Men and women scurried backwards and forwards between different units in the cold, carrying messages and organising last-minute details with the urgency that goes with being on a very tight budget.

Funding for the film had been scraped together from a rag tag mix of government grants, angel investors and desperate appeals on open-source websites. Even the film editor's second cousin once removed had been cajoled into contributing, with promises of tickets to the premiere and film credits. Most of the people scurrying around the forecourt were volunteers from film schools angling to get experience in an actual movie. They survived on student loans and money donated by their long-suffering parents, but primarily they lived on their enthusiastic love of film and, of course, on hope.

Queenstown residents were quite blasé about film crews. The spectacular locations nearby were sought after for everything from action movies to Bollywood romances, and it wasn't unusual to round a bend on a river only to be turned back by crews hoping to get their best shot before the light faded.

The area had the added advantages of an international airport, a small population, and a town large enough to service most demands. Its easy accessibility – if not by road then by helicopter – in both winter and summer, also helped. As well as these natural advantages, there were well-trained Kiwi crews asking internationally competitive wages, not to mention mouth-watering tax incentives from the New Zealand government.

The film being discussed around the kitchen table in Unit 7 at the motel was different. Tim James, the forty-something, stunningly handsome action hero and star of the biggest-grossing blockbusters of the last decade would be arriving before week's end to shoot a small cameo role. His films were some of the most successful ever made, but the excellent work he had done over the past fifteen years was overshadowed by the public's fascination with his not-so-private life. Details of his loves and leavings, his escapades in exotic locations, not to mention his blazing rows with directors, were reported in salacious detail in women's magazines and on gossipy TV programmes. "More social media fodder than real movie star" was how one reviewer had described Mr James.

Tim had agreed to take the part mainly because he liked the script, but also as a favour to the movie's director, a young New Zealander making his first feature-length movie, whose father had just happened to have provided twenty-five percent of the financial backing for the last three Tim James blockbusters.

The crew had been sworn to secrecy, but of course news of his imminent arrival had got out – leaked not only by the director, but also by the marketing department, the local tourism board and the producer.

It went without saying that Tim wouldn't be staying with the crew at their basic and overcrowded motel. Rooms had been reserved for him and his entourage at one of New Zealand's most exclusive lodges – a haven of luxury built on a secluded promontory looking out across Lake Wakatipu to the Remarkable Mountains.

Tim's private secretary, personal trainer, hairdresser/make-up consultant, PR team and a personal masseuse had arrived in advance of the star and were already making waves in local businesses with their demands for immediate service made on behalf of a Mr Smith. The nom de plume fooled no one.

The paparazzi had arrived at the weekend, occupying scarce rooms in busy hotels and motels. It was the height of the ski season, and planeloads of skiers were arriving from Australia and South East Asia several times a day. Some of the photographers had had to find accommodation in neighbouring towns such as Arrowtown and Wanaka, driving into Queenstown and then another thirty kilometres to the gates of the lodge to stake out their vantage points. Others waited patiently at the airport, hoping to get a shot of the star as soon as his private jet touched down. Part of the excitement was that no one knew if Tim would be travelling alone, or if his wife and baby son would be coming too.

Every morning at first light, the photographers took up their positions outside the wrought iron gates of the lodge, blowing warm breath into cold hands and stamping boots on packed snow to get blood flowing to frozen feet, chatting away to each other in different languages or talking by phone to the other side of the world. Each understood the etiquette. Once their quarry had arrived it was every man or woman for themselves, the cheerful camaraderie disappearing as soon Tim James appeared, signalling that the battle for the best shot had commenced.

In the late afternoon a black Porsche Cayenne drove down the access road towards the lodge and the waiting pack. The photographers surged around as it slowed, cameras raised high above their heads in a continuous cacophony of clicking shutters and rolling video, pushing each other out of the way, only to capture a startled middle-aged man trying to swipe his security card through the machine.

Lucy shrank back into her seat as the crowd banged on her window trying to get her to look up. Terrified, she hunched forward, head down. Mark was less concerned. Unflappable – a useful trait in a cardiac surgeon – he knew that as soon they realised the occupants of the car were nobodies, they would lose interest. Which was indeed what happened. One minute the car was surrounded by a baying mob; the next the gates were open and they were free to drive to the front door in peace.

"How was the snow today, Sir?" asked a staff member as Mark and

Lucy stood warming themselves by the stone fireplace dominating the entrance hall.

"Brilliant," said Mark, still flushed with adrenalin. "We spent the morning skiing the back basins at Coronet. Superb. Have you had a chance to go up yet?"

"I went up Saturday, Mr Holmes. Best snow we've had in years, and more on the way I hear. Can I get you something from the bar?"

"I think I'd rather go straight to the room, Mark, if you don't mind," said Lucy.

"Could you send some champagne to the room and we'll have it there?"

"It's already done, Sir," came the reply.

The rooms, which were really small cottages, were set discreetly and separately in the grounds and were connected to the Lodge by sheltered walkways. A central stone fireplace between a living area and the bedroom provided both heat and ambience in the generous space. The doors leading to a private terrace overlooking the lake were made entirely of glass and the view was breathtaking. Comfortable armchairs and a sofa were ranged in front of the fire, and on a sideboard, the champagne sat waiting in its ice bucket flanked by two flutes on one side and an antipasto platter on the other.

Lucy plumped down in the chair by the fire and played her fingers on the armrest. She looked out and across the lake to where straggling beams of winter sun lit up rocky spurs on the peaks, throwing others into shadow as night closed in.

"Who do you think the photographers are for?" she asked, accepting a glass of cold champagne from Mark. He sat in the chair opposite, the sofa stretching between them.

"No idea," he said. "And I don't really care. Whoever it is will want their privacy as much we want ours." He raised his glass and their eyes met. "*Salut.* To another absolutely wonderful day with the woman I love."

They sat watching the firelight, content to drink the wine and say nothing.

The silence was broken by a discreet buzz indicating a call to the room. Mark reached back and picked up the receiver. A woman's voice invaded his peace – loud, relentless and dominating.

"Mark. I've been trying all day to get you on your mobile, but you never answer. What's the point of having a phone if you don't answer it?" She paused then hurried on. "Thank goodness your PA knew where you were staying. I need to know when you're going to be home. We've been invited to the Adamsons' next Saturday and they need numbers for the caterers. Tell me you'll be home in time because I'm tired of going to everything alone. No one believes that someone could be so dedicated."

Mark looked at Lucy and made a face.

His wife laughed before launching into the next subject. "How is the conference? Presented yet? I have no sympathy for you having to stay at The Lodge, somewhere you know I haven't been and where I really want to stay. Sophie tells me it's wonderful."

Mark held the phone away from his ear and grimaced again at Lucy, who shrugged silently in reply.

"Yes, dear," she went on. "The children are fine and looking forward to seeing you, but they may not recognise you. They keep asking me what their father looks like. They're both out; Mathew's at tennis and Hilary's gone shopping. I'll give them your love and explain that Daddy does have to go to conferences. Let me know about the dinner? Soon? Love you, sweetie." And with that the phone went dead.

Tears welled in her eyes as Lucy got up. Mark reached for her hand and pulled her into his lap. He cradled her in his arms, her head on his shoulder, and gently stroked her hair. They sat like this in the firelight waiting for peace to return, trying not to think about real life going on without them far away in Auckland.

"We have so little time," said Lucy.

"That's where you're wrong," said Mark. "Soon we'll have the rest of our lives to be together. This time I promise. I will leave."

Mark's mouth found hers and he kissed her gently, encouragingly. Lucy hesitated but only for a moment.

CHAPTER SIX

"It's colder today than yesterday, if that's possible," huffed Maggie, walking on the spot as she waited for Elka to get organised and out of the car. "I think we'll be OK on this road."

They walked in silence for ten minutes, then Maggie couldn't bear it any longer. "For chrissakes, Elka, stop and tell me what they said in Dunedin."

"It's not good, but it's not hopeless," said Elka, slowing her pace but not stopping.

"Meaning what, exactly?"

"It means they can operate. A few days in hospital and then home. Of course, doctors always hedge their bets. They told me they couldn't be certain about anything till they'd had a good look inside. Made me feel like a car."

"I suppose that's good. When do you go?"

"End of next week."

"Perfect, a couple of days in Dunedin is just what I need. I'll drive."

Elka put her hand on Maggie's arm and they stopped in the lee of a small hill. "I'll understand if you can't come. Really. It's silly I know, but I'm more afraid than I thought I'd be. I'm homesick too, for Germany of all places, which is even sillier considering there's no one left there."

"Which is why I'm coming with you. I can feed you sauerkraut and sausage after the operation, just like they would in Germany, to make you feel at home while you recover."

Elka grimaced. "I can do without the German cuisine – why do you think I left? But, thank you, I don't want to do this alone. I don't think I could." She stopped and bent over to pull her sock out of the bottom of her shoe. "Come on," she said, straightening up again. "This couldn't have come at a worse time – Betty dying and her funeral to come, plus it's peak season and the film crew needs feeding on top of everything else. Not at the restaurant, either, but forty kilometres up the road at Glenorchy. I've been thinking, maybe Kate could help?"

"Of course she will," said Maggie. "I'm pretty sure she doesn't have anything else to do, and it'll be good for her to get out of her bedroom and back into the swing of things."

"We should ask her first. She may have other plans. Who knows, she may have work up north or in Australia. After the rave reviews she was getting before she left London, maybe she has a job already organised. Word has got out about her and chefs are a gossipy bunch – especially the good ones."

The sun was high enough in the sky now to clear the line of hills in front of them. Suddenly blinded by its glare they had to stop, just as an Audi roared around the bend. It swerved and missed hitting them only because the two women jumped for their lives into a shallow ditch full of freezing slime-filled water.

"Are you OK?" asked Maggie. "Tell me you're OK." Her teeth were chattering with the cold.

"I'm fine," laughed Elka. "Wet but fine. You?"

"Yeah, I'm OK. Not that the bloody driver seems to care. He could have killed us. He didn't even stop to make sure we're OK. Typical–"

"Don't say it, Maggie," warned Elka.

"What? Don't say what?" said Maggie, scrambling up the side of the ditch.

"Don't say 'Typical man!' Because he isn't. There is no such thing as the typical man you blame for everything that happens to you. Some men are good and some are bad. You got hooked up with the bad, but that was a long time ago. Get over it. Betty and I have been trying to tell you this for years. The driver probably didn't see us in the glare, or maybe he was driving fast for a reason. But one thing I do know, whatever else this was, it wasn't personal. It was just an accident."

Elka got out of the ditch and carried on walking, her shoes squelching a trail of water down the road.

Maggie stood stock still on the grass verge, absolutely stunned. "Don't hold back will you? Tell me what you really think," she yelled. "OK, have it your way," she muttered, running to catch up. "But only because you're having surgery."

Elka made a face.

"I bet he *did* see us, and didn't stop because he was afraid," said Maggie. "Hardly the caring sort."

"Caring sort? That's exactly what he is, Maggie. I thought you knew. That was the new doctor – Ben Goodman – the one who has been so kind to Betty."

Maggie kept walking, hoping Elka would stop chortling beside her. She pulled her beanie tight over her ears and walked faster. Who knew Elka could laugh for so long?

CHAPTER SEVEN

All Lizzie could see from her flat was the back of a hill. But even if she'd been able to see the mountains, it wouldn't have made one whit of difference to how she was feeling. She was hungry, her morning delivery was late, and she wasn't just unhappy – she was furious.

Yesterday hadn't helped. The home help was a temp and didn't know her likes and dislikes. It was irritating that instructions hadn't been written down and handed out in advance to new people. A simple enough procedure, she'd have thought. After all, they had been coming to her flat every day for ten years. How hard could it be to communicate?

She'd yelled at the girl when she'd made the heinous mistake of opening the windows to let in fresh air. That was just the beginning. It was as if this girl had never cleaned the home of an invalid before. The last straw was when she'd tried to put the last pizza box in the rubbish when there were still two perfectly good pieces inside it. The yelling that had accompanied the girl's tearful exit down the stairs could be heard out on the street.

At least, that's what the district nurse had said as she *tsk tsked* her way into the room.

Supercilious bitch. What does she know about pain? About losing everything in life that meant anything?

Neither of them had spoken as the nurse washed her where she sat and helped her into clean clothes.

When her hair was combed and the dressing on her leg changed, the nurse finally spoke. "She was only trying to help. You know the woman who used to come quit. Said she couldn't cope any more. There are only so many home helps in Queenstown and you've driven most of them away. If you don't start being nicer to people, there will be no one who will look after you."

"I. Don't. Care," said Lizzie.

"I. Don't. Believe. You," replied the nurse.

"You. Should," said Lizzie.

"Now you're being childish. Let's talk about you testing your blood sugars again. Then you'd know when to eat and more importantly, when not to eat. You have to lose weight, Lizzie, or one day I'm going to come up the stairs and find you dead."

"I don't care and I'm not doing it. How many times do I have to say it? You have informed me and I do not give my consent. Simple."

The nurse started to talk, but when Lizzie put her fingers in her ears, poked out her tongue and started humming tunelessly, she gave up. Packing up her equipment she shook her head and left. Lizzie had felt bad, but only until the bumper bucket of KFC arrived.

Because of her weight, Lizzie could only sleep sitting up. Lying down would have crushed her huge abdomen up against her lungs and slowly suffocated her. She spent her days and nights exactly where she was now, on the sofa, in front of the TV screen, her remote controls and laptop within reach.

The new doctor, Ben Goodman, had recommended a machine to support her breathing, but like anything that might help her, she wouldn't have a bar of it. Instead she slept badly, waking up often to get her breath and to move to a more comfortable position. Pain woke her every morning. She managed to use the commode, but this was an effort and made the pain in her leg unbearable. Memories of the accident came flooding back with the pain, and for twenty minutes until the medication kicked in, she was held captive by them, replaying in her mind every minute in terrifying detail. It was the worst part of her day. Later, the only thing to look forward to was the arrival of hot food.

This morning when the food didn't arrive, anger added to pain. Her throbbing left leg turned red then purple; sweat poured off it but it felt like a block of ice. She was furious not just with the incompetence of the delivery service, but with everything and everyone in her life. If it hadn't been for the accident and the incompetent surgeons who hadn't fixed her leg properly in the first place, she'd still be New Zealand's golden girl. The injustice of having everything she'd worked so hard for taken away in a moment of carelessness had never left her. If only the driver had paid attention and hadn't been going so fast. If only they'd got her to a proper hospital where the staff spoke English and there were specialist surgeons. If only the wound hadn't become infected. None of this was her fault, and yet she was the one paying for it. She'd lost the gold medal. She'd lost Oliver. Everything! And the fucking food was still not here.

Where the bloody hell was that new man? Maggie's son. He'd looked like a smart guy. Why wasn't he here? She'd finished the last of her emergency stash early that morning to help get back to sleep, and now all she could do was wait. Lizzie felt alone, hungry, and her pain was intensifying with each unfed second. The deliveries had been set up precisely so that something like this didn't happen again. What was it with businesses in this town, that something so simple could be fucked up so badly? Like everything else in this tin pot bloody country they couldn't even do what they were paid to do.

She punched the numbers on her phone and for the zillionth time heard the nauseatingly patronising automatic voice asking her to leave a message. She obliged, taking some comfort from imagining the look on the face of whoever listened to what she had to say. But she was still hungry and still alone. She hated bloody phones, anyway. Maybe there was a fault and people couldn't hear her. Hurling it as hard as she could, the phone shattered on the wall just above the TV.

Next she went online and left a foul message on the delivery company's website, haughtily stating that in future she would be taking her custom elsewhere and suggesting everyone else should do so too. An empty threat, because there was no other service in this one horse town she could afford and from which, incidentally, she hadn't already been banned.

Nothing.

Silence.

In the kitchen a clock dared to tick more loudly than before.

Tears rolled down Lizzie's face. Tears of frustration, anger, despair and pain, with lashings of deep loneliness thrown in for good measure, pouring down her plump red cheeks as she sat alone in her poky little flat. She sobbed for all she had been and all she might have been, but mainly she sobbed because she was hungry.

CHAPTER EIGHT

"Where's Mum?" asked Nick.

"Stables," said Kate, not looking up from the sofa where she was watching the news, still in her pyjamas and dressing gown. "Not much happens here, does it? I mean here, in New Zealand. This is more gossip than news. Where this car accident was and which type of cow was hit and how the snow is making it difficult to drive to Dunedin. Hardly life and death, is it?"

"I guess it was for the cow," replied Nick.

"You know what I mean. I'd forgotten how small we are. How far away New Zealand is from the rest of the world." Kate took a sip of water from the glass on the table in front of her. "It's hard to take this stuff seriously." She paused. "And the accent. I'd forgotten we have an accent. After London – it's the people on TV who are worst. That Jonathon guy is a hoot. Kaaaaa-kee-taaaayyyy, indeed."

Nick knew her well enough to know that if he said anything he'd be stuck defending his position for another hour if not two.

"Kate," he said, bending over her. "Are you going to sit there pleading the longest case of jetlag in the history of modern flight, or are you going to get up and help out? Mum and I have worked all day today, all day yesterday and all day the day before that, while you, dear sister, have done nothing but sleep. We've been looking forward to eating London haute cuisine cooked by world-renowned chef Kate Potter, and so far, nada. Not even a curry!"

Before he'd finished speaking Kate was off, bolting for the door, thundering up the stairs, dressing gown flying behind her like Batman's cape. Nick heard the bathroom door slam shut. He waited but the door stayed closed. No sound, nothing.

Sisters! He decided to try his luck with his mother. "It's only me, " he called, poking his head into the workroom.

"I'm getting Betty ready, so stay there. What do you want?"

"Nothing."

"OK. Keep me company while I do this then I'll make us something. I'm surprised you never eat while you're at work."

Nick sat down at Maggie's desk and started fiddling on her laptop. "I know how they cook it."

"And don't play with that. I'm working on something and don't want to lose it."

Nick ignored her and opened the Patience app.

It was late in the afternoon and Betty, dead for thirty hours, was already a hollowed-out semblance of the live woman. What little flesh the cancer had left on her bones was cold and doughy. Maggie had to be careful not to break any bones while she washed her. Softly, she cleaned around the orifices before plugging them to prevent seepage.

She filled a basin with water. Nick had seen his mother wash clients' hair many times, and often remarked on how carefully she did it. A bald corpse is not the look we're after, she'd explained. Families prefer hair.

"Guess who I saw today?" he called out.

Maggie carried on working as she waited for the answer. It was rare for her son to say more than a few words at a time, let alone actually seek her out and chat, and she didn't want to put him off.

"Tim James, the movie star," he said, looking up from the laptop. "You remember he's here for that action movie being shot up the Dart? The poor guy was driving through town around lunchtime with a line of cars following him, each one packed with photographers. He couldn't even stop to get petrol without those guys leaping out and taking pictures of him filling his tank. Felt a bit sorry for him till I remembered how much he makes. Odd that he had to get his own petrol, isn't it? You'd expect he'd use a driver."

With the hairdryer on cool, Maggie fluffed up Betty's hair into its familiar style, and then used gallons of spray to ensure not one hair dared move out of place and ruin the hard-won effect. Betty had said she wanted to look as lifelike as possible.

Once her hair was done, Maggie laid her make-up brushes out on the trolley beside her. "He's quite good-looking, isn't he?" she said.

"Some people think so," said Nick. "Starting to look a bit past it if you ask me. He must be nearly forty by now.

"Ouch."

"You don't look forty, Mum, you look great – better than him, anyway."

"You *are* hungry, aren't you?"

"Maybe. Talking of food, you should see this woman I deliver to now. She is *huge*, I mean, absolutely *enormous*."

Only half listening, Maggie gently massaged cream around Betty's neck and face. When she'd finished she took some wadding and pushed this into Betty's cheeks to help take away that "just-had-cancer" look, and then put her false teeth back in.

"Today I delivered six extra-large stuffed crust pizzas and six two-litre bottles of coke. Every day she eats that many pizzas and more and drinks all the coke. The woman can barely move she's so big – honest. I don't think she's left her flat in years. God knows what would happen if there was a fire, because she'd be stuck. No one could get that woman down the stairs without a crane. Elka told me she used to be a skier in the olden days when you were young, but I can't see it. There isn't a tow on the planet that would've had a hope in hell of getting her up a mountain."

Maggie stood back and looked at Betty. *That foundation isn't right,* she thought. Taking a cotton pad she started wiping it off, and chose a lighter colour from the box.

"That's Lizzie Martin. We were at school together. I thought she'd gone up north."

"Yip, Lizzie Martin. Enormous and not very nice with it. Whoever said fat people were jolly has never met this one. This morning I was forty-five minutes late with her delivery. There was a problem with the ovens. When I got there and before I could explain, she was yelling and throwing things at me. *If this was the best service I was capable of she would bleep-bleep take her order bleep-bleep someplace else,*" he mimicked. "On and on she went, until she got a whiff of the food, that is. Then right in front of me she grabbed the boxes and started wolfing the first one down while I was standing there. Not a pretty sight."

Maggie finished the foundation, pleased she'd changed it, and slipped the eyecaps out of Betty's eyes. She got out her tweezers and did a quick eyebrow tidy up and then applied a light brown powder to make them more visible. Betty had said green eyeshadow and lots of it. She wanted colour, and Maggie duly obliged before adding a thin layer of mascara to her lashes and slipping the caps back in place.

"Surely you're exaggerating. Lizzie would have won gold at the Olympics if she hadn't been hit by a car. She was beautiful and very fit. She wouldn't let herself get fat."

"No, it's her. Both you and Elka have confirmed it. Unless this fat person has eaten the real Lizzie and has her trapped inside her body. She could be a zombie."

"Uh huh," replied Maggie, concentrating on painting Betty's lips in the colour she'd chosen to go with her casket. Betty had joined an online Coffin Club as soon as she was told the treatment wasn't working, and had asked Jim to build one for her. She had made the lining herself – pale pink with shocking pink frills – and had then bought a lipstick to match.

Nick finished another hand of Patience. "The worst of it is, despite her being so nasty and rude, she is actually helpless – angry and horrible, sure, but totally helpless. I meant what I said about a fire. She would be so cooked." He laughed, but Maggie could tell he was also concerned.

"Her home help arrived just as I was leaving. She was worried because Lizzie hadn't answered her phone. I had to tell her this was because the phone was in pieces on the other side of the room. Lizzie got me to pick up the bits for her. And then that new doctor arrived just as I was leaving. Gave me a filthy look when he saw me and realised I had brought food."

"Why would he be horrible to you? He doesn't know anything about you." Betty was done and looked as though she could wake up from a nap at any moment. The family, especially Susan, would be pleased. Maggie tidied everything away and took off her gloves.

"Mum, this woman is enormous, and I'm one of the people taking her bloody pizzas and coke every day. The doc looked at me as though I was her drug dealer. Maybe I am."

"Really? Bit strong, isn't it?"

"Maybe. Maybe not. When I saw her this morning, so upset because her delivery was late, it made me think. She's addicted to food, actually sugar, in the same way other people are addicted to drugs. The last thing that woman needs is food."

"But if she didn't get it from you, she would get it from someone else. Everyone has to eat and food is legal, Nick."

Maggie held a mirror up to Betty so she could see how she looked. "You look great," she whispered.

"What did you say?"

"Nothing, just talking to Betty. Come and see how she looks."

Nick looked around the corner and nodded appreciatively. "She looks exactly the way she would want to. Great job, Mum."

Maggie pushed her friend back into the cabinet, and after shutting the door took off her apron. "It's a hard one, Nick," she said. "I don't know what to say, but you have to feel OK about it and if you don't then let someone else do her orders."

Nick squirmed. "I sort of feel OK and I sort of don't. That's the problem. And to make matters worse she gives the best tips and I need the money."

"Ahhh, I might have known there would be filthy lucre involved, corrupting my innocent child." Maggie put her hand on Nick's shoulder.

"On the one hand she gives great tips, and on the other hand, giving a fat lady something you know is killing her makes you feel bad. And on the third hand, what right have you to tell a grown woman she can't have what she wants and has paid for?"

"If it helps," said Maggie, "she was my friend at school and I wouldn't have wanted to get between her and something she wanted, ever. We were in the same class for a while but she left to train in France. No one saw her for ages but we heard all about her. After winning the World Title she became New Zealand's golden girl of skiing. And she deserved it. She was a fantastic skier and would have won gold at the 1988 Olympics if she hadn't been injured."

"You're kidding," said Nick. "That huge enormous woman wasn't just a skier, she was a world champion?"

"Brilliant sportswoman – totally fearless, and beautiful too. Everyone loved her, until the accident. Stepped out in front of a car late one night in France. The rumours were she'd been drinking and got a bit aggro with someone. The car completely shattered her right leg and she was lucky not to lose it completely. No one heard anything about her for ages, until she came back to New Zealand ten years ago. She didn't want anyone to know she was back. Someone recognised her and told the press. The papers tried to make a big thing of it, golden girl returns in tragic circumstances, but she wouldn't have a bar of it. Even hit one reporter with a crutch after he stuck his camera in her face when she answered the door – Jonathon Bramble, I think. I thought she'd gone to ground up north somewhere. But obviously not.

"Right it's been a long day and I'm starving, but I don't want to hear the word pizza. Your story has put me right off. Do you think Kate has cooked us anything, or are we going to have to defrost something I prepared earlier?"

"I suggested she cook but she ran out of the room and slammed the bathroom door."

"I hope she hasn't picked up a bug somewhere. You'll work out what to do about Lizzie. No one from her past ever managed to tell her what she could or couldn't do. Not even her parents, poor things. Maybe talk to her, get to know her a little better? And another thing, don't take any stick from that doc. If anyone is supposed to help her, it's him, not you."

Maggie turned out the lights and locked The Stables' door, an act that always amused her, considering the building's inhabitants weren't going anywhere, and a less likely place for a burglar she couldn't imagine. They walked towards the light of the warm house across the yard, Nick thinking about his problem with Lizzie and Maggie thinking again about how much she missed Betty. She would have known exactly what to say to Nick.

CHAPTER NINE

The house on Suburb Street was crammed wall to wall with family, friends and townspeople. The shadows of sadness had lingered amongst them after the service and burial, but only until those gathered to celebrate Betty's life had consumed one or two glasses of wine. Now they were gaily swapping Betty stories, which were getting funnier and more honest as the afternoon wore on.

"Mum looked great," said Susan, taking Maggie aside. "For a moment I thought she was going to sit up in the middle of the service and start telling us what to do."

Maggie squeezed Susan's arm. "If only she had."

"I'd better go and check on Dad," said Susan, merging with the throng of guests jostling for space in the front room.

A young neighbour co-opted to help out was doing his best to get wine to thirsty guests, but no sooner had he appeared with a tray of full glasses than they were snatched away and he had to go back to the kitchen for more. The mourners at the back of the room were starting to feel the strain of enforced sobriety and despatched the new girl from the council planning department for supplies, with orders not to return empty handed.

Maggie waved across heads to Kate, who was being swamped by people pleased to see her home. Like Betty, many had taken an interest in her progress. They wanted to know what she'd been doing and if she was back from London for good, hinting it was about time she found a man and settled down to have babies. Before long several of the older women had made plans for her to come to dinner and meet their grandsons.

Kate looked exotic in a loose tunic dress made from colourful silk she'd insisted to Maggie was the height of fashion this year in London. Maggie was just pleased to have Kate home again. She felt guilty there hadn't been time for them to sit down and talk properly about Kate's time in London, and, more importantly, what she was planning to do next. Whenever she'd looked for her daughter it was to find her fast asleep in her room.

Memo to self, Maggie thought. *Organise lunch with Kate at Elka's.*

She'd discovered when Kate was going through her teenage years that she could be more forthcoming about all sorts of subjects if they met in a neutral, public space, sitting side by side rather than face to face. With Elka present, Maggie hoped she'd have a better chance of finding out answers to her growing list of questions.

The conversation around Maggie turned from Betty to Tim James, who was making his presence felt in town. Nick had seen him stop off at the local garage to fill up his 4WD, and someone else had seen him looking at paintings at an art gallery. He'd already agreed to donate merchandise from his last movie to the local school hall fund-raising effort, and the principal was swooning in her snow boots. No one had a bad word to say about him.

Visiting movie stars usually kept to themselves, flying by helicopter from the airport to one of the lodges, where their every need was met with discretion, no matter how unusual. Sometimes the only sign that anyone famous was in town was an unmarked jet parked to one side at the airport. And if a star did venture out to a restaurant, they were always surrounded by an entourage who kept the curious at bay.

Tim James was proving to be the exception to the rule, and as a result his popularity rating amongst the locals was at an all-time high.

One of the men in the group was not so enamoured. Listening to the glowing talk, Bruce, a car rental agent, turned to Maggie, raised his eyebrows and gently shook his head. "Don't believe the hype. I don't like him," he said quietly. "This guy is just like all the others – used to getting exactly what he wants when he wants it, and woe betide anyone who doesn't deliver. I was five minutes late with his Audi. You know what the traffic's like now. I tried to explain but that made him worse. He went ballistic in front of everyone on the tarmac. At least you don't need to worry, Maggie. I doubt if he'll need your services while he's here." Bruce spotted his wife and, grabbing the last glass of wine from a passing tray, went to join her.

Maggie now found herself in a circle of men talking about who would make it into the next All Blacks test team. Having little interest in the national sport, she went in search of Elka who was predictably hard at work in the kitchen. Rolling up her sleeves, Maggie started on the dishes. The clean glasses were whisked away for refilling while they were still warm, and the nearly dry platters were loaded up again with steaming hot pastries and taken out to the ravenous guests. The pair worked together silently and efficiently, until demand slowly tapered off and they could relax.

"Can I bring Kate to the restaurant for lunch?" asked Maggie, stripping off her rubber gloves. "I get the feeling she's avoiding me. She talks more freely when you're there."

"Of course you can. How about the day after tomorrow? I want to hear everything about London. Working under Chef Eric must have been incredible."

"It expect so, but I wouldn't know. I've been so busy with Betty's funeral, and then when I had time to talk she was fast asleep in her room. Today is the first time I've seen her dressed since she got home."

A waitress came in and with a loud sigh put an empty platter down on the bench. "That's the last one," she said, daring Elka to contradict her. Taking off her apron she undid her top button and fluffed her hair, before marching into the living room. Someone had put Betty's favourite music on the stereo and the party seemed to be starting in earnest.

Elka shrugged. "She's one of my best waitresses. We're so busy at the restaurant, she's one of the few who can keep up. Anyway – Kate. She'll be exhausted after working for Chef Eric right up until leaving. He's one of the greats, but his reputation amongst staff is awful. And she spent eighteen months in his kitchen. Don't be too hard on her, Maggie. Six months' sleep might just about be enough to get over that man."

"It's your world. Speaking of famous men, I have to say Tim James has never appealed to me," said Maggie, finishing the last of the drying. "They were talking about him before. Raving over him. Well – everyone except Bruce, who said he was appalling."

"He does his own stunts," said Elka. "That's sexy. I like that he doesn't expect other people to put their lives at risk to make him look good."

"I suppose. Unless you're a stuntman looking for work. I don't get why so many women run after him. Sue evidently made a right idiot of herself when he donated his stuff to the school. I know he looks good. Hair: check. Teeth: check. Muscles: check. Smile: Really?"

"So, if he asked you out for dinner, you would turn him down."

"Absolutely," said Maggie, bending down to put a large dish in a bottom cupboard. "Well, maybe. I would only go because I'm curious, not because I'm attracted to him. I haven't been attracted to a man or anyone else for years. And you know I've tried. Tried hard, in fact. Remember six years ago there was that fireman from Timaru?"

As she straightened up, she saw the look on Elka's face. "What's wrong?"

"I suppose she wants to tell you I'm standing right behind you and she thinks you might be about to say something a stranger shouldn't hear," said a male voice. "We wouldn't want to breach the privacy of the fireman from Timaru, would we? Sorry – I took a short cut through the kitchen; I didn't mean to interrupt."

Maggie shrank into the neck of her turtleneck jersey, her face flushed with colour. She turned around to look at the man standing right behind her. He was very tall, so she had to look up to see his face. Judging by his tan, and the rays of white lines sweeping out from the corners of his dark brown eyes, he had spent a lot of time in the sun. Clean shaven and clear eyed, Maggie had to admit he was tolerably good-looking, but that was as much as she was willing to concede.

And then it struck her. "I know who you are. You're Ben Goodman. I've heard about you from Betty. And others. You drive too fast and you nearly killed us on our morning walk a few days ago."

"I did what?"

"You ran us off Lower Shotover Road into a ditch two mornings ago. And the ditch had water in it. Cold, deep water."

Ben looked at Elka. "Perhaps it's time you introduced us, Elka? I like to know the names of the ones who got away."

"Maggie Potter, meet Ben Goodman – Dr Ben Goodman meet Maggie Potter."

"You're the undertaker," he said.

"Funeral director," corrected Maggie.

"Exactly. Betty talked about you. She wanted us to meet. It was all she ever talked about."

"That's strange. She didn't say anything to me about you."

Standing behind the doctor, Elka wagged her finger at Maggie.

"No doubt we'll meet again, Maggie Potter," said Ben, looking towards the door. "Not too often in a professional capacity, I hope. It won't help me build up my practice, if patients see us together. They might think we have an arrangement." He flushed. "Like Dr Harold Shipman, I mean," he finished lamely.

"It was the funeral director who caught him, wasn't it?" said Maggie.

"You're right. It was. Apologies, and also for the other morning, if you really think it was me."

"Of course it was you. Elka recognised your car. Do you think I–"

The door into the living room swung shut behind him.

"The cheek. You know it was him," said Maggie.

Elka looked at her. "You know you're blushing. I haven't seen you look so uncomfortable in such a long time. And telling that huge Betty fib. I bet if we opened the back door we would hear her roaring with laughter from the cemetery. Wait till I tell her how red you've gone. Don't worry, I'm sure he didn't notice."

"Oh hardie har har!" Maggie pointed at the last pile of dirty glasses and platters on the bench. "We'd better get these done."

"I wish Betty was here," said Elka. "She would know exactly what to say."

"Nothing happened. Leave it alone."

Elka found two clean glasses and splashed some pinot noir into them before raising her glass. "To Betty."

"To Betty," Maggie replied. They emptied their glasses and Elka poured again.

CHAPTER TEN

Tim James pulled his lips out from his gums and peered at the reflection in the mirror. Earlier he'd seen his reflection in a window and noticed his smile looked toothier than usual. This wasn't good. His smile was part of the Tim James brand, and its perfection could not be marred by any hint of receding gums. He didn't want to wake up one morning to find the jackals in the gutter press had started focusing on the faults in his appearance and worse, were linking them to his age. Action heroes didn't get old and they most certainly didn't have receding gums. Apart from Liam Neeson, and he was more of an action-dad than an actual hero.

Looking this way and that he reassured himself his teeth were fine and there was nothing to worry about. They were even and very white; his gums were where they should be and his smile was undimmed. It must have been a trick of the light. He did a quick inventory of his skin, eyes and hair, nose and jawline to ready himself for his waiting make-up artist. Everything checked out. He ran his face through a gamut of expressions, from thoughtful to uncontrolled laughter. At the same time he hummed through several octaves, focusing on the base notes. He studied his face and body thoughtfully in the mirror as a craftsman would check his tools before a job. Putting his shoulders back, he straightened his light blue cashmere sweater, turned on his heels and, swinging the door back with a flourish, made his entrance.

The others in the living room looked slightly startled, but recovered quickly and hurried to his side. His personal make-up team was set up and waiting for him. Jonathon Bramble, New Zealand's ageing prime time TV host, was already seated in front of a pop-up mirror, tissues sprouting from his shirt collar. Tim walked across the room, his hand outstretched, his smile aimed at the man who was about to interview him.

"Jonathon, I presume, he said. "They tell me you're 'the man' in this country."

Jonathon Bramble turned awkwardly in his chair and shook the outstretched hand firmly, unwilling to be the first to let go. They eyeballed each other and after a few seconds of sizing each other up, released simultaneously.

Tim sat down in the vacant chair, staring into the mirror while Gwen, tucked tissues into his sweater. Jonathon was having mascara applied and was therefore at a disadvantage, a fact not lost on Tim.

"So what's the plan, my man?" he asked heartily, reaching over and planting a hearty slap on Jonathon's shoulder.

As a result of the sudden jolt, Jonathon copped a streak of waterproof mascara just below one eye. It proved difficult to remove, and left a dark shadow that couldn't be evened out by his make-up. (Later that night Jonathon's greatest fan, his mother would turn to one of the residents in her rest home to say how tired her son was looking. Interestingly, she would also comment on how toothy Tim James was nowadays.)

"Got the questions, Jonathon?" asked Tim, making sure his PR team had briefed this guy properly.

"I have them right here, Mr James."

"None of this Mr James stuff, Jonathon. Call me Tim. Has someone offered y'all a drink, something to eat maybe? I hear you guys have travelled all the way from Auckland just to interview me. Well folks, I am honoured."

Tim nodded to each individual in the room, causing them all to stop what they were doing, make eye contact and nod back. There was a small round of soft applause, led by one of Tim's people.

"Matt, have you looked after these good people?"

"Certainly have Mr James – I mean, Tim", replied a tall man in his early fifties, stepping from the shadows to beside the star's chair.

Tim crooked his finger and Matt bent down as Tim turned away from Jonathon, who was picking the tissues out of his collar. "Just make damn sure the film picks up the bill for anything they order and it doesn't come back to me," he muttered quietly.

Looking nonchalant, Jonathon tried to hear what was being said, but couldn't. He bent forward to look at his reflection, and didn't particularly like what he saw. Despite the best efforts of a skilled make-up artist, he still looked old and, dammit, disreputable. His skin was coarse and his nose bulbous. His hair was dyed and looked it, and his teeth, in comparison to the row of Hollywood pearls beside him, were uneven in both form and colour. *Damn the fags*, he thought, flicking his tongue across his top teeth, as if this would remove the nicotine and coffee stains with one swipe. Wishing he could nip out now for a quick cigarette to calm his nerves, he instead went to his seat for a lighting check and took the opportunity to read over the questions Tim's people had kindly provided for him.

Jonathon had been the host of a prime time news show for nearly ten years. But his format was tired and his once solid fan base amongst big-spending high-living baby boomers was being eroded by the offerings on other channels. Not to mention the Devil's spawn – Netflix. Viewers were ditching his programme in their droves, instead binge-watching *Downton Abbey*, or worse, *Game of Thrones*. When even his own mother had said she was hooked on *Narcos* and didn't bother with the news now, he knew his days were numbered.

"It's not the competition that's taking you out, Jonathon old boy," his agent had said. "The women's mags are the real culprits. Next time you decide to cheat on your wife, please don't do it in a public car park and don't do it with your wife's little sister. You're lucky your father-in-law has enough money to keep most of it out of the press."

However, enough had been leaked by a freelance blogger for management to put him on notice. His agent had read him the letter this morning, while he was in the business lounge at the airport. He had a week before his contract was reviewed. A week to prove to management and the viewers he still had what it takes.

He took his notes out of his pocket and went over them again. The old lady had provided the sort of stuff that only comes along once in a career, but he needed to play it just right if it was going to save him.

He peeled his shirt away from his skin, praying the sweat wouldn't seep through and form dark patches on his suit. Commandeering a box of tissues, he sidled over to a quiet corner and dabbed his forehead to stop his make-up from running into his eyes. *Slow your breathing*, he told himself, *practise mindfulness*. He could hear his counsellor's voice. *Focus, Jonathon. Think about the view. Look at the mountains and the lake. Breathe, breathe. Find your inner peace.*

"I know it's hot in here, Jonathon," said Tim loudly behind him. "I told the crew you wouldn't mind if I put the heating up. Having just come from summer, I need to keep the temperature high so I can acclimatise slowly to your winter. Love the heat, hate the cold."

"No problem," replied Jonathon, looking around for more tissues.

"The questions we gave you. Standard stuff. The interview won't take long. My team has regular focus groups finding out what my fans want to know. These questions give them enough to keep them happy but keep them wanting more – that's the golden rule in show business, ain't it?"

Jonathon nodded his agreement. The interview was to take place in front of the windows. The lighting would be tricky, but the cameraman had assured him it was possible. It had to be. One of his sponsors was the Tourism Board. Tim James sitting in front of the mountains and lake was pure gold to them, and he needed to keep every one of his advertisers happy. After tonight, he hoped they would be deliriously, six-figure-contract-for-ten-years happy.

Ten minutes and several retouches later, Jonathon's make-up had finally succumbed to his anxiety and slid off his face onto his collar. He found a private area behind the lights and quickly changed into a fresh shirt. He had to get control of himself. Tucking his shirt in, he looked up to find the crew waiting.

Tim was ready and making small talk with the cameraman. "In your own time, Jonathon," he called out cheerily to the amusement of the whole room.

Jonathon clenched his jaws only to feel a filling loosen in a lower back molar. *Great*, he thought to himself. *Another dental bill from that robber on Queen Street. Dammit, the bloody station can pay for it. Work injury.* His tongue was drawn irresistibly to the sharp surface of his tooth, as he took his place in the opposite chair.

"When you're ready, Mr James, Jonathon," said his director from behind the lights.

Jonathon removed his tongue from the side of his mouth and flashed his best smile at the star sitting comfortably across from him. For the first five minutes, he stuck to the list of patsy questions he had been given by Matt. Tim was happy to tell him, modestly, that he was the star of the seven highest-grossing movies of all time. Yes, he had broken his leg at least three times doing his own stunts. And the Oscar had been a fantastic surprise because the other nominees were so much more talented than he was.

Outside the sun was setting, so they took a short break as the cameraman adjusted the lighting. Tim relaxed, and reached over to pat Jonathon's leg and tell him how well he was doing. He got Gwen to give his face a quick dusting and they were good to go.

Jonathon opened with a photo of Tim, his wife Jenny, and their twelve-week old son, Isaac. Tim effused his love for this miracle child who he missed more than anything, but then, looking away from Jonathon and directly into the camera, he told New Zealand how he had made a commitment to a friend and that he was a man of his word. As much as he missed his family, he had to come to this wunnerful country, to make this movie. Kiwis were such wunnerful people and one day they would return as a family.

Tourism board – tick.

"Yes," said Tim, suddenly turning his full and glittering attention back to Jonathon. "I'm in your beautiful country for a week then I'm back to the States to film the fourth movie in the 'Possible Harm' series. The movie I'm doing here, *Breakneck*, is a favour for an old buddy. He assures me his son knows what he's doing."

In answer to Jonathon's next question, Tim employed his quiet prudent voice. "My company owns the most successful series of action movies ever made. And yes, that does make me a very wealthy man. But I like to think I do good with that money. Possible Harm Ltd employs more than three hundred people in the States. In our overseas locations I donate to local charities. But I don't think it's right to talk about this in public. I prefer to do this work in private. I do it because it is the right thing to do and not for the publicity." Tim was now looking deeply into Jonathon's eyes, knowing his intensity would be captured by the camera focusing on him from behind his host.

Jonathon shifted in his chair. He took a long slow breath and, feeling calmer than he had all day, asked his next question – one of his own. "You have wanted to be a movie star since you were six years old, when your father abandoned you and your mother and ran off with another … person. Is that correct? How did that feel? Do you think being abandoned is the driving force behind your need to make your audience love you?"

Tim's smile froze on his face. His eyes flicked to Matt, standing off to the side, but Matt looked just as shocked as Tim. No one around them moved, the room was deadly quiet apart from the flames flickering in the fireplace.

Tim looked down, then turning to one side looked up at Jonathon, smiling. He cleared his throat, and in those few seconds Jonathon guessed he was considering whether to get up and walk out, or to just ignore the question and its unsavoury implications. Jonathon breathed a sigh of relief as Tim opted to answer the question

"You have done your research," he said slowly. "Yes, my father left us when I was six for another 'person' ..." Before Jonathon could capitalise further, Tim went on, "And out of respect for my mother's feelings, I believe I should say no more on that subject, Jonathon?"

"Quite," replied Jonathon, willing himself not to grin triumphantly. Suddenly he wasn't sweating any more, he was even enjoying himself. He waited an extra beat before asking his next question, enjoying the change in the balance of power in the room.

"Is it true you didn't invite your mother to your wedding, and that she has never met your wife, the mother of her only grandson?"

He knew Tim must be seething, but again the movie star smiled. It was too late now for him to get up and leave. He watched as Tim adopted a tortured look, evidently going for the pity angle. Jonathan suspected that later, he'd have Matt's guts on a plate.

"Yes, it is true," said Tim, his voice laden with sadness. "My mother and I are estranged, as you must know. She has chosen to pursue her own interests. There is nothing I can add, other than that her actions are deeply painful to me and my wife, Jenny."

Jonathon contemplated how long it would take for the footage to go global, after the interview aired in an hour. He felt like leaping onto his chair and jumping all over it, punching the air with victory, but he couldn't. He wasn't finished with Tim James.

"Your mother tells a different story, Mr James. I spoke to her this afternoon, and she tells me that after she brought you up and helped you to become the actor you dreamed of being, you cut her off without a penny. At the age of sixty-six, your mother is still waiting tables in San Diego, working mainly for tips. I have a clip I can roll for you."
Tim had had enough. Unhooking the microphone from his ear, he stood up, towering over Jonathon who was lamely holding an iPad out to him.

"I think you've taken enough of my time, don't you, Mr Bramble?" he said. "I'd heard Kiwis were polite and showed visitors due respect, but obviously this is not true in every case. I'm sure many of your countrymen and women will be very disappointed about the intrusive questions you have asked me today. Now you must excuse me." Tim stepped awkwardly over several cables until he was out of shot, leaving his microphone dangling on the arm of the chair. This was his living room, his suite, and the only available refuge was his bathroom on the other side of the massive fireplace. He slammed the door, but then had to stay there and wait for them to pack up and go. He heard Matt demand the footage from Bramble, along with the words breach of contract, but as Tim expected, no quarter was given, and certainly no film. He could only imagine how delighted the little TV troll was with himself.

As he sat on the laundry basket Tim thought about how pleased his mother would be with the interview. He could hear her laughing when the segment went to air and then laughing again every time she played it back for her own amusement and that of her fucking friends. Damn the woman. There was no way in hell he'd ever give her one cent of his hard-earned money now. She could and would die poor!

Once the door to the suite had shut behind the last techie, Matt knew what was coming. He poured himself a large whisky from the bar and gulped it in one swig, before knocking quietly on the bathroom door to indicate the all clear.

Tim emerged, every fibre of his body tense with fury.

Matt stood stony faced as the star vented his rage at the interview, at the interviewer, and finally at Matt for allowing it to happen. Next he started on the bloody country for being so small that everyone would see the clip on the evening news, and then ended with a bitter rant about his mother, the bitch who would never, ever go away.

Matt heard but didn't listen. He was used to the ravings of his boss, and had learned long ago to show no emotion at all. He didn't want to incite the man who paid the mortgage on his second home in Mexico.

His boss was mean, and everyone knew it. But it was his job to make sure no one who knew the truth actually talked about it.

The Bramble bastard had gone rogue. He'd ignored every briefing, in his vainglorious attempt to promote himself and his goddamned show.

Matt looked past Tim out the window, taking note of the approaching darkness and watching snow start to fall. It was beautiful in the world outside this room. He stood still until Tim stopped venting and then excused himself, leaving the miserable bastard alone.

CHAPTER ELEVEN

Elka was busy. Too busy to meet Maggie for their morning walk, and far too busy to take time to relax and relieve the slow build in pressure she'd been feeling since booking her operation for the following week. She'd been awake most of the night, tossing and turning, unable to stop her mind running through various disaster scenarios, until she eventually drifted off just before her alarm woke her.

It was a grumpy start to the day, and thankfully everyone was waiting for her when she arrived. She was not in the mood to repeat instructions to latecomers.

Filming on *Breakneck* was beginning, and the logistics of getting food for ninety people to the Dart River valley, up to two hours' drive away at the head of the lake, while still maintaining high standards in the restaurant, was stretching the resources of all concerned.

She still had no idea if Kate would agree to run the restaurant while she was in Dunedin. But if not Kate, then who? Her staff were good but needed direction. And what if there were complications and she had to stay away longer than she anticipated? The downside of being a hands-on boss, she thought, as she ticked off the next job on the long list of things to do. *Kate just has to agree*, she thought. *And if she doesn't then I'll deal with that tomorrow.*

The sound of a lorry backing up to a side entrance distracted her. For the first time since she had opened the restaurant, the wine delivery was on time. Today of all days. Elka wiped her forehead and went out to greet the driver.

Maggie was happy to forgo her morning walk, as it gave her an extra hour or two to get her life into some sort of order. A woman's body had been brought in by the police that morning, with little supporting information apart from the name, death certificate and a contact number for the ex-husband, a lawyer in Auckland. She recognised the woman's name, but with so many newcomers to the district she had never actually met her.

Over the past fifteen years there had been an influx of wealthy Aucklanders, who shuttled between the northern city and the southern country, with grand homes in each place. The police told her this woman had moved permanently to her house beside Lake Hayes five years earlier, but like Maggie, they hadn't had any dealings with her as she had kept to herself and hadn't become part of the community.

Her name was Jilly Levant, and judging from her body, which had been brought to The Stables that morning, the years had not been kind. She had died alone in her sleep in her Lake Hayes home, and had been found several days later by her cleaning lady.

"Not unexpected," said the young policeman. "The cleaning lady said she'd never known anyone drink so much. There were bottles everywhere when we arrived. Full and empty."

Maggie looked at the emaciated body on her trolley. Alcohol – and by the look of the nicotine stains on her fingers, smoking too – had ravaged the woman. She may have been attractive once, but Jilly was wrinkled beyond her years and completely yellow. Myocardial infarction was the cause of death on the certificate, but Maggie wouldn't have been at all surprised if it had read liver failure.

It took all of her dogged persistence over the rest of the morning to track down the lawyer whose contact details had been supplied with Jilly's frail corpse, so she could find out what she was supposed to do. Eventually, between appointments, Mr Levant had taken her call and impatiently agreed to make the necessary decisions, before transferring her back to his PA who was instructed to tidy everything up as quickly as possible. Maggie went over the list of what needed to be done, and the PA politely instructed her to go ahead – purchase a plot anywhere in the nearest cemetery, and proceed with the burial as quickly as possible. All accounts were to be sent to the firm's address on Queen Street.

Jilly had made a will, in which she left everything to her daughter, and Mr Levant would make sure the legal formalities with regards to the cashed-up estate were completed. Maggie was further informed that as Jilly had alienated all her relatives and friends during late-night drunken phone calls, no one would be attending the funeral.

The PA, who never did give her name, also instructed Maggie to arrange the sale of the house at Lake Hayes. Maggie tried to tell the officious woman she was busy enough already, and was not in the business of sorting out the financial affairs of her clients, but it was pointless. The woman ploughed on regardless of her protests, dispassionately informing her she would be paid for her work and so didn't see why there would be a problem.

Maggie was too flabbergasted to protest further when the PA then suggested she could go to the house to sort out the woman's personal belongings and organise their delivery to the firm's address in Auckland. Her boss was in the middle of an important court case, and Jilly's only child, a daughter, was skiing somewhere in South America where she couldn't be contacted. There was no one else to do it, and the PA reminded Maggie once again and ever so patiently that she need only submit her account and she would be handsomely rewarded – as if money really could buy anything.

And then she hung up. Maggie was left looking in amazement at her phone.

"The mystery is not why you drank," she said to Jilly as she pushed her stretcher into the cabinet, "but how you lasted so long." She closed the door and went back to the house for a strong cup of coffee.

When everything was taken into consideration, it seemed there was no alternative but to do as the PA had asked. It wasn't as if she could package Jilly up and send her to the firm's address on Queen Street. The poor woman had to be buried, and Maggie did have the time –

The Stables had been unusually quiet this winter. She blamed the competition and the flu vaccine. The money would certainly come in handy.

In all her years as a funeral director, Maggie had never met a family – well, an ex-husband and his PA – who were so matter of fact about the death of a woman they both knew. The dismissive attitude of Levant, who must once have loved Jilly enough to marry her and build a life with her, was just more evidence in Maggie's ongoing private prosecution of men. As for the daughter who was nowhere to be found, and who according to later reports from the cleaning lady had not been in touch with her mother for years, Maggie held her in even less regard than her father. She couldn't begin to understand how or why a daughter could abandon her own mother.

That afternoon Maggie opened the front door of Jilly's home set high on a hill overlooking Lake Hayes. She knew the house was empty and that she had permission to be there, but felt she was intruding into a world she knew little about.

Leaving her snow boots at the door, she explored in her thick woolly socks, grateful the cleaning lady had left the underfloor heating on. She resisted the temptation to go for long slides on the polished concrete floor, instead, and more responsibly, slowly worked out what needed to be done and how best to do it.

The house was amazing. Brilliantly designed to suit its hillside setting, every room took full advantage of the surrounding scenery, maximising the views to the mountains in all directions and below to the lake, its steel blue stillness ringed with willow and poplar trees, their branches bare in winter. The sheer luxury of each detail in this huge home took Maggie's breath away, having seen houses like this only in magazines or films.

There were thick-piled Persian carpets throughout, highlighting the tasteful mix of antiques and modern classical furniture which worked together to create a home which, although firmly 21st century, implied a heritage of privilege. There were elegant sofas and chairs deeply and invitingly upholstered in gold and red velvets and brocades, their colours contrasting with the snowy countryside outside. Paintings varying hugely in style hung on every wall, sometimes at weird angles; others were stacked on the floor one against the other, some still in their dealers' packing materials.

Throughout the house, the devastation of Jilly's recent past was writ large against the opulence. Maggie had known the woman was a drinker, but was still surprised at the quantity of wine bottles, some half full and others empty, scattered across the floor and on the bedside tables. Dregs of red wine had stained some of the rugs and in places had leached into the concrete. Bottles bore the labels of the better local vineyards, with Gibston Valley wines featuring strongly. Cases from other well-known New Zealand and Australian producers were piled dangerously high against the wine racks lining one entire wall of the entrance hall.

Ash from overloaded ashtrays drifted onto surfaces as she moved from room to room. The house felt sad. Although the décor was impeccable and expensive, the rooms were unused and devoid of family. Designer furniture and lamps did little to create the homely atmosphere Maggie preferred, although, she had to admit, the state of her finances permitted her little choice in the matter.

The few personal possessions she found consisted mostly of old photographs of happier times long past, and wardrobes stuffed with clothes, some with price tags still attached. Unopened delivery boxes from net-a-porter.com were stacked against one wall of Jilly's dressing room, testifying to her ability to spend money thousands of miles from the designer shops she patronised.

Maggie whistled when she looked at the prices, knowing most of the clothes had never been worn. Jilly had been an XXS. Maggie was a definite M, so everything would have to be bundled into rubbish bags and dumped unceremoniously at the charity shops in town. If they were smart enough to sell the pieces online, they'd be in for a bumper year.

The only parts of the house that showed signs of habitation were littered with rubbish. The kitchen, Jilly's bedroom and her bathroom were strewn with empty and half-empty wine glasses. Pill bottles sat beside ashtrays on singed surfaces, competing for space with luxurious tubs of face cream promising salvation from the ravages of time. Her thousand-count bed linen was stained and smelly, and would have to be incinerated.

Amongst the clutter were many photographs of a young girl, some askew on the walls, others in tarnished silver frames on dressing tables and chests of drawers. In one the girl was solemn in school uniform; in others she was laughing with friends. A large photo showed her in cap-and-gown regalia, the formality contrasting with later photos of the now grown-up young woman lugging a backpack in front of Notre Dame. In another photo, the same woman was sitting in her business suit in an office, the unmistakable skyline of New York in the background. It seemed Jilly had been a part of her daughter's life after all, if only through photographs.

There were earlier pictures too – faded images of a man and woman laughing together beside their daughter, their eyes meeting above the blonde head of the child.

Maggie slipped some of the photos she judged would have been the most treasured into her handbag.

Looking over this beautiful but dejected house, Maggie was overwhelmed by the sadness of squandered opportunities. Jilly had lived here for nearly ten years, but once the cleaner had been through, and the photographs and jewellery had been packed up and the wardrobes emptied, there would be no trace of the woman's existence. The house would be sold just as the architect had designed it and the interior decorator had furnished it, wine stains in the concrete her only legacy.

Jilly Levant no longer existed.

"Get rid of the lot," the PA had said briskly, caring little, if at all, that she was talking about a woman's life. "The clothing can go to the local op shop and any photos or jewellery can be parcelled up and couriered north. You can tell the agent the house is to be sold as is – furniture, appliances, wine and paintings – the lot." She had then given Maggie bank account details for depositing the funds from the sale.

Never having bought or sold a house before, Maggie had no personal experience of any of the local real estate firms, but she had heard of Estelle Parker, one of Queenstown's more flamboyant agents who seemed popular with both local worthies and city visitors. Before leaving home that morning, she had arranged to meet her here at the house. Given carte blanche by the PA, Maggie had no interest in spending time getting competitive quotes, negotiating commission, or even in finding out how much Estelle would charge to market the house. If the family didn't care, why should she?

The doorbell rang just as Maggie was mentally ticking off the list of tasks she could do herself, and those she would delegate to others. There were a few people in the community who would be glad of the extra income to finish the cleaning up and clearing out.

Deep in thought, Maggie barely registered the doorbell or the cursory knock that followed, but she couldn't ignore the loud and melodic "Cooee" that heralded the arrival of Estelle Parker.

Without waiting for an invitation to enter, Estelle clicked grandly across the living room in her high heels, only pausing on her way to the windows to air kiss Maggie, taking care to avoid actual physical contact. Turning dramatically with both arms raised, and framed against the snow-covered mountains and the lake behind her, Estelle announced her thanks breathily to the woman in black standing near the fireplace.

"We've never officially met, have we, Maggie? And yet ..." she paused for dramatic effect, "you bring me this. The best house with the highest commission I will make all year. I will, of course, never forget your consideration." She paused again, and squinted. "But who knew you were so beautiful – much too beautiful to be an undertaker, my dear."

"Funeral director," corrected Maggie. "I prefer that. It's less gruesome, don't you think?"

Estelle smiled painfully. She had done everything she could to ward off the ageing process and was an active patron of many alternative health therapists, both in and outside the district. Right now she was in the throes of having her chakras balanced and felt them wobble as Maggie said the word *funeral*. She would make an appointment when she got back to the office.

Estelle was afraid of only two things: ageing and death. She was trying as hard she could, regardless of the cost, to prevent both, spending thousands of dollars on regular retreats to exclusive spas in New Zealand and overseas, where every inch of her body inside and out was analysed, massaged, alternately fed and starved, exercised and thoroughly cleansed.

In return for her efforts Estelle was gratifyingly alive and well, and looked several years younger than her real age, which served to confirm her faith in her chosen therapies. The spas had the added advantage of providing opportunities to meet the partners of rich men – women desperate to maintain a semblance of eternal youth as their best insurance against divorce and the relative penury and social banishment that inevitably followed. The good thing about divorce, Estelle had realised early in her career, was that whereas a married couple needed only one house, a divorced couple needed two houses.

Estelle sighed. She hadn't known Jilly but couldn't help knowing about her. They used the same wine merchant. If only Jilly had found my path, she thought, she wouldn't be dead before her time and looking like shit, by all accounts. And a stranger would not be selling her house.

"Look at this view," she said. "You know the lake was named after Bully Hayes the pirate, don't you?"

"That's what a lot of people say, but it's not true," replied Maggie. "I suppose it's more romantic to think it was named for him, but the old families remember an Australian called Hays who came here before the gold. He was looking for sheep country but this wasn't it, and he left."

"Dear me. How dull. I prefer the pirate story," Estelle said, walking out of the room.

She did a quick tour of the house and garden before joining Maggie for a cup of coffee at the black granite bench in the kitchen.

Maggie was relieved to see she wasn't the only one in awe of the home and its contents. It was gratifying to know that Estelle, who was surely used to this sort of place, was also impressed.

It didn't take long for the two women to conduct their business together. Estelle was remarkably understanding and sympathetic, which surprised Maggie who, knowing the woman only by reputation, had imagined she would be overly businesslike. She surprised herself by accepting an invitation to Estelle's next cocktail party, to be held the following month at Elka's – but not as surprised as Estelle had been when she'd issued the invitation.

Estelle had assumed Maggie would be dour and solemn, as she imagined all undertakers needed to be. She was genuinely attracted to Maggie's warmth and humour and bemused to find herself drawn to this woman in black. That she was delighted Maggie had brought her this great house to sell went without saying. A party invitation was the least she could do in return.

Sitting companionably in the kitchen they shared the necessary addresses, contact details and other relevant information to make sure everything could be achieved with the minimum of fuss. Estelle planned to stay on after Maggie left to draw up an inventory of the contents and take photographs for her portfolio of properties. She waited for the inevitable question from a client – which was how she now viewed Maggie.

"Around the $5 to $6 million mark I think," said Estelle, watching Maggie's face register her surprise. Then Estelle corrected herself.

"Actually, with the paintings and furniture, I think the market could – no, will – pay more. This is one of the few locations left on this road which can't be built out, so it will always be private. It's also on the right side of the airport."

"So how long do you think it will be before you find a buyer?" Maggie asked her anxiously. "I don't want this to drag on any longer than necessary."

Estelle paused, considering carefully whether to divulge the fact that she already knew of two possibles, before concluding Maggie was essentially harmless. There was no way she could affect the sale process. "Within the week, I think. I've got two buyers I'm going to call now; I'm hoping they can come out and look at the place this evening."

"But it hasn't been cleaned," Maggie said, clearly shocked at how quickly things were moving. "Poor Jilly only died a few days ago and there are bottles everywhere. I didn't know her, but we can't let people see how low she sank."

Estelle relented. Maggie was right, but for the wrong reasons. No buyer with that much money wanted to witness another human being's total degradation in what would be their new home.

"Good thinking. I'll ask them to come tomorrow afternoon. Do you think the cleaners will be finished by then?"

"I'll talk to them. Who are they, your buyers? Do I know them?" asked Maggie

"A couple staying at the Lodge told me they were thinking of moving here and. wanted a property in the country. This would suit them perfectly. The other buyer you might know, so you don't breathe a word to anyone, or I will have to hunt you down and kill you." Estelle smiled dramatically, but her intent was clear. "It's the new GP, Ben Goodman. He wants something just this, and of course with his family money, he can afford it."

Estelle was amused at Maggie's feigned indifference, but said nothing. She wouldn't have been good at her job had she not been able to read faces. It suddenly occurred to her this woman might be attracted to the doctor – much good it would do her, poor soul. Ben Goodman had a reputation for being very selective when it came to women, especially since his divorce from the glamorous Sarah.

Stepping out of the warm house into the cold, Estelle watched as Maggie pulled her down jacket around her before turning with an outstretched hand to say goodbye.

Closing the door, Estelle was surprised at how well she coped with physical contact with a purveyor of the dead.

CHAPTER TWELVE

Mike had done his best to explain the finer points of driving a jetboat to Tim James, but even he, known for being one of the calmest men on the lake, had given up. Tim knew everything about everything, and rather than listening to advice was instead telling Mike about each and every race, chase, and stunt sequence he had ever done. He raved on about how he had personally designed most of them, driving boats of all descriptions on rivers as diverse as the Nile and the Hudson.

Mike didn't like to point out the rivers mentioned were actually very similar, the only difference being they were on different continents. Both the Nile and Hudson were deep, predictable bodies of solid water, providing grip and resistance to a boat's propellers. Not only that, but they were also wide bodies of water, which made them forgiving and manoeuvrable.

The braided shallow river courses of the South Island were completely different. Shallow and constantly changing, they were far more challenging, and unless Mike somehow managed to get this through to Tim, the potential for disaster was huge. Jimmy, the young director, had again pleaded with him to try and make Tim understand that the boats were different and needed to be to cope with this type of river. This was the most expensive sequence in the movie, and the insurance premiums were exorbitant. Mike knew Jimmy had considered writing out the Tim James scenes altogether, but the backers had insisted he keep them in. Tim had the star power to pull in audiences around the world, and the backers demanded a film that repaid their investment not only in full but with interest. Or, as Jimmy's father had told them, "This is your only chance. Cock this up and it's over."

Mike felt sorry for the young director, and so, when he'd cooled down, he approached Tim again. Differently this time. "Let's walk down to the boat, shall we?" he said.

As they reached the riverbank, where the boat was tied up to a heavy log, he said, "You and me, we're men of the outdoors. We have a natural affinity for the world around us. I watched you kayak those rapids in the last Possible Harm movie, and I was gob-smacked. I told Susie, the wife, 'There's a man after my own heart.' It's just a pity Health and Safety gets in our way."

"I know exactly what you mean – Mike, isn't it?"

Mike nodded.

"It's just that when someone speaks to me like I'm an idiot who has no appreciation of risk, that's when I turn off. You'd be the same."

Mike nodded again. He couldn't decide if this guy was all right, or if he was a total asshole taking the piss.

"So go on, tell me what you have to, Mike, and I'll listen. Then you can go back to our young nervous director over there and you can tell him the Health and Safety box has been ticked."

Asshole. Definitely.

Taking a deep breath, Mike went over everything he had told Tim before, but more slowly this time. It was good to see the guy fidget with irritation.

"The Dart – this river," he said, pointing at the water behind him, "is like all South Island mountain–fed rivers. It's always changing. Rainfall high in the ranges behind us," he said, sweeping his arms towards the peaks rising high behind the bush, "comes down here in a rush and the sandy gravel bed means it picks up speed – nothing to slow it down, see. This makes it aerated or bubbly, not as "solid" as the water you've been on before. Less–solid, that makes it harder for a propeller to push against, and the variability in flow, depth and currents compounds the problem."

Tim was fiddling with a stick he'd picked up, smoothing it this way and that. He looked up when Mike stopped talking. "I get it. I do," he said. "Go on."

Mike decided this asshole deserved the long version, the one he gave in schools. "Just after the Second World War, which saw the development of the jet engine, a New Zealand high country farmer–engineer designed and built an impellor system, or an inboard version of a jet engine, for boats."

"What was the guy's name?" asked Tim.

"Hamilton," said Mike. "That's why they're called" he paused and pointed to the logo on the engine, "HamiltonJets."

"Don't get snippy with me, Mike. One, I don't have to be here, and two, I was only asking."

"I'm sorry, Mr James. I'll make this as quick as I can so both of us can get out of here. The boats are fast – very fast – and that's because they rise to the top of the water. This makes them manouvreable, but it's also dangerous because they can slide out from underneath you just when you least expect it. You have to constantly be looking ahead, reading the river to get the best out of these beauties."

Tim had dropped the stick and was kicking the sand out from under an old log by the time Mike had finished. A cold mist had sunk low between the dark bush-clad hills, creating an eerie atmosphere in the stony river valley.

"Listen," he said to Mike, fingers to his lips.

Mike breathed out slowly, saying nothing.

"Amazing," said Tim. "Nothing but nature. I hear nothing but the sounds of nature. What a beautiful country."

Mike could only assume the sounds of a movie crew of ninety people going about their business in various vehicles beside the river were, to Tim, an integral sound of nature.

Mike looked over to Jimmy and lifted his shoulders, hands upraised in capitulation. "I tried," he mouthed to the desperate director standing a little way off up the bank.

Jimmy walked down to the boat. "Mike, why don't you get some coffee while I explain to Tim here how his scene is going to work."

Mike didn't need to be told twice. He disappeared in the direction of the food truck before Jimmy had finished speaking.

"You know, Jimmy," said Tim, still kicking the sand away from under the log, "I don't appreciate being treated like some rookie on his first film. I've done more chase scenes than that guy has had hot dinners. And I don't need him to tell me how to drive a goddamned boat."

Jimmy sighed. It was going to be a long day. "Of course, you're totally right, Tim. I'll tell him to back off."

"I'd appreciate that, Jimmy," said Tim, turning to face him. "Now tell me what you have in mind and maybe together we can come up with something great."

Jimmy reached for the storyboard again. He'd already been over this with Tim several times, but what the hell, maybe this time he might listen.

"Your character, the key to the whole movie, is escaping the bad guys. They surprise you in their helicopter, you jump into your boat and get down the river as fast as you can, dodging bullets along the way before you reach the lake and safety. Mike will go over the route with you. He'll be flying the chopper behind you and letting you know which channel to take through your earpiece, at the same time. His co-pilot is the stuntman, who will be shooting at you."

"And the cameras?"

"I'm planning to have one camera running continuously on the side of the chopper, and another in the chopper itself. Your boat shots will also be filmed by drones flying on either side of you, and of course the camera on the boat. Remember, Tim, because you insist on driving the boat you need to be absolutely focused on Mike's instructions. Your only job is to watch the river ahead and follow Mike's directions. And every now and then pretend to duck a bullet. Do not look away from the river. These boats are tricky beasts, as no doubt Mike has told you, but I promise the sequence will look amazing."

Jimmy finally had the feeling the guy had taken his instructions on board. Maybe, just maybe, it would work out all right.

"Sounds good, mate," said Tim in an ersatz Kiwi accent. As the actor laughed uproariously, Jimmy thought it only polite to join in.

They walked up to the food truck where Tim asked for a coffee rather than going back to the privacy of his trailer. Early in his career he had learned how important it was to mingle with the crew. He knew that if he offended anyone on set, they could and would work against him. Rumours of what a pain in the butt he was would surface in the pages of the trades before seeping into the popular press, and before long he'd be known as "demanding and temperamental". The best crews in the business would suddenly be too busy to work on his films. "Look what happened to Christian Bale when he lost his cool on set," he'd said to Matt only last night.

"Christian who?" Matt had said, right on cue.

"You're good, Matt. You're good."

Tim was good with being known as approachable and friendly, as far as it went. Dammit though, he was a star – a huge star, and a star who always did his own stunts. Usually that got him some credit from the crew. That guy, Mike, had treated him like a child, explaining about bloody rivers and who invented the goddamned boat, for chrissakes. As if he cared. He'd assumed this crew from the back end of nowhere would know and respect his work without him having to spell it out. After all, who better to make Tim James look great while keeping Tim James safe than Tim James himself?

There was also a flippancy creeping into the team, which made him anxious. If he was going to put his neck on the line, he needed everyone to back him, and the jokes the Kiwis made at every opportunity were starting to grate. Their not-so-subtle references to his interview and his mother didn't help. He was in the goddamned middle of nowhere, and still his mother made his life miserable.

The director had assured him he'd be needed for only two days of filming, and Tim was looking forward to getting back on his plane and getting the hell back to the States, his debt to Jimmy's father well and truly cleared – but everything was happening frustratingly slowly. One of the grips had said something about the weather up in the mountains being bad. The river was running too high, or some such nonsense.

Back home there was a new movie to plan. Jenny and Isaac were booked for a photo shoot with Annie Leibovitz, no less. He needed a boost to his star tank after the last few days, and he didn't want to piss about in this underpopulated backwater for any longer than necessary. For the first time on a foreign set, Tim was homesick.

"More coffee, Mr James?" asked the caterer.

"No thanks, I'm good. Best darn coffee I've ever had." He handed the mug back to the woman and smiled his famous smile at the people standing awkwardly beside him.

"Mike?" he called. "Why don't we cut the bullshit and take the boat out? We could even have some fun."

Mike shrugged. Tim, keen to get moving, was already walking down to the river's edge. They climbed in and Mike took the wheel. He turned the key and the engine rumbled into life, water bubbling up behind. One of the guys untied the rope and Mike throttled gently into reverse, backing the boat into the current. He eased the throttle forward and they were off, picking up speed, the prow rising till they were planing across the surface, driving upstream. Even Tim had to admit this was a totally different and very thrilling kind of ride.

Mike swerved the boat to negotiate bars of gravel and sand midstream, at times turning almost directly into them so the back of the boat swung out behind before catching the deeper draught, enabling him to power forward and around. Ahead of them, Mt Cosmos dominated the glacial valley, a source of the pounamu or greenstone that his people had used for tools and jewelry long before the arrival of Europeans. This sacred mountain had been attracting Maori, then Pakeha, for centuries. On each side of the valley, waterfalls cascaded vertically over rock faces high above the dark southern beech forests lining the lower reaches. The sun broke through the clouds and the mist had now gone – it was, after all, a fabulous day to be working.

Mike slowed the boat until it sat low in the channel, the idling engine gobbling water. He held the wheel, indicating Tim should take it, and they swapped places awkwardly. Once more Mike quickly went over the controls with Tim, and this time the guy seemed to be paying attention. Tim eased the throttle forward, gradually getting used to the boat's response. Ahead was a long uninterrupted stretch of relatively deep fast–flowing water. Without checking with Mike first, Tim pushed the throttle hard down, putting the pedal to the floor, feeling the prow rise up, the full–throated roar of the engine reverberating between the valley walls. Tim banked into his first turn, copying Mike's moves exactly, and positioned the boat beautifully for the next bend. Mike had to admit the guy had natural ability.

It was the log that bobbed up in the current at the last minute that ruined the morning. Mike saw it in time, but Tim, less used to reading the river, didn't see it until it was too late. The boat hit the log at full speed, front on, knocking the hull off line. Tim did his best to slow down and almost made it, but by then the hull had tipped into a sandbank, stopping momentarily and throwing Tim sideways into the solid metal bar across the top of the windscreen. Mike reached over and grabbed the controls, pushing Tim out of the way, and steered to a spot where he could nose the boat out of the current and rest it against a gravel island in the middle of the river.

The damage was obvious – copious quantities of blood were pouring down the famous face from a large cut across the forehead. Tim would need medical attention and stitches. A lot of stitches.

Mike found the first aid kit, and once the bleeding was staunched with a large swab and a badly applied but tight bandage, he turned the boat around and they returned to camp in silence.

CHAPTER THIRTEEN

Lizzie said nothing about the late delivery and her tantrum the previous morning when Nick arrived with her food. She was surprisingly chatty, not only pausing her game but going as far as to put down the remote on the sofa beside her. Today, the living room was tidy and a small window at the back of the room had been left open so the normally musty room smelt fresh.

"Would you mind shutting that window for me, Nick?" Lizzie asked as he deposited the food on the table. "I can't reach it from here."

When the window was closed she said, "I'm assuming your mother's told you all about me. She is Maggie Potter, isn't she?" When Nick nodded she continued, "Maggie was one of the better girls at school, not like some of those other bitches. Someone famous once said, 'Anyone who says women should rule the world instead of men obviously never went to high school.' She was talking about our school." Lizzie lifted out a slice of pizza from the box closest to her and took a huge bite. "Tell your mother to come and see me," she said through her food. "I need to discuss something with her."

Lizzie ate her way efficiently and quickly through the first piece of pizza and started on the second, all the while talking to Nick, who eventually had to look away as half-chewed food dropped from her mouth, bounced off her shelf-like bust and came to rest in the folds of the voluminous filthy lap below.

"So, what do you do – apart from delivering food to disgusting fat cripples, that is," she asked.

The protest stopped on Nick's lips and he decided to let it go. "Just this. Trying to earn as much as I can to pay for design school in

Wellington next year. CADs. One day you might be playing one of my games."

But he could tell Lizzie's interest in him had waned. She'd eaten enough and was eager to get back to her game. Her fingers twitched, her eyes turned again to the screen and it came alive. A slim, agile young woman was leaping past every conceivable barrier to freedom.

"OK then," he said to Lizzie's back as he packed up the empty pizza box. He'd drop it in the bin at the bottom of the stairs. "See you tomorrow."

There was no word of thanks, no acknowledgment.

CHAPTER FOURTEEN

Maggie and Kate arrived separately at Elka's at two o'clock. Most of the lunch crowd had left, which suited them both. Maggie wanted to be able to talk openly; she didn't want their conversation overheard by nosy neighbours.

Elka waved to them from her table near the kitchen, where she was working on her laptop. "Kate and Maggie, my two favourite women in the world," she said, closing her computer. "Sit, sit," she called after exchanging kisses and a long hug with Kate. A waitress placed glasses of Prosecco in front of them while another staff member brought out an antipasto platter.

Elka raised her glass to Kate. "A toast, to the return of Kate, my favourite goddaughter. Welcome back."

"Your *only* goddaughter, I thought," said Kate.

"Exactly."

Elka fixed Kate with a beady stare and commanded imperiously, "News, Kate. And if you leave anything out, we will know!"

Kate took a tiny sip of the crisp clean wine then a deeper draught of water, and smiled. "What can I say? In a nutshell, two years ago I left, as you know, and travelled through Asia, as you know. I had a great time, broke up with Brett in Vietnam because he was more interested in Tiger Beer than he was in me, as you know. Went across Russia and Europe, as you know, and took the first job I could get in London, which was at Eric's restaurant in Mayfair, and I have been there ever since, as you know."

"And?"

"I worked like a dog. He didn't even know I was there, the place was so big. The sous chef gave me all the horrible jobs, and I mean horrible.

My poor hands. But 'head down bum up', as you always told me, and I slowly worked my way up the ranks. You must have read about the huge fight they had. Eric and Charlie. It made all the papers. Unlucky that the guest got in the way and ended up with a black eye. Lucky for Eric he'd ducked and it was Charlie who'd decked him. It meant Eric could call the police and fire poor Charlie on the spot. We were so busy after that – you know what they say. Any publicity is good publicity. Eric didn't have time to advertise and I was suddenly sous chef in a three-star restaurant. And then he opened the new place and I was left in charge. You've read my reviews, haven't you, Elka? Did I make you proud?"

"So proud. So very proud, Kate." Elka reached out and squeezed Kate's hand.

"But my two-year working visa expired and here I am, home again. No job and feeling a bit cast-off, to tell you the truth. I thought … well, never mind. Didn't happen."

The waitress came back and removed their glasses, checking first with Kate because her wine had hardly been touched. She brought fresh glasses and poured an excellent pinot grigio. The entrée consisted of three platters of freshly shucked plump deep sea Bluff oysters. On one platter, the oysters were au natural, on another they had been quickly battered and deep fried. On the third platter they were grilled with a salsa dressing.

Elka and Maggie started eating the oysters immediately. Kate nibbled on a piece of sour dough bread and creamy butter, both made daily in the kitchen.

"So," said Elka when she had had her fill of oysters. "Two questions. One, why didn't Eric, or the Master as he likes to be known, sponsor you to stay, and two, what are your plans?"

Kate flushed. "It's a long story so I'll only bore you with the good bits. He was really rude, even worse than Charlie. He didn't know who I was but he used to hurl hot pans at me when I wasn't looking, and yelled at me if anything wasn't up to standard and then he yelled at me when they were. When I was promoted he made fun of my Kiwi accent. I'd take him a new dish, which he'd rubbish, and two days later I'd find it on the menu. His menu. No credit to me. I so hated him, but he was – is – the most amazing cook. He's everything they say he is and his instincts for food are mind blowing. I put up with him and his tempers so I could learn from him. After he worked out there was nothing he could do to make me quit, he taught me so much. In the end I like to think he respected me, and that after a year we even got to be good friends."

Kate shot a glance at her mother. "Actually, more than good friends. For a while, that is, until I told him I had to leave. But only if he didn't sponsor me to stay, and he didn't. End of story."

Maggie and Elka exchanged looks. They hadn't expected this. Now her days in bed made sense. Maggie's heart wrenched to hear the sadness in her daughter's voice. She knew what it was like to have your heart broken. Bloody, bloody men.

"You know what you need, don't you, Kate?" said Maggie cheerily. "Work."

Elka shook her head fiercely, but Maggie took no notice.

"Kate, I've told you Elka has to go to Dunedin for an operation. You need a job, something to take your mind off this bastard, and Elka just happens to have one going, starting in the next few days. You need to get back in the kitchen where you belong and stop thinking about him."

Kate didn't look up. A tear dropped onto the tablecloth.

Elka sighed. "It's all right, Kate. You don't have to do it. I don't know what to do with your mother sometimes. She wants to organise the world despite what those around her might be feeling."

"I do not," said Maggie indignantly, rustling around in her handbag for tissues and handing one to Kate. "It's just that this makes sense all round. You need someone to look after the restaurant, and who better than Kate, who just happens to need something to take her mind off that bastard."

"Don't call him that, Mum."

"And I want you to stay with me so I can spoil you and look after you. You can't go traipsing off to Auckland or Wellington to work by yourself. We – Nick, Elka and I – are your family. We love you."

Kate blew her nose loudly on the tissue. Red-eyed, she looked up first at Elka and then at her mother.

"And I need to buy you some new clothes."

Kate groaned and rolled her eyes at Elka.

"The ones you brought back from London don't do you any credit at all. Kate, the sackcloth and ashes look does not become you!"

"At least I don't only wear black, Mum. Morning, noon and night." She turned to Elka, laughing, and said loudly, "You do know *everything* she wears is black – underwear, pyjamas the lot! And she dares to give *me* advice on how to dress."

There was a snort of stifled laughter from a table on the other side of the restaurant, and the three women looked over to see Ben Goodman trying unsuccessfully to look serious. He buried his head deeper into his paper.

"Sorry, Mum, I didn't mean to yell," said Kate quietly, and then signalling them to come closer, she whispered, "especially in front of the most eligible bachelor to hit town in years."

Now it was Elka's turn to smirk at Maggie's obvious discomfort. "Don't kick me," she said to Maggie. "She's your daughter."

"Mum's daughter and your stand-in chef," said Kate. "She's right, Elka. I do need something to do while I figure out the rest of my life, and since you taught me to cook, the least I can do is look after the place until you come back." She stopped and looked questioningly at Elka. "You are coming back, aren't you? I mean, this operation is nothing serious is it?"

"Of course she'll be back," said Maggie.

"I have no intention of leaving everything to you just yet, Kate."

Kate rubbed her hands together with relish. "I'm going to enjoy having my own kitchen while you're away. I have all sorts of ideas I want to try out but couldn't in London. It's going to be huge fun."

"I hope I'm not interrupting," said Ben, now standing behind them.

All three jumped.

"Clearly you are," said Maggie. Immediately she regretted her tone. Why was she always so abrupt and defensive when this man was around?

Elka glanced at Maggie with amusement. "Lovely to see you, Ben. You've met Maggie, but I'm not sure if you've met Kate, her daughter. She's just come home from London and is my saviour! This famous international chef, Kate Potter, is going to look after Elka's while I'm away. But I'm forgetting my manners – is there anything I can get for you?"

"No, Elka, I'm fine. You have to stop thinking about everyone else and relax. Kate and I have met briefly, as a matter of fact, and of course it's nice to see you again too, Maggie. I've had my questions answered. Just wanted to make sure you were set for Dunedin."

"Thanks, Ben. With Kate looking after the business and Maggie there for support, and with you to look after me when I get home, everything is under control."

"Wonderful," said Ben quietly.

There was an awkward silence as no one was quite sure what to say next.

"Goodness, is that the time?" he said, looking at his watch. "I have surgery in an hour and visits to do before then. Nice to see you again, Kate, Elka, Maggie." And nodding to the waiter to put his espresso on his account, he left the restaurant.

"What did he mean, Kate – *nice to see you again*? When did you meet him?"

Kate ignored her mother. "Did you see his watch? Eric, the bloody Master, bought one of those beasties to celebrate his third Michelin star, but he was poor for six months after and was too afraid to wear it. He never stopped talking about it, though, which is why I recognised it. This doctor is a bit of mystery, because methinks being a country GP does not pay that well, even in Queenstown."

Maggie wondered whether to say anything about the house at Lake Hayes, and Estelle's comments about family money, but thought better of it. Any money Ben Goodman had was his business.

Pudding was brought to the table and, having arranged their world to their satisfaction, the women tucked into the perfectly caramelised tarte Tatin served with fresh vanilla ice cream, something Elka had made in honour of Kate's return.

Kate was normally one to enjoy a great pudding, but she tasted just enough to tell Elka how good it was before passing on coffee and suggesting they visit the kitchen so she could meet the staff. Suddenly her daughter was all business, and Maggie listened while the two chefs organised the next few days.

After returning from the kitchen, the two of them pored over menus and talked food. As Kate quickly picked up the details around suppliers, ordering, and other necessary aspects of the business, Maggie watched her daughter with a mixture of pride and sadness. So grown up, so clever and so beautiful, and that bastard Eric had broken her baby's heart. The things she would say if she ever met him.

Nick arrived just as they were leaving. "Thought you'd be here. It's my day off tomorrow, Mum, the weather's supposed to be good and there's fresh snow. Can I tempt anyone to a day on the mountain?"

Kate and Elka both excused themselves.

"Mum?"

"You only want me to come so I can pay. All right. I don't have anything booked for tomorrow. A day on the mountain with my son is just what I need."

Nick gave Maggie a big hug. Now that he was taller she had no choice but to be hugged, not that she minded.

"By the way," he said as he let her go, "Lizzie Martin told me to tell you she wants to see you. No idea why, but she wants to ask you something. Not urgent. Come on, women, I need dinner and one of you has to cook it for me."

Just around the corner from Elka's, Mark and Lucy were standing in the doorway of the estate agents, with Estelle.

"It's a wonderful house, Estelle," said Mark. "It's exactly what we're looking for. A brilliant location and perfect for us. Make sure you tell the vendors the offer is cash with final settlement in a month, and if they're good with that, we'll come in after skiing tomorrow and confirm. Thank you for showing it to us."

"Mark, Lucy, an absolute pleasure," gushed Estelle. "I'll talk to them this evening and I'm sure there won't be a problem. It would be lovely to have you in the District. Good luck with your offer. I'll call you as soon as I hear anything."

Estelle watched Mark and Lucy walk arm in arm towards their car in the gathering darkness. They stopped, and Lucy framed Mark's face in her hands, bringing his lips gently down to meet hers.

Cynic though she was, Estelle found herself smiling at their happiness. She hoped it would last and they could indeed buy the house.

Her phone beeped and, wrapping her light pink pashmina tightly around her shoulders, she hurried inside to take the call. Thirty minutes later, flush with the adrenalin of a likely sale, she turned out the lights of her little office and locked the front door. On her desk in the dark, a big red Under Offer sticker had been placed across a photograph of the Lake Hayes house – a house that had been on the market for less than twenty-four hours.

"What recession?" she muttered to herself as she stepped onto the street, eager to buy herself a celebratory gin and tonic at Elka's before going home to her cottage and cat. There would be no one at home to share her triumph, which to Estelle was the one and only disadvantage to being single. She wanted a drink but not alone – not yet, anyway.

CHAPTER FIFTEEN

Maggie's father had taught her to ski. Her brother Simon was a natural, and impatient with it, so he'd left his father with his younger sister at the first opportunity, disappearing up the chairlift with this friends, only coming back at the end of the day to get a ride home.

Learning to ski with her father was Maggie's only fond memory of him. He was different on the mountain. He'd told her once that this was where he felt free to be himself, free to smile and laugh, away from the watchful gaze of the town. He knew the Coronet area backwards and his mountain craft was second to none.

Methodical in his instructions, he taught her the basics first. When he was sure she could negotiate any slope in any conditions, he took her over the summit and into the back basin where the powder was fresh and they could yell their exhilaration to the wind as they raced to the bottom.

If only he'd been like that at home, things might have been so different.

"What's done is done," Betty had said when Maggie, feeling bogged down in motherhood and work, had gone to see her. "Be grateful for the times you did have together. I remember your father when he was young, before he married your mother. Life wasn't kind to him, either. Do you think he wanted to be an undertaker?"

"Funeral director."

"Sorry. You know what I mean. There aren't many who get the life they dream of. He was an artist, a bit like your Nick, but after your grandfather died I never saw the paints again. Packed everything away and took over the business. He had a wife and two children to provide for. With no education to speak of and living in an out-of-the-way town, as it was then, what choices did he have? Be grateful you saw your father happy, even if it was only on the mountain. Now stop feeling sorry for yourself and go and look after your children."

Maggie remembered Betty's words as she drove into the car park. The place was packed and they were lucky to find a space. Her father wouldn't recognise the ski field now. The facility was huge, and attracted visitors from all over the world. Four- and six-person chairlifts radiating from the base area had opened up acres of runs of all levels. When her father had started skiing back in the fifties, the solitary rope tow could be frozen to the pulleys first thing in the morning, and skiers had to climb to the top carrying their skis just to get a run.

"Your grandfather would never believe it, if he was here now," Maggie said to Nick. "The snow-making machines take *my* breath away. I can't imagine what he would say."

"I win," said Nick, lifting their skis off the roof rack. "Kate owes me ten bucks."

"What for?"

"She bet me you'd have stopped talking about how it was different when Granddad started skiing, and I bet you hadn't. Thanks, Mum. Coffees are on her."

"God, I hate being so predictable. I'll give you twenty to tell her I never said a word."

"Done."

It was the sort of day when it's impossible not to feel alive and invigorated by the sun, the blue sky and the wonderfully crisp mountain air. Keen to get going they took the express quad up to the summit, and after checking bindings and goggles skated over to a ledge before effortlessly dropping off into one of the black runs to the left of the track. Nick, the better skier, took the lead. Maggie had been forced to concede that both her children had surpassed her skiing abilities by the time they were teenagers. Both had natural flair, but their courage came from her.

Maggie's skis sliced cleanly and evenly through the new snow, and they quickly arrived at the top of the more crowded Exchange drop before relaxing into the intermediate-level West Gates run and back to the tow queue. It was midweek, so the field was free of the crowds of university students and skiers from Dunedin who arrived at weekends, and the line was minimal. They were whisked back to the top of the mountain before Maggie had time to catch her breath.

From their vantage point on the chair, Nick pointed out a particularly good skier, his expertise making him stand out from the crowd as he carved his way down the mogul field beneath them.

"Great run, Doc," yelled Nick.

Ben Goodman skidded to a stop and looked up. "Wait for me at the top," he yelled back.

"There goes peace and quiet," said Maggie. "What did you do that for? I wanted to spend the day skiing with you, not someone I barely know. Plus he's really good!"

"Scared we'll leave you behind?" said Nick, punching his mother gently on her arm. "He's all right, Mum. You'll cope. You're not as old as you look."

Maggie retaliated with a punch of her own. Damn. There would be no getting out of a day with the boys.

"Nick, you lead the way," said Ben, as he skied off the chair towards them.

At least there was to be no small talk. *That's something*, Maggie thought as she waited for him to go past, assuming she would bring up the rear.

The rest of the morning passed in a blur of fast runs down the more difficult trails, with Nick and Ben taking it in turns to lead. As experienced and brave on the snow as Maggie was, she enjoyed watching the beauty of the two men skiing in front of her. Ben was afraid of nothing, and followed Nick's lead without hesitation, sure in his ability to ski his way down anywhere he was taken. Maggie was content to take alternative routes to their high-flying short circuits. More than once she saw both skiers find air, landing with a plump in a deep drift before lifting themselves up and out of the powder and heading straight down a chute, turning twice if at all.

The chairs carried between four and six people, so there was plenty of room on the way up. Maggie sat back and listened as Nick and Ben worked out their next route down. It was relaxing hearing them swap stories. Nick had the local knowledge, but Ben had skied all over the world. Working as a ski instructor had helped pay his way through medical school. There was no continent he hadn't skied. Nick asked question after question, and Ben's answers were detailed and entertaining. Maggie even detected a tinge of sadness in his voice when he talked about having to choose between skiing and medicine, and how he still wondered whether he'd made the right choice.

"You're very quiet, Maggie," said Ben, suddenly turning to her.

"Yes, Mum, not like you," taunted Nick. "Either you're going deaf or you're quietening down in your old age."

"Not many 'old' people can ski like your mother, mate," said Ben, rising surprisingly quickly to her defence. "Good to see you're consistent, even on the mountain, Maggie."

"Not sure what you mean."

"Black-black skis, boots, jackets, pants. The lot. Looks great, I have to say."

"Mum always wears black," chipped in Nick, unaware he was contributing to a discussion his mother didn't want to have.

"So I've heard," said Ben, "even to bed!"

"It's easier," said Maggie, defensively. "I don't have to think about clothes when I get up in the morning, or in the middle of the night or when I go skiing."

"The fact you look great in black has nothing to do with it, of course," he said staring straight ahead. "Just because black suits you, showing off your blonde hair and blue eyes to perfection – that doesn't mean anything."

Maggie looked at him. How infuriating he was.

"No, I do understand, I do," he said. "It's your work. You have to wear black, doesn't she, Nick?"

Maggie felt herself colouring. "I warn you, Nick, uninvited comments about my choice of clothes can make it hard to get down the mountain at the end of the day."

"Don't worry, Nick," said Ben. "The doctor wearing red can drive you home in his blue car. Wouldn't want to see you stranded just because your mother has gone a bit dark."

Maggie and Nick groaned in unison as the chair reached the top.

"Lunch after this run?" asked Ben, and skied off before either could answer.

Maggie watched him make his first turn. No man had noticed what she wore – far less commented on it – for years. It felt strange, but it also felt nice. Just this once she would let it go. Her tummy rumbled loudly. Until now she hadn't realised how hungry she was.

Later, in the queue at the cafeteria, Ben leaned forward. "Autumn colours would suit you as much as black," he said, reaching forward to ladle soup into a bowl. "Think about it."

Maggie was flabbergasted. She barely knew this man, but more to the point he barely knew her. She'd let it go once, but twice would be encouraging him. She had to stop it now. But as she turned to say something, she accidentally knocked his arm, and hot soup spilled onto his hand. He dropped the bowl, which shattered on the floor, sending soup everywhere.

Maggie grabbed some serviettes and handed them to Ben. "Here, use these. I'm sorry I knocked your arm but I guess I've had enough advice for today." She picked up her tray and left him to clean up the mess.

The cafeteria was full of hungry skiers eager to talk about their morning. Sun poured in through the windows, melting the snow carried in on boots into puddles on the concrete floor. In one corner a group of elderly Chinese tourists, there to see the view rather than to ski, looked around uncertainly, overwhelmed by the noise. In another corner, three Australian families had commandeered tables where the mothers were busy handing out food to a pack of eager children, while their older siblings sat facing the wall, heads down, mortified at having to eat in public with them. Fathers were kept busy going backwards and forwards to the servery for more food and a stream of hot drinks. Outside, the tables on the veranda were less busy due to a cool wind, but doors still swung open and closed as orders were made and delivered.

Nick looked from Maggie to Ben as they ate their food, wondering how the mood between them could change so quickly. Sitting across from each other, they might as well have been on opposite sides of the planet. Eye contact was studiously avoided, and neither spoke as they consumed their lunch as efficiently and quickly as Nick had seen anyone eat. Ever.

Nick was just about to clear away their trays and suggest they head back up, when a request for a doctor came over the public speaker system.

Ben stared down at the table in front of him.

"Aren't you going to go?" asked Maggie.

"Only if no one else volunteers. It's bound to be nothing the ski patrol can't handle, if they think about it."

"It didn't sound like nothing."

"I haven't been on a ski field yet where there weren't at least ten doctors around. One of them can go. This is my day off."

A tow operator appeared at the table. "I knew I'd seen you here, Doc. Can you come and help?"

Ben got up and smiled. "Of course. I was just coming."

Maggie snorted.

Ben ignored her. "What's the problem – Pete, isn't it?"

"Yip, Doc, that's me. Arthur our paramedic went off to fetch a broken leg down the mountain and hasn't come back, and now something else has come up. Sorry to bother you," he added, heading for the door.

Nick and Maggie had finished their lunch, so they followed on behind in case there was anything they could do to help. Both had done ski rescue work in the past and were used to dealing with minor injuries.

It was a short walk to the tow shed at the bottom of the quad lift. Once there, an attendant pointed up at a chair slowly making its way down the mountain. It was the only one that wasn't empty.

The attendant, who quickly introduced himself as Luke, spoke with an American accent. He was young with an unruly mop of blond hair held back with a blue bandana. Intelligent brown eyes framed a darkly tanned face, his white neck just visible at the top of his jacket.

Squinting, he pointed towards the chair which was now on its descent.

"Something weird is going on with those folks," he said. "They went all the way to the top and came all the way down again, and rode around here and didn't get off. They're skiers, and not tourists, because they're both wearing ski boots, but they haven't got skis or poles. It's a couple and she looks like she's hugging him and he's not moving. I called out, but nothing. I've closed the tow while I was waiting for help."

The radio on his hip crackled. "*Hey Luke, there are skis and poles under the chair about halfway up. It looks like they flicked them off.*"

"When they get here, I'll slow the chair then stop it," Luke replied. "They better not be messing around 'cos if they are, I'll feed them to this ugly crowd behind me."

Luke ducked across to talk to the queue. They heard him telling some very irritated people to go to the other tows because this one would be closed for a while. The crowd murmured fretfully, but it wasn't long before most had left, only a few remaining to see what the fuss was about.

When the couple's chair was two pylons from the bottom, Luke slowed the tow down to walking pace. Five pairs of eyes stared up at the pair as the chair came slowly closer and stopped.

A woman looked at them over the shoulders of a man slumped in her arms. There was silence as the engine cooled and cut out. Ben walked over, knelt down in front of them and lifted the woman's arm from around the man cradled against her. He reached up to the man's neck and felt for a pulse.

"He's dead, isn't he?" the woman asked, her face streaked with tears.

Ben nodded.

Maggie looked at the pale lifeless face slumped against the woman's chest. Ben reached in to separate them, and the man's head dropped lifelessly backwards, his lips blue. A string of saliva dangled slackly from the corner of his mouth. The woman bent forward and put her head in her hands.

"I'm Ben. Can I ask who you are?"

Without looking up, the woman said, "Lucy. I'm Lucy and this is Mark. Mark Holmes."

A great gulping sob escaped her as she reclaimed her man, grasping him and rocking him in her arms, not ready to let him go again.

Luke swallowed and brushed his eyes. Looking around for something to do, he walked over to the barrier and shooed away the gawpers and sightseers hanging around to see what was happening.

Maggie's first instinct was to wrap the poor woman in her arms, but all Lucy wanted to do was to hold onto Mark.

"What happened?" asked Ben quietly.

"We were talking about the house we're buying when Mark just stopped," said Lucy. "One minute we were working out how to find more money and then nothing. He looked at me and nothing. I couldn't believe it. We were right in the middle up there, about twenty metres above the snow. There was nowhere to get help. The chair kept moving. There was nothing I could do. I couldn't get us off at the top and the guy didn't see me. So I reached down and flicked our skis off. I thought if I held him, he would be … By then, we were on our way down again and I knew there was no hope of getting help in time. I knew he was gone."

"I'm so sorry," said Ben. "You're right, there was nothing you could have done. We can't stay here, Lucy. I need to ask you to help us."

Lucy looked at Ben and nodded.

"We'll get him off the chair and then down the mountain. Maggie, behind you, is going to help." He looked at Maggie. "You have your vehicle here don't you, Maggie? It'll be easier than calling an ambulance or helicopter."

Maggie reached into her pocket for the keys and tossed them to Nick so he could fetch the 4WD.

"Luke? Have you got a stretcher and a blanket?" asked Ben.

Maggie helped Lucy to a seat, holding her hand while Luke and Ben gently lifted Mark's body onto the stretcher. Then Nick, Ben, Pete and Luke carried it down the slope to the first aid station where they sorted out forms and worked out what to do next. Ben meanwhile called the police, and it was agreed it would be best to take Mark down to The Stables.

While this was going on, Lucy sat hunched up against a wall unable to speak, staring at the body under the blanket on the stretcher beside her.

"Do you know anyone here in town?" Ben asked when he put down the phone. "Is there someone we can call to meet you?"

Lucy shook her head wearily. "No one apart from Estelle, the estate agent, but I don't think this is quite her field, do you? No, Mark's the only person I know here. We're staying at the Lodge."

Nick appeared in the doorway to let them know Maggie's 4WD was outside. Lucy followed the stretcher out before looking up in horror to see a hearse.

"I'm a funeral director," said Maggie weakly.

When everything was secure and Lucy was tucked up in a blanket in the front seat, Ben gave Lucy's car keys to Nick and suggested he collect up their gear and meet them back at Maggie's. Ben would follow them down.

"Just one question before you go, Lucy," said Ben, leaning through Maggie's window. "Are you from Auckland?"

Lucy nodded.

"Your husband isn't a surgeon, is he?"

"He's not my husband, but he is a surgeon. Cardiac."

"I thought I recognised the name."

Lucy didn't look up. She was shivering in the draught coming through the open window.

Maggie saw the exhaustion on her face, "Let's go, shall we?"

Ben stepped back and she closed the window, turned the heater on full blast and drove down the mountain, Lucy crying quietly beside her.

CHAPTER SIXTEEN

By the time Ben arrived at The Stables later that afternoon, Nick and Maggie had put Mark's body in one of the chillers. Maggie and Lucy were sitting in front of a roaring fire drinking freshly brewed coffee while Nick refilled the large wood basket. The room was warm and Lucy's colour had improved considerably, but there was no mistaking she was both numb and exhausted by the events of the day.

"I called into the police station on my way here," said Ben, explaining why he was so late. "I've organised most of what needs to be done, but Lucy, I'm sorry, a constable will be here soon to ask you a few questions. I know it's a bad time, but I'll take you back to the Lodge as soon as all the official stuff is over. I forgot to ask, Maggie, but I hope that's all right with you?"

Maggie watched bemused as Ben, confident that everything he did would be fine with those round him, poured himself a coffee before sitting down in an armchair in front of the fire. He looked so at ease in her kitchen she had to remind herself it was the first time he'd been to her home.

"There are a few things we need to ask you, Lucy. I'm sorry," said Ben. "From what you've told me I'm guessing there are other people we need to contact, such as Mark's wife."

Lucy and Maggie exchanged looks. They'd been talking before he arrived, and once Lucy had started, it was if a dam had broken. Maggie was apparently the first person Lucy had ever told about the affair. There was no one in Auckland she could confide in, she said, because for the past five years her social life had revolved solely around Mark. She felt guilty about the deceit but what could she do? She loved him, and he'd said he loved her and had begged her to wait.

Lucy was also a doctor – an anaesthetist, she'd explained. That was how they'd met. His wife knew about the affair, but preferred to pretend it wasn't happening. Mark had felt duty bound to stay with her for the sake of their children. Of course he felt bad about the sacrifices Lucy had made, but had promised to make it up to her.

They'd been about to buy a house at Lake Hayes; there had been some last-minute problem with price and another bidder, but nothing they couldn't have sorted out.

And now, just when it had seemed everything was going the way they'd dreamed, he'd died and left her alone with nothing. She wouldn't be able to share their relationship with anyone, or grieve for him in public.

Maggie hadn't reacted when Lucy talked about the house. Instead she'd held Lucy's hand, and when the woman started to cry again, tried to comfort this person she barely knew, attempting to sooth some of the pain away.

"Did Mark have any health issues, anything he'd seen a doctor about recently?" asked Ben.

"None. He would have told me. We had no secrets. No medications, nothing. He's a runner and really fit." She looked up at Ben. "He'll need a post mortem, won't he, to find out why?"

"Most likely," he said. "The coroner usually requests one in these situations, but I suppose it depends ultimately on what his wife and his doctor back home say."

Lucy flinched as if she'd been struck. "I'm sure she won't add anything I don't know. They weren't close. It was me he loved, you know, not her."

Maggie and Ben looked awkwardly at each other.

"Lucy, I know how stressful this is for you and I promise I'll get you back to the Lodge soon," Ben persevered gently, "but his wife is his next of kin, and she'll most likely need to come down and identify his body.

After that he will go through to Dunedin for the post mortem. Look – I'm sorry, but I think I know his wife."

"You know her? How?"

"Jude and my ex-wife are best friends."

Maggie heard the words "ex-wife" and something inside her froze. *Don't be so silly*, she thought. *What does it matter to you?* But her heart, beating heavily in her chest, told her otherwise.

Ben was talking; he hadn't noticed her lapse in attention. "They were friends at school. That's why I recognised Mark's name. I never met him, though. We were both too busy working when I was married to Sarah, and our paths never crossed. I can imagine Jude will want to take charge as soon as she gets here."

"There'll be no room for me then," said Lucy angrily. "She knows about us. Three years ago she threatened to leave and clean him out financially if he didn't end our relationship. It was all talk on her part. She had no intention of leaving. He was her meal ticket. The kids didn't come into it, she was only thinking of herself. But it's too late now. He's gone and she's his widow. That woman who made him so unhappy will own his memory as well as everything else."

Maggie and Ben let Lucy talk herself out. There was nothing either of them could say or do that would help. Maggie's thoughts turned to Ben again. *Ex-wife, ex-wife* reverberated through her head until she called a halt. *Of course he's been married. He's too old to be single and he's not gay, so of course he has history. History, which is none of your business.*

To everyone's immense relief, a young policeman finally arrived with the necessary forms from the coroner. He confirmed Mark's wife's contact details and said he would organise for someone at the Auckland station to visit her.

"Are there children?" he asked. "It helps the person in Auckland to know what to say." Despite his callow appearance it seemed he understood Lucy had not shared a public relationship with the deceased. Nevertheless he took her contact details, telling her he'd be in touch tomorrow, as he needed a statement before she returned to Auckland.

The formalities over, Ben helped Lucy into his car.

"Rough day," he said to Maggie through the open window as he turned the ignition. "I'll call later to make sure you're OK."

"There's absolutely no need. I'm fine."

He looked at her carefully then shrugged. "If you say so."

Back in the house, Maggie put more wood on the fire, stirring the flames higher, grateful for the extra heat. Standing with her back to the fireplace she smiled at Nick as he ventured downstairs, now all the fuss was over.

"Ben hoped you'd follow him out to the Lodge in their Porsche and give him a ride back to town."

"No problem," he replied. "Funny way for the day to turn out."

"Certainly was," said Maggie. She looked at her watch. "Good grief, is that the time? I've got to get some things together for Jilly's funeral tomorrow and it's late. Poor Jilly. Don't you let me be buried without someone there to say goodbye, will you Nick?"

"I thought you wanted to be cremated?" he said.

"I do, but not without the traditional wailing, beating of chests and rending of clothes. There has to be some acknowledgement of my passing to show the world I existed. Don't you forget that – rending and wailing at the very least, even if you don't mean it. And make sure you let Kate know what's expected. I want the full show at my funeral."

"I'll drop the car back and no hurry, by the way."

"For what?"

"Your funeral."

CHAPTER SEVENTEEN

It was one in the morning in Los Angeles, but Tim James wanted to see his son. He figured it was only the night nanny's rest he was disturbing, and he wasn't paying her to sleep.

The Skype connection was annoyingly slow and kept freezing before skipping ahead, totally frustrating his long-distance attempt at fatherhood. His son had the good grace to look confused at the larger-than-life face of this strange man making goo-goo noises on the giant screen in his nursery.

"Don't tell Jenny about this," he'd said to the nanny when she'd gasped at the bandage on his head above his swollen eye. "It looks worse than it is and I'll tell her, but not yet." He hoped the press didn't get to her first.

Jenny had been out when he'd called her earlier, and then the day's events had overtaken his good intentions. He wanted to make sure she was alone and no one could overhear their conversation when he told her about the accident. Jenny was the only woman apart from his mother who could tell when he was lying, so he'd have to come clean about it. So far Matt had been able to keep things quiet, even though some of the news-hungry paps were still camped outside the gates of the Lodge.

He had been lucky that Doc Goodman was at the Lodge already when the helicopter had landed on the lawn. Bringing back another guest whose partner had died, he was told, but Tim didn't care. All he cared about was the repair job on his face and from what Tim had been able to see, it looked like the doc had done a brilliant job hiding what would be a scar in one of the "character lines" on his forehead. It would mean an end to the botox, which was a pity. Although he could grow his hair – that would cover it.

He'd hoped to spend a few days recovering quietly at the Lodge, but his insurance company required him to fly up to Auckland the next day to get a second opinion from a plastic surgeon. His face was his fortune and any scar would be magnified in every close-up shot, so it had to be the best repair possible.

"Now hold up my little guy so I can get a good look at him," he ordered the nanny.

"But he's asleep."

"He is not."

"Well, he isn't now."

"What did you say?"

"Nothing, Mr James, here he is. Isaac, say hello to your daddy, who is all the way across the sea in Australia."

"New Zealand."

"Aren't they the same?"

"No they are not." Tim was getting impatient with this nanny. Too chatty by half. He wanted to talk to his son, not her.

"Damned isolated country with goddamned slow internet," he cursed as the screen froze again. He didn't want to upset his son, but the painkillers were wearing off and he had one hell of a headache. Truth be told he also felt a bit foolish. He should have paid more attention to Mike, and everyone from Jimmy down to the caterers knew the accident probably wouldn't have happened if he had.

The baby took one look at his father's bandage-clad face grimacing at him and broke into howls of tears. For a brief moment he stopped crying to take a breath, and opened his eyes, but his daddy's unfamiliar face still loomed over him and he screamed and writhed in the nanny's arms, inconsolable.

The nanny was obviously displeased and suggested maybe Mr James should call it a night so she could settle his son. Tim could only acquiesce graciously. She could wait. The screen went blank as she cut the connection. He would see that young madam when he got home. If he wanted to see his son at any time of the night or day, he expected the staff to make sure it would be the best father-son bonding experience money could buy. When he called home he didn't expect to have to deal with a screaming baby and a stroppy young woman telling him his time was up.

Tim had been enchanted when, twelve weeks ago, the baby had been put in his arms to hold while Jenny's abdomen was stitched up. Isaac had looked at him with the blurry eyes of a newborn and Tim's heart had melted. Since then, he had hardly seen the boy. He'd been finishing a film in Spain and had flown home for the birth before going straight back for another month. The few days in LA on his way to New Zealand had been spent in meetings and attending social functions.

"I have to be seen and so do you," he'd told Jenny. "We can see Isaac later."

But the days had passed quickly and the next minute here he was in New Zealand with a bandage over his forehead.

Tonight, though, had provided one consolation to the distant father. Peering closely at the frozen-screen baby Isaac, Tim had caught sight of a small pear-shaped mole he hadn't seen before on the back of his son's neck. When he'd seen the blemish, his own hand had moved unconsciously to rub the very same mole on the back of his own neck. Headache forgotten, Tim's heart had lurched with joy and with the overwhelming relief that indeed the boy was truly, and beyond doubt, his boy.

"I really, really am a father," he whispered.

Against Doc Goodman's orders Tim poured himself a congratulatory whisky and stepped out onto his snowy veranda to smoke one of the bespoke hand-rolled Cuban cigars he allowed himself each night to compensate for being away from home. The doctor had advised no stimulants and lots of rest, but what did he know? Truth be told, Tim relished his after-dinner cigar but employed a myriad of excuses to convince himself he was actually a non-smoker.

It was a calm, clear evening, and the sky above the lake was scattered with stars. They were brighter here, far away from the lights of the civilised world. Taking his time to exhale a cloud of thick luxuriant smoke redolent with the scent of the tropics, Tim let the stillness envelop him. The nicotine surged through his blood, giving him the brain hit he craved at this time of day, but making his headache suddenly much worse. Even the whisky had turned against him. Instead of soothing his palate, it burned his throat and was making him nauseous.

He tossed the still lit cigar onto the lawn in front of him and tipped the single malt into a plant box. Feeling distinctly unwell, he heard the sound of a woman's muffled sobs from one of the other cottages.

Knowing that another guest, a man, had died skiing that afternoon, he surmised the sounds of distress coming from next door, must be from his wife or girlfriend. Tim shivered at this uninvited proximity to loss, his awareness heightened by his own near miss in the boat this morning. He went inside shutting the door tightly behind him, and after tossing down some more painkillers settled in front of the fire to do some work.

Later, when he'd almost forgotten about the whole business, one of his staff, dropping off a script for his approval, made an inane remark about the death of his neighbour, and how important it was to seize each day because you just never know what's going to happen next. Tim had snapped at the young guy, telling him to keep his T-shirt philosophy to himself.

People had said the same stupid thing at the few funerals he'd been unable to avoid attending, and it always irritated him intensely. He always made a point of seizing each day so tightly he was afraid that if he seized it any harder it would kill him. For as long as he could remember, he'd extracted every single precious moment not only from his life but also from the lives of the characters he played. He had no patience with passive passengers on life's great journey.

When he was alone again, he tried to settle in front of the fire and check the requested additions to the script. The noise of the woman wailing next door was just audible. Obviously the thick floor-to-ceiling curtains on the windows and the solid walls of the buildings were not enough to block out the loud crying of a woman in grief.

The man was dead, for chrissake – nada, nothing. His body would rot or be burned in the next few days, leaving the world to the living.

It was the way of things and it terrified Tim. He couldn't imagine not being alive, here on earth, making things happen. The thought of not seeing, hearing, feeling, breathing, fucking his wife, or anyone else's wife for that matter; of the world going on without him as if he didn't matter, filled him with dread. Rationally he knew, of course, that his own death was totally inevitable, and he wasn't so stupid as to not understand that. But it drove him each waking moment to strive even harder to be the best, the winner in the only game in town, the man who was not forgotten, and would never be forgotten. He would live forever in his films. Tim was prepared to consider the possibility of death only when he decided he'd had enough. His accident today was a wake-up call to be more careful.

Thoughts of his mother arrived unbidden and unwelcome. If anyone was going to die, it should be her – his ageing but very lippy mother. It was her turn next, and then maybe he would get some peace from her public jibes about how mean he was with money and what a bad son he was. Ungrateful bitch. He'd made her famous and now she was tittle tattling about him to the press.

Did she think the cheap women's magazines whose pages she frequented would take any notice of her moans of neglect and deprivation were she not the mother of the multi-award winning, world famous, fabulously wealthy and handsome actor, Tim James?

He'd put up with her snarky comments for years before deciding he had to cut her off so she wouldn't bleed him dry. Then she really *would* have something to moan about. It had worked up to a point. Having to work for a living meant she had less time to hassle him and the scum journalists who believed her, so gradually her whines of poverty and neglect had drifted into the ether of rumour and back-handed asides. He'd bought her a house so she had somewhere to live, and his conscience was clear, but that didn't make for a story. No one wanted to know what he had done for her, just what he hadn't – and his mother had a list as long as your arm.

Her life wasn't that bad, he thought, as he fingered the bandage on his head. We all have to work. Working keeps you healthy, especially at her age. She should be thanking him, not bad-mouthing him.

Tim turned on the TV, but the face of that annoying little jerk Jonathon Bramble filled the screen. Rather than flick through the channels to find something worth watching, he clicked it off.

The silence was broken by the sounds from next door.

Normally he would have called management and complained, but he knew how it would look if he did. It was such a small town, and no matter how much discretion was promised it would be bound to get out that he was a callous and unsympathetic bastard who didn't respect a woman's grief.

Returning to his armchair beside the open fire, he picked up the house phone and spoke to the duty manager.

"Tim James here. I know it's late, but you guys are fabulous and can do anything," he schmoozed. "Would you please send a very large bouquet of flowers to the poor woman in the cottage next to mine? I feel I have to do something. Yes, it has to be tonight. Just a small card, and if you could write, 'With sympathy for your loss, Tim James', I will be more than grateful. Whatever it costs," he added, leaving the rest to the duty manager's imagination.

"Of course, Mr James," came the reply. "My name is Geoff Banks and I would be happy to organise that for you. And may I say how thoughtful of you. It will be done within the hour. Good night, Sir."

Tim gave himself a mental pat on the back. Word of his kind gesture would no doubt spread, but possibly too slowly to be of use, particularly if there was no guiding hand. He messaged his PR manager and explained why there would be an expensive bill for flowers on his account. He knew Matt would understand the point of the message – and soon the rest of the world would know he had sent flowers in the middle of the night to a grieving widow.

There was no point in working now, so he went to bed. Just as he drifted off to sleep, the crying stopped.

CHAPTER EIGHTEEN

Maggie punched a code into the number pad set into one of the stone pillars at the bottom of Jilly's drive. The gates swung open noiselessly. Driving up to the house she was puzzled to see lights blazing from every room. It was supposed to be empty. She didn't see another car but the garage door was shut, so maybe someone had put their car inside out of the cold. Perhaps it was the cleaning lady forgetting to turn things off, she thought. She peered through the windows into the brightly lit interior looking for anything unusual, but nothing seemed out of place.

Dressed in her usual black she was instantly absorbed into the shadows, almost invisible to anyone looking out. Sticking to the dark patches around the house and clutching her phone for security, Maggie tiptoed around the outside of the house looking for signs of an intruder, her heart beating heavily in her chest.

You're an idiot, she thought. What if someone is here?

She looked toward the gates and the snow falling softly on the gravel drive. Her heavy snowboots meant running wasn't an option. Not fast, anyway. And there was no way she could climb those gates, even if she did get that far.

If there *was* an intruder, the best place to be would be the car. She'd have to get back there, lock the doors and call the police. Maybe sound the horn for the neighbours.

Good plan, she thought, and tiptoed round the next corner only to trip and fall over a garden hose. She sat on the ground for a minute, waiting to see if she'd been heard, but there was no sound; no footsteps of someone coming to find out about the noise. She was alone. She got up, dusting the light snow off her jacket, and started walking back to the front door. *Get what you need from the house and skedaddle*, she said to herself.

Suddenly two strong arms reached around her from behind, pinning her hard against a man's chest. Too surprised and terrified to scream, Maggie's survival instincts and self-defence training took over. She lifted one boot and crunched it down hard on the man's foot behind her, kicking the other backwards into his shin. His vice-like hold on her loosened and leaning forwards, she tumbled free and was off, back to her car. Locking the doors she fumbled for her phone, and at the same time pounded on the horn shattering the still night air.

The man came hurtling round the corner after her, his shape silhouetted against the house lights, and thumped hard into the front of her car. It shook, but Maggie didn't look up. She was concentrating on trying to stop shaking so she could punch in the emergency number. This was easier said than done as she tried to hit the correct numbers on the tiny screen, but to no avail – she had to try again. She huddled over the gear stick, willing herself to get it right, refusing to look outside her safe zone. She knew he could see her in the light from the screen, but she couldn't see him. He was just a very scary shape looming in the dark outside, trying to get to her, to do God knows what.

It took another moment or two of sheer panic for her to slowly register that her attacker was calling her name.

"Maggie. For goodness sake, Maggie – it's me! Open the door!"

Maggie took her hand off the horn and peered through the window. Ben Goodman's pained and panting face was looking back at her. It took another minute for her to process the fact that it was indeed the good doctor, the man who had been drinking coffee in her living room that afternoon. She didn't know him particularly well, and it *was* possible he could be an axe murderer, but on balance she thought she was probably safe.

"*Fire, Police or Ambulance?*" a voice asked from her lap.

"It's all right," said Maggie, putting the phone to her ear. "Pocket dial. Sorry."

She unlocked the door and got out of the car. Ben stepped back and let her go first into the house. She jumped at the sound of the door closing behind her.

"What are you doing here?" she asked, trying to sound confident.

"I could ask you the same thing," he said, bending down to rub the front of his shin. "What are you doing sneaking around my house and peering in the windows at this hour of the night? For an undertaker you sure get around."

"Funeral director," said Maggie.

"Ah yes, funeral director. That makes all the difference, doesn't it? Come into the kitchen and warm up. Then you can tell me why you're here."

Maggie perched on a stool, keeping the bench between them, willing herself to stop shaking before he noticed.

"You look very pale," he said. He took a glass from one of the cupboards, filled it from the tap and passed it over. "Drink this."

Maggie didn't need to be told twice. She sipped the water slowly until it was all gone and her shaking had stopped. She felt him staring at her, and looked up.

Ben was leaning back against the fridge, his arms folded across his chest. "Is it good luck for the first guest in your new house to be an undertaker – sorry, funeral director – do you think?"

"*Your* house? But Lucy told me she and Mark had bought this house."

"They certainly made an offer, but I was able to top them and my offer was formally accepted by the vendor this afternoon, just after I dropped Lucy off at the Lodge." He paused and looked around. "I've had lots of houses, but this one ... there's something very special about it, don't you think?" His eyes sparkled and Maggie heard the excitement in his voice.

Damned if she was going to get caught up in his mood. All she could see was Lucy crying in her living room only a few hours ago, lamenting the loss of her lover just as they were finally going to be happy together in this very house.

"It's stunning. It's the most fabulous house I've ever seen." Then, before she could stop herself, "Lucy loved it."

Ben froze. "Yes, but–"

"But what?" said Maggie. "It must have been an interesting drive back to the Lodge this afternoon. Just long enough for you to convince her to withdraw her offer so you could step in and buy it. And here you are, triumphant. Mark not dead twelve hours. The woman's broken heart just a stepping stone for you to get what you want."

"It was nothing like that."

"Really?"

"Yes, really. Do you think I would do something like that?"

"I don't know you."

"No, you don't." He sighed, the excitement in his voice gone. "So what are you doing here? Shouldn't you be tucked up in bed, sound asleep in your black pyjamas?"

"What I wear to bed is none of your business."

"Then why are you here, creeping around in the dark? Did you follow me?"

"That's ridiculous. Of course I didn't follow you. Why would I? I'm not interested in you."

"You've made that perfectly clear. So? Explain."

"I came to get Jilly's things for her funeral tomorrow. Not that it's any of your business. Why are *you* here? You may have signed the contract, but that's all you've done. Estelle should be shot for giving you a key."

"It's not her fault. I persuaded her against her better judgement."

"And you always get what you want, don't you?"

"I give up, Maggie. You do what you need to. I'll be in the garage."

Maggie watched him leave and could have kicked herself. *Why am I such a bitch?* But she knew. It was better to ruin any chance of something good happening in her life, before it happened. No more broken hearts, no more disappointment. Much better to be safe than sorry later.

So why was she feeling sorry now? *Stop it*, she thought. *As if he would ever be interested in you. How could he ever be? Now hurry up and get out of here.*

She was pleased to see the empty wine bottles in Jilly's bedroom had been taken away, even if the cleaning hadn't been done. Pushing aside dress after dress in the crowded wardrobe, she couldn't help thinking about Ben talking Lucy out of buying the house when she was so vulnerable. Because that's what he must have done. Lucy was so sure they'd bought it. Were doctors allowed to take advantage of distressed patients? She'd check later, she thought. But I'd better hurry or I'll never get out of here, and he'll think I'm hanging around just to see him.

Finally she decided on a simple blue sheath with long sleeves and a collar heavy with gold embroidery. Perfect, elegant, and simple but rich – just like she imagined Jilly must have been before alcohol stole her life.

Hunting through a chest of drawers for underwear, Maggie caught sight of her reflection in the mirror above. The woman looking back at her took note of the black clothes and waggled her finger warningly, before smiling back ruefully. I look fine. Damn him, who cares what he thinks?

There must have been at least twenty photos from Jilly's life displayed on one of the walls, in a spare bedroom, the early ones in black and white. Her baby photo and her first day at school; a photo of her in a ball dress being presented to a bishop, and next to that, one of the Auckland lawyer and Jilly on their wedding day, eyes only for each other. There was a professional photo of the two of them bending over their daughter's bassinet, their love for the baby unmistakable.

The holiday snap of the three of them at the beach marked a different era. Their daughter was looking up at them as they stood apart, smiles forced. After that, the photos were only of Jilly and her daughter, the lawyer noticeable by his absence. In her daughter's graduation photo,

Jilly was thin, her face lined and her hair grey and in need of a wash. Her daughter looked as if she couldn't wait for it all to be over.

The last photo was the same as the one in Jilly's bedroom, and showed a successful businesswoman sitting at a desk in front of a window overlooking Central Park in New York. Her daughter had written on it, "*To Mum, If I can make it here ...*"

Maggie chose the one or two photos in which Jilly looked truly happy. Stripping them from their frames, she tucked them into a tote bag with the underwear, picked up the dress and a pair of matching shoes she'd found in their box in the bottom of the wardrobe, and walked back through the silent house to her car.

The light was on in the garage. She called out goodnight to Ben, and he replied but didn't come out to see her off.

Maggie thought she'd feel relieved when the house gates shut automatically behind her and she was on the road back to Queenstown. But all she felt was regret, and she didn't want to let herself think about the reasons why.

CHAPTER NINETEEN

"Kate, have you got Lizzie's order ready yet?" asked Nick, poking his head through the door to the kitchen.

"Over there," she said, inclining her head in the direction of the pizza bag and the box of coke, before turning back to talk to Elka.

"Don't worry," she said, "I promise I'll look after it as if it's my own."

"That's what I'm afraid of," replied Elka. "You'll do so well and make such a name for yourself, there won't be room for me when I'm ready to return. I know what you young chefs are like."

"Elka, one of the most important things Eric taught me was the importance of consistency. There are two sorts of diners who come here. The first are the regulars – they know what to expect and that's why they keep coming back. The second are the new customers, the tourists who have heard or read about Elka's and want a special night out. They'll love it no matter what, just on your reputation, great food and excellent service. So as long as I follow everything you've shown me, it'll be fine. They come for the Elka experience, not the Kate Potter one. So please, I don't want you stressing out before your operation. I'll be working hard to make sure every customer who walks through that door gets the Elka experience with maybe the chance to try a little Kate Potter dining on the side."

Elka held open her arms to Kate. As they hugged, she said, "You're a wonderful girl, young Kate. I've been so worried."

Stepping back from the hug, Elka looked quizzically at her. "You've put on weight. It's all very well enjoying your food, but be careful, no room in a small kitchen for a fat cook."

"That's a bit harsh, even for you, Elka. It's because I haven't been working for a few weeks. Can't wait to get busy again and get rid of it."

"Just keep it the way I've left it. No heroics."

"Done. Now go home and pack. Mum's excited because she hasn't been to Dunedin for ages and wants to go shopping. She says she needs new clothes. Please, Elka, talk her out of buying more black. It's so depressing, isn't it Nick?" said Kate.

Nick nodded, unsure what he was agreeing to. Then following Kate's lead, they shepherded Elka outside to her car. Nick wrapped Elka in a big hug, told her he loved her and would see her soon. Kate followed suit. Elka shut the car door and set off, as the two young people she had watched grow up waved her off down the road. She tried to reassure herself again that Kate understood and respected her fears for the restaurant. If only the operation was over and done with and she could get back to normal life – cured.

Until now she'd never had a day's illness, something she'd put down to giving up cigarettes, keeping fit and staying away from doctors. Now this horrible thing was lurking inside her and she had to depend on strangers for help. There had been a lot of stories of surgical botch-ups in the papers recently, and she was worried. What if something went wrong? Thank goodness Ben had given her some sleeping tablets, with strict instructions to take one if not two tonight so she got a good night's sleep. She planned to do just that. She just needed to clean her house from top to bottom first.

Kate felt Nick looking at her as, arms raised, she waved goodbye. She knew what her predictable brother would say next, and he didn't disappoint.

"Kate, you definitely put on weight when you were away."

Taking a deep breath, she chose not to react the way she usually did when he made comments about her appearance. Normally he had to quickly duck the blow that followed – Kate had never believed in pulling her punches, no matter how many times Maggie had told her off. Today, all she did was shrug before loosening her apron over her chef's clothes and muttering something about never trusting a thin cook, before she disappeared back into the kitchen to oversee the prep work for tonight's specials. Since filming up at the lake was on hold, they had been given a respite from the demands of catering for ninety hungry crew members. Kate was pleased about the less frenzied introduction to her new role. She said it would give her time to work on the new recipes she had in mind.

CHAPTER TWENTY

Lizzie was her usual self when Nick delivered her order. Tetchy, but pleasant enough.

"When's your mother going to come and see me?" she demanded. "I hope you told her."

"I asked her two days ago," said Nick, "but she's really busy, and tomorrow she's going to Dunedin with Elka. She's got a service today and you would have heard about the man dying on the chairlift yesterday?" He was sure at least one of her carers would have told her the gossip.

"They said something about it being lucky Ben Goodman was there," said Lizzie. "I don't see why, when the guy was dead."

"I was there too, so was Mum. We looked after the guy's partner. One very upset woman. His wife is arriving on the afternoon flight from Auckland, so Mum is going to be busy with her. She asked me to tell you she hasn't forgotten and will come and see you when she gets back from Dunners."

"I suppose I don't have much choice, do I, other than to sit here and wait." Lizzie restarted her game and dismissed Nick with a wave.

As soon as she heard the door click shut behind him and his feet on the stairs, Lizzie froze the screen. Pulling her walking frame around in front of her she edged forward inch by inch, then heaved herself bit by huge bit out of the sofa. Just standing up made her breathless, and she had to wait until the stars in front of her eyes went away. She shuffled the walker in front of her, taking little steps, wincing each time her damaged foot took her weight. Reaching down to the box that Nick had left on the table beside her sofa, she grabbed two of the coke bottles by their necks and swung them into the basket hanging on the front of her walker.

Slowly but surely she moved, clumping the frame down in front of her and hauling the wasted right leg behind her. When she got to the sink, she leaned heavily on the bench before picking up one of the bottles, unscrewing the top and emptying the contents before refilling the bottle with water. It took over three quarters of an hour to empty and refill all six bottles with water and put them back beside the sofa out of sight of curious eyes.

"No one's business," she said to herself. Exhausted by the unaccustomed effort, she sank back into the sofa and snoozed for an hour before resuming her game. The pizzas were cold when she woke, but she ate them all.

CHAPTER TWENTY-ONE

Now and then Maggie dealt with someone who died without family, or without family who cared. Believing that everyone deserves some recognition of having been on this earth, she would hold a small ceremony for them at The Stables and would then accompany the casket to the cemetery for burial. If cremation was the chosen option she would put their ashes onto the "relic shelf", where they stayed until they were claimed. Six-monthly reminder letters asking for the urns to either be collected, or for alternate instructions to be given, were sent out routinely, but usually these sad letters were returned marked address unknown. When there were too many urns and the shelf was in danger of collapsing, she had another one built. It would be someone else's problem when she died – what to do with the relics.

This morning the ceremony was for Jilly. The Auckland PA had informed her Jilly had hated the thought of cremation, so Maggie had purchased the next available plot in Queenstown cemetery from the council and made the necessary arrangements for a burial. And lots of flowers! And a singer!

The Presbyterian minister was always happy to come and say a few words. Neither of them knew if Jilly had been a believer, but Maggie always erred on the side of better-to-be-safe-than-sorry. She had copied the photos she had taken from the house and printed off a short order of service, to show anyone who turned up that Jilly had been happy once. It was really none of her business, but she would send several copies with her account to the PA and her boss, just to show them how their money had been spent.

She put the original photographs in the casket beside Jilly, who looked fabulous in her blue gown. When she'd finished making Jilly look as close as possible to the earlier versions of herself, Maggie took photographs of her lying peacefully in the white-silk-lined casket. It was not something she normally did, but this time she made an exception, just in case anyone was interested.

The Jilly in the casket looked very different from the sad woman who had been brought to The Stables a few days ago. Maggie had relished the opportunity to make someone she barely knew look as beautiful dead as she had once looked alive. Jilly looked great, even if Maggie was the only one who knew.

The minister had finished his short eulogy when the door opened and Ben Goodman slipped quietly into the reception room. Maggie had never been more surprised to see anyone, especially after last night.

"I thought I should pay my respects," he whispered as he edged past her to an empty chair, nodding to the minister and Jilly's only other mourner, the cleaning lady.

One of the town's more gifted young singers had just enthusiastically launched into her version of *Amazing Grace*. Ignoring the fine voice, Ben leaned down disconcertingly close to Maggie and whispered quietly in her ear, "After all, I will be living in her house." Maggie's gasp at the cheek of the man was thankfully muffled by the song.

The girl finished and made a quiet exit back to her day job as a receptionist at a nearby hotel, very happy with the large cash payment in the envelope from Maggie. Thankful to get away from Ben, Maggie busied herself opening the double doors, and with Nick's help, wheeled the casket out to the waiting hearse. The flowers Maggie had ordered smothered the interior, putting to shame the modest bouquet from her ex-husband, no doubt courtesy of his PA. There had been nothing from Jilly's daughter.

The meagre funeral cortege, made up of Maggie and the minister in the hearse, Ben in his car, the cleaning lady in her small Suzuki, and Nick on his scooter bringing up the rear, wound its way through the town and up to the cemetery, which was tucked into the base of a hill dark with pine trees.

Jilly's grave was waiting for her. The frozen ground had been back-hoed first thing this morning, and the machine was parked diplomatically a few rows behind, ready to refill the hole when everyone had gone.

The minister read Psalm 23 as the casket was lowered into the ground, and once Jilly was in her final resting place, Ben, the minister and the cleaning lady made their awkward farewells before wandering back to their cars. The digger moved in and started work, heavy clods of earth thumping onto the wooden casket. Together Maggie and Nick ferried the flowers from the hearse to the graveside, their bright colours sitting pretty against the dark mud of winter. Maggie was pleased she'd ordered them, and something inside her told her Jilly would have been pleased too, and bugger the expense.

When she got back to The Stables, there was an email waiting for her from Helen Holmes, Mark's wife, informing her she would be arriving just after three and would come straight from the airport to talk to her and to see her husband, before they went to their hotel. Maggie assumed this meant Helen was bringing a friend.

There was another email, from Lucy, thanking her for her kindness the day before and to say she would be flying back to Auckland this afternoon. Maggie hoped the women wouldn't run into each other at the airport.

CHAPTER TWENTY-TWO

It was after four when Helen and Sarah finally arrived. Maggie learned that the only hire car available had been an orange Suzuki Swift, which Helen had immediately told the young Irishwoman staffing the counter just wouldn't do.

"It's the only way to deal with these people," she told Maggie later. "So we waited at the counter, our luggage bundled all around us, for about ten minutes. There was a queue of course, but when I told them my husband had just died, people were very understanding. So ... where was I?'"

"'The girl came back–...'" prompted Sarah.

"That's right. She came back and told us a black Porsche Cayenne had just that minute been returned, a day early. We knew all along she'd had something but was just too lazy to get it for us until we insisted. Typical Irish. Probably thought we would give in and make do with the Suzuki." Helen had looked at Sarah then and snorted, "As if."

Maggie had recognised the Porsche as soon as it had pulled up outside The Stables. For a moment she thought Lucy had forgotten something on her way to the airport. But of course, Lucy would be mid-flight by now, returning home alone, after arriving less than a week ago with such high hopes for her future.

It was unsettling when Helen and Sarah walked into her office. Both were wearing sunglasses and snug-fitting shearling jackets over black leggings tucked into English riding boots. They were only spared the accusation of mutual flattery by imitation, by the different handbags they carried, and because Sarah was wearing a large square of brightly patterned silk under her jacket, while Helen, the grieving widow, was more simply adorned with several gold rope necklaces draped against her white cashmere jersey.

Maggie's first impression was that they were the same age, but after a few seconds she realised Helen was a good ten years older than her friend.

Maggie stepped forward, hand outstretched, before realising too late this was not the usual way these women greeted people. However they were too well-mannered to ignore her, and each awkwardly clasped the tips of her fingers before disengaging. She invited them to sit down, relieved she had her desk to hide behind. If only it were tidy – dusted, even.

As they made themselves comfortable, Maggie couldn't help staring at Sarah. She was beautiful. Of course she would be, but in a refined way she hadn't expected. His type would be, she thought, as she waited for them to sit.

"In your email, Mrs Holmes," Maggie began, "you said you wanted to come and see Mark on your way to the hotel. I can take you to see him now if you like, before we go over the details. Or we could do that later."

Helen slumped suddenly in her chair and put her hand over her face. She reached out for Sarah, and finding her arm, squeezed it.

Her face full of concern, Sarah covered Helen's hand with her own and patted it comfortingly. "You wouldn't have a glass of water, would you?" she asked Maggie. "It's been a long journey in very sad circumstances and it's all getting a bit much. The car business at the airport didn't help." She reached over and lifted Helen's face – her dry face, Maggie noted. "You do look dehydrated, my sweet," said Sarah. "We have to look after you. For the children's sake."

As she filled a jug with water, Maggie wondered who was looking after the children while their mother was here.

When she returned to the office a few minutes later, Sarah was kneeling in front of her friend. "It will be all right, Helen. I'm here for you," she said, standing up and taking a glass from the tray, she filled it from water from the jug.

"It's tap, but it'll be OK," said Maggie.

Helen looked up and took a sip, then sighed loudly. "It's just so hard, Sarah, but I suppose I must be brave." She looked at Maggie. "We want to know what happened. Don't leave anything out."

Maggie did her best to tell them everything. However, she saw no need to mention Lucy. Neither woman cried, but Sarah did reach out and put a comforting hand on Helen's arm again. Thankfully neither asked who Mark was with when he died, though Sarah looked genuinely surprised when Maggie talked about Ben.

"So he *is* here," she said.

"You don't have to see him, Sarah. Remember, we talked about this," said Helen quickly. "I suppose we might as well go over everything now, Maggie. I can't see the point of getting settled at the hotel and then traipsing back here. And then I suppose I'd better see him. It'll be good to get it over and done with in one fell swoop."

"Are you sure, Helen dear?" asked Sarah gently. "You don't have to, you know. We can always come back tomorrow, can't we Maggie?"

Maggie nodded.

"No, let's get it over. Then we can have a drink when we get to the hotel. I need a gin. The whole thing has been horrible. Answering the door to that policeman who looked barely older than my son. Thank God you were there, Sarah. Anyway, I've been told my poor husband has to have a post mortem. He would have hated that, wouldn't he Sarah?"

"Yes dear, I'm sure."

Helen looked up at her friend to make sure she was truly sympathetic.

Sarah reached over and squeezed Helen's arm again. "He will be missed, sorely missed. A great man and a wonderful husband and father," she said soothingly.

The Helen and Sarah act was starting to annoy Maggie.

"Unfortunately we can't do a PM here in Queenstown," she said. "It has to be done in Dunedin, and then the coroner has to be satisfied that everything is in order. Once that happens you can take him home."

A flash of annoyance crossed Helen's face before she quickly resumed the role of the grieving widow. "We want to take him back to Auckland tomorrow. This ruins everything. There must be a way around it. Sarah, what was the name of that nice judge we met last week? A judge trumps a coroner, surely. If I called him, I'm sure he'd sort it out."

Maggie bit her tongue. It was the only way she knew to stop herself from saying something she shouldn't, but it didn't always work. This time she kept biting, while counting slowly to ten. When she stopped her tongue hurt and she could taste blood.

"I'm sorry but there's no way around the law. Even the Governor General herself couldn't trump a coroner, as you put it. With your permission I was going to take him through to Dunedin tomorrow. You could follow in your car. I've spoken to the pathologist, and he thinks he can speed things up at his end for you. If everything is straightforward you could take him back to Auckland the day after that. He told me to tell you he'll move things along as a personal favour to an esteemed colleague."

Helen cheered up a little at this hint of special treatment. "That could work, couldn't it?" she asked Sarah.

Sarah nodded.

"Settled," said Helen. "I suppose I'd better see him now. The sooner we get to the hotel the better. What time do we meet you here in the morning?"

Maggie suggested a nine o'clock start, at which they both gasped until Sarah said, "Needs must, old girl. We can do it."

When Helen saw her husband's body, she was calm, almost aloof. Sarah, whom she insisted came with her, told her repeatedly how brave she was. It was Sarah, though, who reached out to touch one of Mark's hands and who quickly recoiled at the coolness.

Having done her duty, Helen indicated to Maggie she had had enough and walked back to the office. She chose a simple functional casket for her husband, before tidying the paperwork away into her handbag and thanking Maggie for her help. Rarely had Maggie seen a widow so composed. It made her own job much easier, not to mention quicker. Having to counsel a distraught widow took time and was not easy, but it was part of the job. Helen's absence of emotion was unnerving.

As they were leaving, Helen asked, "You might not know this, but would we have to book to get a table at Elka's tonight? We've been looking forward to dinner there after one of our friends told us it's the best restaurant in Queenstown. Sarah and I thought we deserved a treat after this hellish day, and all this …" She waved her hands back towards where Mark was still lying on the stretcher.

Maggie found the bitten hollow in her tongue and made it deeper. "My daughter is the chef, while Elka is away, so I'm sure if I phoned her and explained, she would organise a table for you."

"Oh, how marvellous," said Helen, enlivened by another favour conferred. Her eyes sparkling, she turned to Sarah. "I told you Maggie was special, didn't I? You were so efficient when we spoke, I knew straight away I could depend on you. I'll tell all my friends what a wonderful undertaker you are."

Closing the door behind them, Maggie muttered between clenched teeth, "Funeral director. "

CHAPTER TWENTY-THREE

"Mum, are you awake?"

Maggie opened one eye. It was dark and she was lying, still dressed, on the sofa in the living room in front of the burnt–out fire. Kate was bending over her, hand on her shoulder, shaking her gently back to consciousness.

Shivering, Maggie sat up and pulled a mohair rug around her shoulders. Kate reached past her and turned on the lamp. Maggie licked her teeth, trying to get rid of that dry furry feeling which comes from falling asleep in an awkward position with your mouth wide open. Dribble was still wet on her chin.

"What time is it?" she asked. Reaching up to sweep her hair back, she found a post–it note stuck to her forehead. It seemed Nick had decided to let her sleep when he'd tip toed past earlier in the evening. Instead of waiting to tell her again to remember to visit Lizzie, he had scrawled *Lizzie* on a note and thoughtfully stuck it to his mother's forehead.

"Just after eleven," said Kate in a loud whisper from the kitchen. "I'm making herb tea. Would you like some?"

"Camomile would be lovely." Maggie stretched up, feeling life flow back into her stiff body. "I'm so tired," she said. "These past two days have been full-on." She yawned. "Tell me, how did it go tonight? Your debut."

Kate put the cups on the table and sat down. "Good," she said. "It was a full house and we took over eight thousand dollars, which isn't bad for a week night, but–"

"Well done. What do you mean, 'but'?"

Kate took a deep breath. "Those women you sent, Mum. They were a nightmare. They were awful. In London we used to call that sort 'sophisticated savages'."

"I'm sure they can't have been the women I called you about. One has just lost her husband."

"Precisely," said Kate. "I told the maître d' about Helen's husband as soon as they arrived, just before they ordered their first cocktails – and then their second and third. For a while it seemed to be going well. They'd decided to see Mark off in style and they certainly knew their wines. I checked, and between the two of them they polished off one bottle of Cristal and a bottle of Pyramid Valley Angel Flower pinot noir – after the cocktails. I could have served them steak and chips, because the food meant nothing after that much alcohol. They managed to hold it together until the end of the evening, and thank goodness most of the other diners had left early because that's when the fun really started."

Maggie shook her head. "They were such ladies when they were here this afternoon. I don't believe it."

"A lady," said Kate, "does not think it highly amusing to jump out at other guests from the coat cupboard, before running the length of the restaurant with her hands over her mouth hoping she'll make it to the loo in time to be sick. And she didn't. Make it. Helen must have thrown up more than four-hundred dollars' worth of champagne and pinot noir. Lucky it only hit the door of the loo and not another guest, but the smell was atrocious. And then she went in and wouldn't come out. All we could hear was more vomiting and lots of loud crying. Not a bad way to empty a restaurant. And don't look at me like that; it wasn't funny. Eventually she emerged, only to sob her heart out on the wine waiter's chest, telling all and sundry how Mark, her husband, had been planning to leave her for some 'anaesthetist bimbo'."

"Did she really say 'anaesthetist bimbo'?" asked Maggie, unable to hide her glee.

"She did say that, yes. I told Brian not to give them the second bottle of pinot they wanted. He thought they'd been drinking even before they arrived. And I know we should have been monitoring them, but truly, Mum, they seemed fine until just after the mains went out. They changed in an instant. One minute we had two well–dressed women having dinner together, and the next minute, all hell had broken loose.

"But wait, there's more – that's not the worst of it!" Kate said dramatically, enjoying the horrified look on Maggie's face. "Around ten o'clock, just when we were trying to ease them out the door, who should call in on the off chance we could do a takeaway pizza, but Dr Goodman. You and Nick went skiing with him yesterday, didn't you? He was there when Mark died? Anyway, he was at the counter talking to me when Sarah, who seemed less 'tired and emotional' than the widow, suddenly saw him and pitched herself across the floor and stood there, hands on hips, yelling. He was surprised, to say the least, and then I swear, he just looked terrified. I would have been too. She had so much hate in her eyes. We all felt sorry for him."

"This is her." Kate got up, put her hands on her hips, and leant unsteadily forwards, swaying, as she imitated Sarah. "Ben Goodman, you rat. How *dare* you divorce me and come and live in this ... backwater! No one does that to me and gets away with it. You think you've escaped. I've got a new lawyer and I'm coming after you!'"

"Then Helen joined in. 'Why didn't you save my husband? He's dead and I have to take his unfaithful body home to our children.' I tell you, it was all on and now all directed at poor Ben."

Maggie listened in shocked amazement. She'd heard about tourists sometimes getting drunk and making fools of themselves in the cheaper pubs and clubs in Queenstown, but the idea that two middle–aged women from Auckland would get so trolleyed was breath–taking, especially as one of them was supposed to be a grieving widow. It wouldn't be long before the story made the rounds. There was nothing the locals liked more than bad behaviour by city visitors. Elka definitely didn't need to know. Her reputation was precious to her, and Maggie didn't want her upset before the surgery.

"Mum, focus," said Kate. "There's more. Poor Ben went white. Literally the colour drained from his face in front of me when they were yelling at him. He just stood and looked at his wife while she went on and on about how she was going to get her fair share of the Goodman millions by hook or by crook. I have to give it to that man. He was a total gentleman. As soon as she'd stopped raving at him, he said, 'It's lovely to see you again, Sarah. Helen, please accept my condolences for your loss.' And then he left."

"It would've been fine if they'd left then, but now it was Sarah's turn to burst into tears and lock herself in the loo. I left Brian to get them out, because I was so over them both. By the time we'd finished cleaning up the kitchen, they'd gone, thank goodness. I think Brian ordered a taxi to make sure they got back to their hotel without falling in the lake."

Kate yawned. "I am so tired. Come on Mum, it's late."

As they walked upstairs, Kate turned to Maggie. "The next time you see Ben, be nice to him. He deserves some kind words after everything he must have been through, married to that woman. I'm going to bed. Give me the quiet of London nightlife after the hurly burly of Queenstown any day."

The next morning, Maggie's phone rang at seven. It was the receptionist at Eichart's Hotel, advising her that Mrs Holmes and Mrs Goodman would not be meeting her at nine o'clock after all, and she was to go on without them. If necessary, Mrs Holmes would meet her later that day in Dunedin.

CHAPTER TWENTY-FOUR

"Tim James."

"Tim James – the movie star."

"Possible Harm – those films. He's that one."

"Oh, him. I thought he'd be taller."

"Nice bum."

Whispers swirled around Tim as he strode through Queenstown airport, his staff clearing a path through the crowds. He was wearing a BreakNeck baseball cap low down over his eyes, and this, combined with his trademark Aviators, hid most of the damage. His make-up artist had been able to cover the rest with plastic skin and concealer.

Tim rarely used commercial planes. His own jet was parked away to one side of the runway, but this was such a short flight and it seemed unnecessary to go to the expense of activating his crew from their unpaid holiday in Queenstown. Buying fuel for an eighty-minute flight to Auckland when the local airline was reasonable and ready seemed such a waste of money.

Smiling graciously and nodding to people around him, he caught sight of a little girl looking at him with huge eyes, nonplussed by all the fuss. Picking her up, he encouraged her mother to take a selfie of the three of them. It occurred to Tim he could've carried the girl off to Auckland without a maternal murmur of objection, if he'd so desired, such was the effect he was having. The girl's father was less star–struck and reached across his wife to firmly extract his child from Tim's arms.

Just then Matt leaned in and whispered that the plane was waiting for him to board. The gathered crowd sighed as he waved and threw them a dazzling smile, before turning on his heels and jogging manfully out and across the tarmac to the plane. Another full arm wave and he was gone.

Tim and his entourage occupied the first three rows on the plane. Used to travelling in his private jet, he was bemused by the flight safety instructions playing on the drop-down screens above him. Always the centre of attention, he mimicked the flight attendant standing at the front of the plane, taking delight in watching her trying not to laugh.

Tim was still smiling after the plane had taken off and another attendant trundled her trolley down the aisle, stopping to ask if he would like tea, coffee or mineral water. He looked at the large pots of cooling tea and coffee and chose water. Unable to resist, the attendant showed him her phone, eyebrows raised in a silent question.

Tim didn't need to be asked twice. "Of course," he said, taking off his glasses and turning to present his good side, and to hide the scar. The attendant put her head as close to his as she could and pressed the screen.

Tim's head ached where the cap dug into the stitches. He replaced his glasses, closed his eyes, leaned back and tried to get some sleep. As soon as he landed, a car would whisk him into Auckland and he would see the plastic surgeon. Once he and his insurance company were reassured that all was well, he intended to spend a few days relaxing in a discreet hotel, seeing what the city had to offer. Jimmy was sweating the small stuff, but he didn't have to. Tim was going to enjoy this forced break in his schedule. It was a pity Jenny couldn't join him, but he knew she'd never leave Isaac for such a short time, so there was no point in asking her to.

Matt had suggested they could fit in some golf and deep sea fishing while he was there. Photos of him enjoying New Zealand's outdoor lifestyle would boost his profile, and the Tourism Board was paying for the hotel, so he guessed he owed them something. There was also some big gala ball in a couple of days, at which Tim was to sit with the young female Prime Minister of the whole goddamned country. A local personality he'd seen on TV earlier that week had been contacted and invited to be his "date" for the night. Tim liked to be photographed with beautiful women, and he knew Jenny would understand. Matt would brief his date about the scar, and if she was as interested in her career as she had professed on the phone, she would say nothing.

The flight droned on. The pilot informed them that the plane had just crossed Cook Strait and was heading up the west coast of the North Island, with views to Mount Taranaki on the left. Tim decided it was time for him to walk the length of the plane to the rear bathroom, where he'd stay for a few minutes (taking care to avoid contact with all surfaces) before walking slowly back, nodding and smiling modestly at everyone. A little public adoration was always good for his soul. Maybe he should do this more often, he thought, as phones snapped as he moved down the aisle.

Having done his victory walk, Tim settled down to look at the photos of his son on the iPad Matt had handed him. The flight attendant collecting the rubbish melted when she saw the devoted father looking at photos of his baby.

Another attendant's voice came over the intercom, giving instructions in preparation for the descent into Auckland. She finished, "On behalf of Air New Zealand, thank you for choosing to fly with us today – especially you, Mr James."

The rest of the plane cheered and clapped when Tim raised his arm in acknowledgment. Two hundred smartphones took two hundred photos.

CHAPTER TWENTY-FIVE

Elka looked fantastic sitting up in bed in her sunny room at the hospital in Dunedin. At least that's what Maggie told her. Armed with glossy magazines and an extravagant bunch of early spring flowers, she had cautiously opened the door to her friend's room, ready for the worst. It had been a long operation – two to three hours longer than anticipated – and she expected to find Elka lying flat on her back hooked up to drips and monitors, with beeping noises punctuating the quiet and nurses hovering around her looking serious.

Instead, Elka was looking at her laptop, ear buds in, laughing at whatever she was watching. There was only one drip, innocently and quietly going about its business; there were no beeps to be heard in a room empty of nurses. On the bedside table was a small machine with a syringe locked into a pump of some sort.

Maggie stood on the far side of the room until Elka looked up, her face breaking into a huge smile of welcome. She flipped her laptop closed and pulled out her ear buds before gingerly holding up her arms for a hug. Maggie unbundled her presents and hugged her friend carefully back, not wanting to squeeze anything too tightly. There was reassurance for both of them in their embrace.

Maggie let go and stepped back to take a closer look. "You look fine," she said. "No pain?"

"That's a morphine pump," Elka said, pointing to the syringe. "It's my friend and it stops all the pain. It is my very good and bestest friend, apart from you. It makes me feel very happy, and I can press this little button when I need to feel happier. I do have this, though." She pointed to a plastic bag of yellow murky fluid hanging from the side of her bed, connected to a tube snaking its way out from under the bed covers. "It's out tomorrow, all being well. They've told me I can go home the day after, once they're sure I can pee without any problems and the pain has settled. You don't mind spending an extra day here do you, Maggie? I know we were supposed to go back tomorrow, but they've only just told me the damn thing has to stay in for another twenty-four hours. Will the others cover you for an extra day?"

"They'll be fine. They owe me, anyway, because I haven't taken time off for ages. The main thing is you're OK. I'll come and watch movies with you and spend time 'laxing', as the kids would say, with one of my favourite people." She looked around the room. "Where do you think I could find something to put these flowers in, before they die in this heat?"

Elka pointed to a cupboard under a handbasin. Maggie found a vase, filled it with water and arranged the flowers before putting it on the window sill. The smell of Early Cheer permeated the room, bringing with it the promise of better weather to come. She added the magazines to the pile on the bedside table.

She was settling into a chair when she saw Elka's face droop and gradually turn grey. Elka squirmed in the bed, trying to find a more comfortable position, but without success. Her eyes shut, she reached for the red button attached to the pump and pressed it twice. The syringe emptied its contents into the IV tubing.

It took no more than half a minute for the colour to return to Elka's face, and for her muscles to lose their tension. For the first time since her lump had been diagnosed, Elka had actually looked sick. She reached for Maggie's hand and squeezed it tightly. Maggie stayed holding her hand until Elka feel into a deep sleep. Digging in her handbag for some paper and a pen, she left a note on the bedside table: *Sleep well. Back first thing in the morning. Text me if you need anything.*

Winter in the southern city can be as dour and cold as the Scots who settled the area in the middle of the nineteenth century. Today was no exception, as Maggie left the hospital and considered her options.

For the past twenty years she'd left Queenstown only when absolutely necessary, and unless she was on a training course, never without Kate and Nick for company. She was used to being on call twenty-four hours a day, and the freedom she felt now was invigorating.

While there was a constant stream of tourists visiting the Lakes District, both winter and summer, the actual population of the town and surrounding hinterland was quite small. It didn't take long for everyone in Queenstown to get to know everything about their fellow citizens, and it wasn't possible to do anything out of the ordinary without word spreading as quickly as the ensuing and inescapable judgements.

Having two nights alone in a city, anonymous and unmonitored, made Maggie feel like a teenager again. Her spirit soared with relief and barely contained excitement. She was free, healthy and single and she intended to make the most of these freedom days. She had a credit card which was actually in credit, and her tax wasn't due for two months. She would forget about death, work, and that man. Life was bigger than the debacle of the other night.

Instead of a moderately priced motel in North Dunedin, she decided to book herself into the new hotel in town, where she could order room service and breakfast in bed, should she want it – but only after sleeping for as long as she liked. The thought of being able to stretch out in a huge bed made with smooth, freshly laundered sheets she hadn't washed and ironed herself almost made her purr with anticipation. Shopping was also high on the agenda, as was visiting some of the local art galleries and the newly renovated Otago Settlers Museum. Of course, she needed to be with Elka too, but Elka needed to rest and recover, which meant Maggie was free. Free to be Maggie Potter, grown-up.

The cold in the southern port city was damp and bone chilling, without any of the invigorating dry cold of the mountains, but she had brought her warmest clothes in anticipation. Leaving her bag in the hotel, Maggie walked to the Octagon in the middle of town and stopped for a double espresso in the warmth of the modern bustling café next to the city's art gallery. She flicked through the latest magazines, which were full of photos of Tim James on location at the head of the lake.

Posters in the art gallery foyer advertised an exhibition of early New Zealand paintings, which she decided would be worth seeing. Besides, it was late afternoon and the sun had dropped behind the hills, taking what little warmth there had been outside with it. It was too cold and too late to go shopping – she would do that tomorrow.

"The gallery is closing soon," advised the gallery attendant. "I'd start at the top and work your way down."

Maggie put on the headphones to listen to the audioguide and took the lift to the third floor. She was soon lost in the world of early New Zealand landscapes, some depicting Lake Wakatipu and surrounding valleys. Deeply engrossed in a view of Mt Cosmos and the river below it, she stepped back and collided with another visitor to the gallery. They turned to face each other, fiddling with the mute buttons on their audio guides.

"Ben!" said Maggie.

"Maggie!" said Ben.

"And then," said Maggie sheepishly to Elka the next day, "well ... you know."

Elka rolled her eyes and just managed to stifle a groan. The likelihood that this had been a chance meeting was a million to one. It was incredible that Maggie didn't see what was staring her in the face.

Maggie paused, evidently trying to find better words to explain exactly what she meant. "That sounds so silly. I mean, something changed. Maybe."

Elka had never heard Maggie speak like this about anyone. She was standing over by the window looking the worse for wear, her breath smelling of alcohol poorly disguised with mints.

"So?" asked Elka.

"So?" repeated Maggie, her voice twisting with embarrassment. "I don't know. It was wonderful but strange. I haven't felt this way for years, if ever." Her voice quivered. "I can't talk about it. Really, I can't. Would you like me to get you coffee? There's a café downstairs."

"I don't think I could bear the smell, but thanks."

"Sorry, here I am going on about me and you're the patient. You look better today and the bag's gone."

"Don't need it, I can walk to the loo now," said Elka. "And I slept after you left – all night. First time in months. Tell me, why is Ben in Dunedin? Seems strange he didn't say he was going to be here when we were talking at the restaurant."

"It was a last–minute decision," he said. "There's a GP conference on and one of his partners said he'd cover for him. He's going to pop up and see you later too, and he hopes he can have a word with your surgeon. Quite a coincidence that I should bump into him, wasn't it?"

"Was it?" asked Elka, but the irony was lost on Maggie.

"The gallery was closing when he bumped into me, so we had to leave together and as we were walking past the café, he asked me if I'd like a glass of wine. He said he was meeting friends and asked if I'd I like to join them, considering I was in Dunedin, and alone." Maggie paused. "So I said yes."

"Of course you did. Were they nice?"

"Who?"

"His friends."

"Yes, they were lovely. All doctors. From different parts of the country, here for the conference. It was quite a reunion. One's a pathologist in Christchurch and had been involved with identifying the people who died in the earthquake, which sounded horribly stressful. And," she said, laughing at the memory, "Ben told him I was an undertaker, but then corrected himself to say 'funeral director'. Something I have been trying to make him understand for ages. He must have been listening after all."

Elka smiled, not wanting to interrupt her.

"We had quite a bit to drink, so it seemed easier to stay there for dinner. Excellent food. You would have enjoyed it. One of the other doctors, a woman GP from Wellington, cornered me in the loo and asked how long we'd been going out, which was a bit embarrassing until I told her we barely knew each other. She said none of them had liked his wife because she was a bitch. She said he wouldn't listen when they'd tried to warn him about her, so they were pleased when they broke up two years ago. After what she did the other night–"

"Don't worry, Kate told me. She did well to get them out by the sound of it."

"Anyway, we talked, ate, and drank lovely wine until ten, when the staff wanted to close up. Ben tried to pay for me but I wouldn't let him, and this caused a bit of a fuss, but I got my way. Bruce, a surgeon from Ashburton, suggested we all go to Poqueno, a whisky bar just around the corner in Moray Place. I was quite merry by this time, as you can imagine, and so whisky on top of all the wine didn't seem like a good idea. They insisted, and one of them told Ben I was the best thing that had happened to him in years, which was VERY embarrassing. It was a fantastic bar with a huge fireplace, and there was a three–piece jazz band playing the most wonderful music. I haven't laughed so much in years, Elka." Seeing the look on her friend's face, she added, "Except when I'm with you, of course."

"It's fine, Maggie. It sounds great. Let me know when you want to come back and I'll organise another operation." She sniffed huffily for effect.

"Ben made me try a whisky called Glenmorangie, which was good but very strong. It was really late when the others left, but we stayed a wee bit longer because – and get this Elka – we're both staying at the same hotel. I'm not sure his friends believed us when we said we were just friends, because they said something to him which I didn't hear and he blushed. Next minute the staff were making *Go Home* noises. We were talking so much, neither of us had noticed that not only had the band stopped playing and packed up, but everyone else had gone and we were the last ones there."

Maggie came over and sat on the edge of Elka's bed. "He is *so* interesting, Elka. There aren't many places he hasn't been. He's a GP but he's trained in Denver in emergency medicine. Good skiing on his days off."

"Maggie. I need to get to the bathroom. Quickly."

"Sorry sorry sorry, Elka, here's me wittering on and you lying there in agony."

Maggie helped Elka slide off the side of the bed, and taking one arm supported her slow shuffle to the bathroom.

"I need you to help me more. Sorry."

Maggie lifted Elka's nightie and held her as she gingerly lowered herself onto the loo. They waited, but nothing happened.

"I'm bursting, Maggie. I know I have to go because it's so sore. Turn on the tap."

Maggie turned on both taps, letting the water run noisily into the basin and down the plughole. Nothing. Elka was turning grey with pain. The walk had been too much for her and she was gripping the handrail so hard her knuckles were white.

"I used to make *pssss psss* noises when I was potty training the children – maybe that will set you off," said Maggie, turning the taps down to slow drips. Crouching down beside her, Maggie stroked Elka's free hand, soothing her, and started making the promised sounds. All was quiet, and then there was a tinkling sound in the bowl, just a little at first, then a stream hitting the porcelain followed by a deep satisfying sigh from Elka. Their eyes met and they burst out laughing. Maggie watched the colour come back into Elka's face and some of the missing sparkle return to her eyes.

"Result!" yelled Elka triumphantly, her fist weakly punching the air.

"You are going to get better, aren't you?" asked Maggie. "You will be all right? I couldn't bear it if anything bad happened to you."

Elka held out her arm and Maggie eased her upright.

"I'm going to be fine. The surgeon told me this morning that the cyst-lumpy thing they removed looked benign, but she needs another week for the histology to come back and then she'll know."

"What's histology?"

"They check it out under a microscope and work out what it is and then what that means. Already I feel so much better, just knowing it's gone. She said I could go home tomorrow as long as I peed today, and now, as we know, I have. Thank goodness you have toilet-training experience or I could have been here for weeks."

Once back in bed and sitting comfortably, Elka leaned over to Maggie and prompted her for the rest of her story with a knowing grin. "You'd left the bar, you were on the way back to the hotel and you were both a little drunk. Tell Aunty Elka everything – and I mean everything! What happened next?"

"Nothing happened," said Maggie. "We shook hands, and that was it. He was a perfect gentleman. We took the lift and he got off at the third floor and said goodnight, and I carried on alone to my room on the fifth floor."

Elka was disappointed. "All that build up and nothing? No kiss?"

"No kiss. We're just friends."

"You're kidding me, right?"

"OK. He is nice – nicer than I thought, but that's all. Really. You look tired after your big walk. I'll come back this afternoon. Do you need anything? A Rolls Royce? A diamond necklace? Tim James, even – it was on the news this morning that he's been putting it about in Auckland at some charity ball. I'm sure I could arrange a welcome home date with him. We know he likes your cooking."

"I don't do movie stars, but I will take the diamond necklace and the Rolls Royce sounds good. But if you can't find them in my size, don't worry. You being here is enough." She squeezed Maggie's hand. "By the way, Kate said Nick wants to remind you to see Lizzie when you get back. She keeps asking for you."

CHAPTER TWENTY-SIX

"Don't do it, Potter," a husky voice whispered from the other side of the clothes rack in the middle of the shop.

Maggie jumped.

The voice whispered again. "You've been warned! Don't do it."

Standing on tiptoes she peered over the top of the clothes, but couldn't see anyone. Walking around the end of the rack she saw Ben, chortling away, delighted with himself.

"I couldn't resist," he said. "I saw you walk in and felt duty bound to stop you from buying another item of black clothing to complement your already extensively dark wardrobe. You need to kick the black habit, Potter."

"Habit? It's a choice."

"Are you sure? As a medical professional I diagnose a pathological deficit in imagination and I'm here to prescribe the cure – colour. This is not the nineteenth century. Undertakers do not have to wear black all the time, certainly not every second of every day. I meant funeral directors, sorry. Do it for your kids, Maggie, show them you have a life outside work. Show them you were a woman once."

"Once? That's a bit off, and just when I was starting to li–"

"You were starting to like me," he interrupted.

"That's not what I was going to say at all. And my kids are fine with how I dress."

"Then why do they make comments about it?"

"They're just being funny – it's a family joke. And it's none of your business."

"I've never seen you in anything but black. I've told you it suits you, but you're not wedded to the job, surely. Relax for once."

Ben's voice faded into silence. Maggie turned and looked at herself in one of the long mirrors. She saw him standing behind her, trying not to smile.

"OK, if you're such an expert, what would you suggest?" she asked, hoping to put him on the spot.

Ben scanned the shop. It seemed there was nothing he liked, so he thanked the disinterested shop assistant and guided Maggie out the door with the lightest touch on the small of her back.

"This shop – come in here," said Ben, opening the door of another boutique just a few doors down.

The contrast couldn't have been greater. There were sisal rugs on painted floors; large mirrors and good lighting. Racks of clothes in dusky pinks and creams, along with exotically patterned silks and soft crepes, were watched over by a smiling, attractive young woman who welcomed them warmly.

Maggie instantly recoiled. None of these clothes would be suitable for work, and if she spilled so much as one drop of tea or coffee on them, they'd be ruined. Besides, she lived in Queenstown, where most people wore merino clothing, ski jackets and boots for warmth. Where would she wear any of these clothes, enticing though they were?

"Just look," he urged, seeing the expression on her face. "It can't hurt to look. What else were you going to do this afternoon?"

"I was going to visit another art gallery and then check on Elka. I do have plans. I can't spend all day in shops looking at clothes I can't afford and would never wear, because where on earth would I wear them? And if I did wear them, I'd be afraid they'd get ruined. I don't move in your social circles, and I don't have your money."

Maggie regretted her outburst as soon as it had escaped her lips. She hoped the shop assistant hadn't heard. Tears sprang to her eyes as she realised she'd probably offended him, and after his kindness yesterday and even today, that was the last thing she wanted to do.

Maggie looked up, half expecting to see him walking out the door, but he was still there.

"Sorry," she said, "I didn't mean that the way it sounded. I know you were just trying to be nice."

The shop assistant broke the awkwardness. "Can I help you?" she asked cheerfully, arriving beside them at just the right moment.

"Yes, you can," said Ben, taking charge while Maggie composed herself. "My friend in black needs some lightening up. Perhaps a shirt or a dress, but definitely something with colour. I don't know, what would you suggest?"

Stepping back, the young woman cast an expert eye over Maggie. "I have two things that would look fabulous, and which you could easily wear with the clothes you have on. You're so lucky with your figure and your hair, you'd look gorgeous in any of the clothes we have."

Her high heels tapped on the white painted floor as she went to one of the racks and pulled out a cream shirt, and what looked like a patterned piece of material hanging limply on a hanger. Handing the items to Maggie, she showed her into one of the changing rooms and offered Ben a cup of coffee.

The pieces the assistant had chosen looked fantastic on Maggie. The soft cream crepe blouse could be worn with the floppy bow at the neck done up or left open. She could see how well it would go with her skirts, or under a jacket for business meetings, and she could wear it with trousers and boots for casual occasions. The patterned silk turned out to be a tunic that could be worn alone or over trousers and leggings. It clung in all the right places, emphasising Maggie's perfect hourglass figure and high breasts.

Having tried them on, there was no way she couldn't buy both pieces. She almost pranced out of the changing room, and watched while the assistant made a fuss of wrapping the clothes carefully in thick layers of tissue paper before easing the beribboned rustling packets into one of the store bags tied with gold ribbon and a red bow for good measure.

Maggie sparkled with pleasure. The smile on her face was contagious as she twirled towards Ben. "Thank you for making me do that. Wait till Kate and Elka see me in these," she said, laughing.

Outside on the pavement she said, "I needed the push. I see that now." And before she could stop herself, she blurted out, "I don't suppose you'd like to come to Port Chalmers with me? The drive is beautiful and we could go to the Spit afterwards."

Ben looked at her quizzically. "The Spit?"

"Aromoana," she said. "When I was little, my family always called it the Spit. It's an old Otago name."

"Not as old as Aromoana, I'd venture," he said, straight–faced.

Maggie stopped and smiled. "No," she said thoughtfully. "You're right again. You're on a roll today, Dr Goodman."

"I can't, Maggie," he said. "I really do have to get back to the conference. It was only by chance I saw you shopping. Now that I have rescued the damsel from her black, I'd better go. You can thank me later."

"You are an idiot."

"Thank you, Madam," he said, drawing himself up to full height. "You're not the first person to notice. I have an ex-wife who often told me the same thing, but perhaps not as nicely."

Maggie winced. It was the first time she'd heard any flicker of self-pity from him. But in a strange way it was comforting to know he could be vulnerable too. And before she quite understood what had happened, he'd suggested dinner later and she had agreed.

CHAPTER TWENTY-SEVEN

The restaurant on the esplanade overlooked the pounding surf on St Clair beach. To someone who'd spent her life miles from the sea, the roar of the waves was exotic, conjuring up images of ships and sharks.

Although it was mid-week, the popular restaurant was fully booked and they had to wait for a table at the bar, where Ben ordered them both a glass of champagne.

"To the new you," he said, raising his glass. "You look very beautiful. I particularly like the earrings, which I believe may be also be a new purchase."

"The Port Chalmers gallery," said Maggie, pleased he'd noticed them. "You're a very observant man, aren't you?"

"Observe, Remember, Compare. It's carved in stone on one of the lintels at the medical school, and I've always remembered it because it's a useful maxim in life. It can be applied to almost anything: diseases, houses, wine – even women."

Maggie blushed and tried to deflect the direction of his conversation to something less embarrassing. "It suits you being a doctor, doesn't it?"

"I don't know of another job which would have been quite so stimulating or which would have taken me to so many places – and I don't just mean physically," he said seriously.

"From what I've heard," Maggie said, unsure how he would take this, "you don't need to work. So why do you, and why something as demanding and I would imagine restricting as medicine?"

The maître d' interrupted them to say their table was ready, and the conversation lapsed until they were seated and had ordered food and more wine.

"So," she said, returning to their previous conversation. "Why *do* you work?"

"Brought up to it. I come from a family that believes in work, and I know this is corny in today's world, but my parents also brought me up to believe that with privilege comes responsibility. As the oldest I swallowed their reasoning hook line and sinker, and never regretted it. My younger sister, on the other hand, was totally resistant to their indoctrination and is completely work-shy, but she gets away with it because she's fun to be with. Work shy but fun. All sorts of people have tried to take advantage of her over the years, and as her big brother it's been up to me to get her out of some very tricky situations."

He stopped smiling. "I believe you met my wife, Sarah. She was very like Laura, my sister, when I first met her, but without the money. Once we were married and she had access to unlimited funds for the first time in her life, it went to her head. I understood how exciting it must have been to be able to buy anything she wanted for the first time, and I let her go wild. I waited for the novelty to wear off, but it never did. And despite all the promises she made before the wedding, afterwards she made it clear that she didn't understand my need to work, or why we couldn't travel the world living in one hotel after another. She ended up making it very difficult for me. No doubt my friends told you. They'd tried to warn me, but love makes you do silly things."

With the arrival of their meals, the conversation stopped until Ben said, "What about you? Why is an attractive woman single and working as an undertak–" He stopped and corrected himself, "a funeral director in Queenstown?"

"Married too young, both Andy and me. Babies too quickly and too much responsibility for him. He couldn't play beach volleyball *and* be a dad, so he left. I haven't seen or heard from him since the divorce, which was arranged through lawyers after I came back to New Zealand. Both my parents were killed in a plane crash, and I had to come home. Kate was eighteen months and Nick was just six weeks old. Simon, my older brother, is a lot like your sister sounds. He handed me the keys to the house and the business the day after the funeral, and left to go travelling. I had no choice but to get on with it and look after the three of us. No one else ever offered."

They smiled ruefully at each other.

"Let's talk about something else, something more cheerful than failed marriages and disappointing partners," said Maggie.

"What do you suggest?"

"Politics?"

"I thought you wanted us to be more cheerful. I know – why don't you tell me about Lizzie? She tells me you were at school together."

"We were, but why were you discussing me?"

"We were talking about Nick, actually, and you're his mother, so ... I know, let's talk about skiing. That's not going to make your hackles rise, surely? You can tell me where the best back country runs are."

Maggie enjoyed the rest of the evening. They shared a similar sense of humour, as well as a love of skiing and mountains. Ben regaled her with tales of his climbing expeditions and travels to out-of-the-way places around the world, while Maggie filled him in on the more amusing exploits of the local identities in Queenstown.

It was late when they got back to the hotel. Tonight the lift seemed very small, and Maggie found it impossible not to be acutely aware of Ben standing tall beside her as they watched the numbers count off one by one before the door finally opened on the fifth floor and the corridor stretched in front of them.

"I thought I should see you to your door," said Ben.

Digging in her bag for her key, Maggie wished she hadn't had so much wine. She felt hot, and the door to her room swam in front of her. She felt his hand on her shoulder, gentle but insistent as he slowly turned her towards him. Her heart beating hard in her chest, she looked into his eyes. Neither said a word, aware of the other's breathing and the tension and heat rising between them.

Maggie felt his hand move tantalisingly slowly from her shoulder to caress the side of her neck before he reached behind, cradling the back of her head, guiding her even closer before leaning down and softly brushing her lips with his. Maggie closed her eyes as his lips became more insistent for her response, his tongue curling around hers curiously and delicately. She could hardly breathe as she leaned into him, her world contracting to the feeling of his breath on hers, to the softness of his mouth, to the smell of him and the power of his arms as he wrapped them around her, pulling her deeper against his body. She almost fell into him when he stepped back, and holding her shoulders with his hands, examined her face hungrily before taking in the rest of her.

"Who are you really, Maggie Potter?" he asked quietly, fixing her eyes in his gaze.

"I'm just me," she breathed, wishing he would stop talking and kiss her again.

He did, but this time more slowly, his whole body pressed against hers, leaving her in no doubt as to his attraction to her. He turned away from her mouth, sliding his lips down to nuzzle the pulse on the side of her neck, till she was barely able to stand.

"Would you like to come in?" she whispered beside his ear.

It was if she'd hit him. His arms fell to his side and he stepped back, away from her. "I hardly know you, Maggie."

She turned, trying to put her card in the door so she could get away from him, to be anywhere but here, feeling so very very foolish. Overwhelmed by her own stupidity, she fumbled, and dropped the card in her confusion. "Go. Just go," she said unable to look at him.

"I didn't–"

"I said *go*. Get away from me or I'll scream."

She listened as the sound of his footsteps on the thick carpet faded away down the hall and the door to the stairs swished open and shut. Only then could she bend down, pick up the card and escape into the safety of her room. Only then could she let her anger explode, as she screamed her disappointment and hurt into the soft hotel pillows.

She was a grown woman who knew what had been happening between them. So did he. He was no innocent virgin. He must have known she would ask him to come in. What did he expect? A handshake? A quick peck goodnight, after what they had just been doing in a public hallway?

"Bastard, bastard," she said, flinging herself onto the bed. "Who the hell does he think he is?"

Embarrassment, and most of all fury at her gullability took their turns in no particular order in a long queue of emotions raging through her. *He must think I do this with every man I have dinner with. And he's right damn it, I do!* "Precisely because," she yelled into her pillow, "he's the only man I have had dinner with in years – and he is the goddamned last."

Maggie held the pillow around her head as she sobbed and raged at his rejection. Finally, when she could cry no more and the pillow was soaked with mascara-stained tears, she pulled herself up and sat on the side of her bed, before peeling off her new shirt. Being cream, it too was streaked with make-up. Even the shirt somehow conspired to make her feel inadequate, something a black shirt would never have done, for damn sure. She hurled the offending garment into a corner, wishing she'd never bought it, along with the dreams of a different life that had seemed to go with it.

In the bathroom she soaked her face in cold water and brushed her teeth between sobs. Slapping night cream carelessly in the general direction of her eyes and cheeks, she dared to look at the red-eyed woman with the puffy face looking back at her.

"Never again," she said to the person in the mirror. "Don't you ever, ever trust a man with your feelings again."

Turning off the light, she went to bed and tried unsuccessfully to sleep.

In his room on the third floor, Ben Goodman had the good grace to feel absolutely awful about what he'd just done to a woman he had started to like very much.

"How could you?" he asked the man in his bathroom mirror brushing his teeth. "How could you be such a complete and total arse to someone who is one of the most decent people you've met in years? Not to mention beautiful."

Ben pointed his toothbrush at his reflection. "Because, you idiot, you know what will happen. You know you will get trapped into a relationship with her before you are ready. They always seem fine at the start, but eventually it's your money they want, not you. They use and abuse you and you're left with the bill. You know that."

OK, he thought, brushing furiously again. She may be different. She certainly seems different ... so far! And she does have such lovely soft lips and she smells so good and she is very beautiful.

One part of him wanted to march straight back to her room, bang on her door, apologise for his rudeness, sweep her into his arms and kiss her again.

The other part – the part that had grown stronger with each unhappy relationship – said, "The way you handled it is to be regretted. But you don't know her and you certainly don't know her well enough to get that close to her. How would it look in such a small town?"

But God, she felt good, all of her.

He stripped off and lay on the bed. *You're too old for another casual fling and too bloody old to make another mistake.*

Turning off the light he lay awake, tossing and turning, for most of the night.

CHAPTER TWENTY-EIGHT

The rumble of tyres on cobblestones woke Elka.

"We're home," said Maggie, shutting off the engine.

"Why are we at your place?"

"You remember, your surgeon said you needed someone with you for the next week. We both know that if you went home you'd wouldn't rest. We're going to look after you. Kate can keep you updated about the restaurant so you won't feel left out, and Nick can run any errands. The Potter Family convalescence service is at your service."

"Please, I don't want to make a fuss. Take me home, Maggie. I've planned for this. It's OK."

"Absolutely not. Doctor's orders."

Maggie walked around to the passenger door and helped Elka out of the car. Kate must have dashed home and got the spare bedroom ready after Maggie's text from Cromwell, because there was fresh linen on the bed and the heater was on. A bunch of yellow daffodils sat in a jam jar on the bedside table, a reminder that it was spring even if the weather was still cold.

"You know where the bathroom is. Call out if you need help. I'll make some tea and bring it up," said Maggie when Elka was sitting up in bed, resting comfortably on the bank of pillows behind her.

Elka lay in bed, listening to a series of bangs and thumps downstairs. Something wasn't right, but Maggie wasn't letting on. At the start of their journey, when she'd asked how dinner had gone the night before, she'd got no response. Maggie, her lips tightly pursed, had started fiddling instead with the radio tuner, trying to get a station. When Elka could stand the hissing noises no longer she pressed the seek button, and the dulcet tones of Katherine Ryan could be heard introducing the author of the latest cookbook.

"You should do that," said Maggie.

"What?"

"Write a cookbook."

"I've thought about it, but I haven't had the time."

"Maybe you could think about in the next few weeks, while Kate's here," said Maggie.

"I'd rather think about why you sound so flat today."

"I'm not flat. Just tired," said Maggie, firmly closing out any further conversation.

Elka took the hint. Her medication was starting to kick in, and although she tried to listen to the interview, within minutes she was fast asleep. She had woken outside Lawrence, the town marking the half way point of their journey. Initially she thought it was the pain deep in her groin that had disturbed her, but that wasn't it. She had been woken by the sound of Maggie crying. Elka kept her eyes shut and her breathing even. Maggie wasn't ready to talk.

The banging in the kitchen got louder. The kitchen door slammed shut and from outside came a muffled curse before it opened and shut again, this time more quietly. Elka pretended she was asleep when Maggie brought her cup of green tea upstairs, setting it down next to the daffodils. She heard Maggie walk over to the window and sigh loudly.

Elka sat up yawning. "Oh good, green tea. Just what I felt like."

"Sorry about the noise downstairs," said Maggie.

"I've been asleep. What noise?"

"Nothing. It's just ..."

"Didn't go well last night, I take it?"

"Nope. Disaster. Then I spent the whole night awake. I couldn't believe–"

"What? Tell me. It might help."

"I can't, Elka. I can't say the words. But if you ever tell me what a nice man Ben Goodman is, ever again–"

"I won't, I promise. I thought he was nice, but look at the state of you, Maggie. He didn't hurt you, did he? Force you, I mean?"

"Oh no, it's nothing like that. I wish he ... No. Of course I don't. I just don't understand how he could have ... Elka, that's the last time I give any sort of love any sort of chance. I'm no good at it. I'm terrible in fact. Whatever I do or whatever I say, it's wrong. I don't know if I can face him. At least when Andy left me I didn't have to see him again, I didn't have to work with him. God, I wish I lived in a city."

"You poor thing. This is *your* home, remember, not his. Maybe I should change doctors."

Maggie walked over and sat on the bed, looking utterly dejected. "Of course you can't change doctors. He's the only one who listened to you. Just warn me when he's coming and I'll make sure I'm out. Maybe if I don't see him for a few weeks then we can pretend nothing ever happened. It's not as if we move in the same circles, is it?"

Elka squeezed her hand. "Why don't you have a nap? It was a long drive and you look exhausted."

"I can't. I promised I'd go and see Lizzie as soon as I got home. And I have to let the others know I'm back. It was good of them to hold the fort when I was away, but... it's back to work. Don't worry. I'm a grown-up. I can do this. It's you we need to look after, not me. Is there anything you need before I go?"

Elka finished her tea and handed Maggie the cup. "I'm good. I'll be up and around in no time. Thank you for having me here. I don't know what I'd do without you."

"Sleep. I'll look in on you later."

Maggie went downstairs. As she rinsed out the mug and put it in the dishwasher, she thought about Elka. They'd been friends for over twenty years – their relationship had lasted. But was a friendship enough? Certainly it was less complicated than a marriage. In a way, they had the best of both worlds. Someone each could depend on when times were tough, but with room to be themselves, to live their lives exactly as they wished. Elka had been there for her through thick and thin, and she had done the same for her in return. It had suited them to be close, with neither feeling smothered by the other. When Maggie thought about the future, and God forbid, old age, it was Elka she was relying on to be there with her.

A wave of acute embarrassment flooded over her when she thought about the scene in the hotel corridor last night. *Why? Why did I do it? Why put yourself at risk?*

You know why. For the first time in years, a man – a decent, healthy, good–looking, charming, funny, intelligent man – paid attention to you. He made you feel like a woman again. Not just a person, but a woman. A desirable woman. And you blew it.

Maggie shook her head. She hoped she wouldn't see him again for a long long time.

CHAPTER TWENTY-NINE

The sun was shining and there was an early spring warmth in the air, despite the dirty snow still banked high in the lee of some of the buildings. Driving was less treacherous today, but the same couldn't be said for Lizzie's stairs, which hadn't fared well in the winter weather. Water had inveigled itself under the treads of the upper steps, and then frozen at night, expanding to rip the rubber away from the wood underneath. Maggie needed to warn Lizzie to get the landlord to make repairs, or someone could trip and fall. She would prefer that it wasn't her son.

She'd heard Nick talk about her old school friend, but even so she wasn't prepared for the mountain of blubber she found sitting on the dirty sofa in this horrible little flat on the dark side of town. The young Lizzie she had known at school, and had seen in photos around the time of the World Champs, had been gorgeous. Maggie had fond memories of a confident energetic teenager with blonde hair and sparkly green eyes excitedly saying goodbye to her before leaving to train in the French Alps.

Lizzie had stunned the country with her performance at the World Champs in the downhill slalom. Everyone had been backing her to win gold at the next Olympics, and there had been full- page photos of Queenstown's 16 sixteen-year- old golden girl on the front covers of national papers, and magazines. The local and international press had clamoured for interviews and photographs, while sponsorships and endorsement requests had flooded in. There were rumours about late nights and wild parties, but no one believed them. How could someone so beautiful and talented risk everything, when sporting glory was within reach?

Taking a deep breath and then regretting it instantly, Maggie tried not to look shocked when she saw Lizzie, or to react to the smell of living decay that smothered the atmosphere in the small room. She dug out one of the strong mints she carried in her bag and popped it in her mouth, waiting for the stringent peppermint relief to float up and absorb the odour of sweaty woman.

"Good to see you, Lizzie," she said, breathing through her mouth.

There was only one spare chair in the room, so Maggie moved it closer to the sofa and sat down.

"Sorry it's taken so long, but you know I was in Dunedin with Elka, and before that Betty died and then Jilly ..." Maggie trailed off weakly. "Actually ... I should have come to see you sooner– much sooner. I'm sorry."

Maggie felt Lizzie examine her. "We don't always do what we should, do we, Maggie? You and I both know that, so let's leave it there." She paused. "You look wonderful – but then you always did."

Maggie was at a loss to know what to say in reply, and it showed.

"I know how I look, so don't say anything," said Lizzie. "Honesty used to be your forte, so don't start with false manners now. I know I look like shit, but that's the way my life has turned out. The doctors didn't do their job properly and I'm the one left with the problem." She sighed, lifting her leg to show Maggie her foot. "My life was taken from me when my foot got broken. Can't walk because of pain, certainly can't ski. That was the only thing I was good at, so what can I do?"

The scarred twisted foot hung in the air between them, seemingly on display, until Lizzie was sure Maggie understood the significance of her injury. Maggie duly commiserated, but she lacked sincerity and both knew it. The atmosphere in the room chilled as Maggie tried to maintain a polite façade, which she could see didn't fool Lizzie for a moment. In full victim mode Lizzie was angry that Maggie was judging her and had found her wanting.

"I heard your life didn't work out that well either, Maggie Potter," said Lizzie spitefully.

"Maybe," retorted Maggie, "but at least I didn't let it beat me, Lizzie Martin."

"I'm not beaten," said Lizzie, defiantly. "This is the way I want to be, at least until someone finds a cure. Unless you've been through this yourself, you couldn't possibly understand what I have to go through every day. No one could."

Maggie could see from the petulant expression on her face, that Lizzie had become more accustomed to thinking about what she couldn't do, rather than what she might be able to do. There would be no purpose in pointing out how others coped with far worse injuries, than she had experienced so she relented and let Lizzie's disability win.

"Why did you want to see me?" she asked.

"You're not the right person after all," said Lizzie stiffly. "You've become very judgemental, Maggie, and I don't know if I like you enough to trust you."

Maggie sighed. "I'm sorry," she said. "I guess I'm lucky, because no matter what else has happened to me, I can walk and I'm not in pain. Of course things are awful for you, Lizzie, and of course I can't possibly know what it's like."

Lizzie picked up a little at this, settling with a resigned sigh into her helplessness within the depths of the stained sofa.

"Tell me what happened," said Maggie. "I remember the accident, but soon after I moved to Australia. Things weren't good with Mum and Dad so I lost touch. Your father was with you when you had your accident, wasn't he?"

"He'd just arrived. There were rumours about my behaviour, and Dad said he'd come over to bring me home and knock some sense into me. The ski scene in Europe was such a shock, coming from little old New Zild. I knew I was out of control, but who wasn't? I was seventeen, had just won the championship and the Olympics were coming up.

Everyone wanted me. They were giving me stuff and saying nice things. After the years of training, the time in the gym, the early nights, it was mind-blowing to go out and party. One day, I'll tell you all about the fun times."

"Anyway, Dad didn't get on with Enzio, my new coach. They had this huge fight about the parties, the money, everything, and Dad stormed out. I went after him to tell him I wasn't coming home, and that's when the car hit me. I'd been drinking and ran straight out across the road. I don't blame the driver. It was my fault, but when the doctors couldn't fix me properly, I lost everything. Dad stayed by my side at the hospital day and night, but he blamed himself. For a while, I blamed him too. I didn't see Enzio again. He made one quick visit to the hospital the day after the accident, then I heard he was coaching an American. Not as good as me, though; got disqualified in '92."

"Why didn't you come home?" asked Maggie.

"I couldn't. I thought the doctors in Europe would be so much better than the ones here, but they weren't, and by the time I found out it was too late. I had four operations but my ankle just got worse. When they told me I would never ski again – well, not competitively – I gave up. Skiing was my life; it was everything to me and it was gone, taken. Dad tried, but then Mum got sick and he had to come home to look after her. I felt really bad about everything I'd put them through. They'd sacrificed so much for me and here I was a cripple and unable to repay them. Sure I had money, but that's not the point is it? I wanted my old life back. I wanted to be Queenstown's golden girl, but I was just some gimp in pain, talking about past glories, with no future. So I stayed there. Mum died first and then Dad a few weeks later, broken-hearted, as someone kindly pointed out in a newspaper. What could I have done for them, Maggie? Nothing. I didn't want to come back when I knew they were sick, and have them look after me. You understand, don't you?"

"I think so. Your poor parents must have missed you, though. You were their only child. How could you let them die without seeing you?"

"Isn't that what you did to your parents? You can't sit there and lecture me about being a good daughter. My father told me you broke your father's heart when you buggered off to Australia with the first ski bum who asked you out."

A big fat tear rolled down Lizzie's cheek. "I know it was wrong, Maggie. I felt so bad, and I still do. I let them down. I know it was different for you. You had no warning of what was going to happen to your mum and dad. Anyway, after my parents died, I knew everyone would hate me for not coming back, so that was another reason to stay away. I couldn't face anyone who knew me in the old days. Still can't. Look at me, Maggie. Imagine what people would say. My life is never going to be the way I want it to be. It's all gone. I have nothing. You don't understand." Lizzie was crying in earnest now.

Maggie knew she should be trying to comfort Lizzie. That she should give her a hug, even, but instead she had to work hard not to get angry with her and tell her a few home truths about how selfish she'd been and how pathetic she was now.

For goodness sake, it was just one bloody foot. There are paraplegics who don't give up and hide away, she thought. *They don't blame everyone else for their problems.* She'd seen people with all sorts of disabilities skiing on Coronet.

She found a paper serviette that had been delivered with that morning's KFC, and offered it to Lizzie, who took it gratefully and blew loudly, before handing the crumpled serviette straight back. She wiped the tears from her eyes with the back of her hand. "I suppose I'd better tell you why I wanted to see you then," she said, "so you can get back to The Stables. I wouldn't want to take you away from your family."

"And Elka. She needs me too at the moment," said Maggie. "She's had surgery and we're looking after her until she gets back on her feet."

"Lucky her, to have feet to get back on to," muttered Lizzie.

Maggie purposely kept her face still. "What is it you want?"

"As you can see, I'm not in the best of health." Lizzie's voice dropped to a whisper. "I wanted to make sure you'll have a coffin big enough for me, should anything happen."

"It's only your foot, isn't it? That's hardly going to kill you. Don't you think ordering a coffin or casket – they are different – is maybe getting a bit melodramatic?"

"I didn't know you had a medical degree as well as being an undertaker," snapped Lizzie. "As you can see, I'm bigger than I used to be. I'm fat, Maggie. Not my fault. It happens when you can't exercise. I have conditions because of my weight, and the new doctor, Ben Goodman, has told me I don't have long to live."

"Have you got cancer?" asked Maggie, suddenly feeling guilty.

"Not yet, but he did say I was at a higher risk of cancer because of my weight."

"What did he actually say? What were his words?"

"He said I could go at any time, if I carried on the way I was. You have to accept that when a doctor says it. It's not good – which is why I needed to see you, to prepare. I know it'll be hard to find anything big enough to put me in and I don't want to be left lying around. I want to get it organised now."

"The obvious question, Lizzie, is why don't you stop carrying on the way you are and then you won't need me? Try exercising – lose some weight, stop eating KFC. Surely that's what Ben was trying to say to you. He wasn't telling you to prepare for your imminent demise."

Lizzie bristled with anger. "Do you want my business or not, Maggie? I could go to the other outfit. I thought of you first, but if you won't take me seriously, then perhaps you'd better leave. Don't bother coming back. Seeing you again has not been as nice as I thought it would be."

"I'm sorry, Lizzie. Of course I'll help. Why don't you go online and look at what's available. A casket would suit you more than a coffin, rectangular shape whereas a coffin goes in at the feet and shoulders, so look at those." Maggie found a clean serviette and wrote down the name of several websites. "I'll get Nick to bring some brochures and then you can let me know when you want to discuss this again."

Slightly mollified by Maggie's apologetic tone, Lizzie nodded. "OK, I will. In case you're worrying about being paid, money isn't a problem. Dad set up a trust for me when I was a baby and it's doing quite well. Plus I get the gaming money."

"Gaming? Are you a gambler?"

"No. *World of Warcraft*, it's a computer game. Oh never mind, ask Nick."

Maggie shrugged and got up, then stopped and looked at the door. "This won't be wide enough to get you out and down the stairs, Lizzie. If you can't lose weight, I'll have to arrange for the fire service to take the side of the house off and get you out that way – but that means there'll be sightseers. Think about it. If you lost weight, we could get you out of here with dignity. Just a thought. Oh, and tell your landlord about the stairs – the tread's lifted on these top ones and they're really dangerous. I don't want Nick to trip."

When Maggie got home, she found Nick asleep in front of the TV. He stretched out as he woke. "All go well?" he asked, yawning.

"Seemed to. I'll go back and see her in a few days. How's Elka?"

"She's been asleep since you left. But I meant to ask, how did it go in Dunedin? Anything exciting happen in the big smoke?"

"Nothing exciting, just the usual," lied Maggie, picking up a piece of paper from the bench. "What's this?"

"There's a guy who keeps ringing Kate, but she's never here when he calls. Wants her to ring him."

"Probably work. I knew it wouldn't take long for people to find out she's back. Put it on the bench by the coffee and she'll see it in the morning. I'm going to bed."

"There's a letter for you too."

Maggie found a thick envelope under the day's paper. "I've been invited to a party – next week at the restaurant."

"Who's it from?"

"Estelle, the real estate agent. She remembered."

"Are you going to go?"

Maggie hesitated. She knew Ben would be there. Next week was too soon.

"Of course she's going," called Elka from upstairs. "I am, and she's got to look after me."

CHAPTER THIRTY

Tim was relieved to be back on set, especially after the fuss that had gone down in Auckland. He was more relieved his scar was healing up. With the help of the make-up artist, filming could start again. The weather had cleared, the river was down, the crew were ready and he was back where he belonged, where he felt safe – in front of the camera.

But he couldn't wait to get home.

The press, led by Bramble, had made his life hell for the past few days. He'd realised too late it was a mistake to go to the charity ball. Seated at a table of people who didn't know how to keep their mouths shut, his every utterance had been reported and commented on, mostly negatively.

Photos of him talking to the celebrity organised to be his date had been uploaded to social media while he was still at the ball, for chrissakes. The only consolations were that she was shorter than him and looked great – you can't go past big breasts and a low–cut dress.

Tim was well aware dancing was his weak point, and usually avoided public displays that would expose his lack of rhythm, so he only had himself to blame when some asshole filmed him taking to the floor with the encouragement of his partner, after he'd had one whisky too many. When he was overly relaxed, his timing and arms went even more to shit, but he'd been powerless to resist the breasts swaying in the cleavage displayed in front of him. The resulting fiasco had made him a laughing stock on YouTube, with the clip getting more than three million hits so far, and climbing. And his PR team could do nothing about it.

Even the footage of him with one of the biggest trout caught in the Tongariro that year made not one whit of difference to the online derision that was growing by the second. The worst of it was, Tim had genuinely caught that trout, reeling it in after a long battle, without help from the fishing guide who admitted to being genuinely impressed with his effort. But did anyone apart from other fishermen watch that clip on YouTube? Nope. Anglers didn't count in his world. Tim's target audience consisted of women and young people who paid to see his movies. Ted Turner had sent him a text saying *Well caught!*, which he supposed was something. Maybe he would hear from Putin, another guy who triumphed in manly pursuits but was always misunderstood.

And still that damned woman kept giving interviews. If he saw one more coy, misleading headline on the cover of another woman's magazine, he would scream. It had been one night, and she was acting as if he was leaving his wife and running away to New Zealand to live with her and make her an honest woman. What was wrong with her? Couldn't she tell he'd been acting? He had to admit, he was a good actor, and she would had to have been very astute indeed to realise she was only a one–night stand. Maybe it was time to cut down on the whisky.

Tim made a mental note to get Matt to call her *again* and explain the facts of life, and if that and a big bunch of flowers didn't work, he might just have to pay her to shut the fuck up.

The only good thing about the week had been Jenny's professional attitude, at home in LA. His wife understood how the system worked and knew her role in keeping his image on the front pages. She'd driven out of the gates of their home, slowing down in the middle of the pack of voracious paps, top down on the car so they could get a good shot of her, head covered, large dark glasses partially obscuring her face, looking sad but furious, before speeding off in a cloud of cheated wife. She'd looked magnificent, and the papers had lapped it up.

And it wasn't just the magazines who were interested. One of the NY broadsheets had run an opinion piece saying he was only interested in other women because Jenny took her mothering too seriously, and wouldn't leave her baby to travel on location with her sexually charged husband. The article had linked his latest escapade to dominant male chimpanzees, with quotes from primatologists and psychologists excusing his behaviour as evolutionary rather than just plain irresponsible. Jenny was cast in the role of alpha mother, tending her child until she could return to his side and again fend off the predations of the women who saw no barrier in the wedding band on Tim's finger. She played her part beautifully, and he'd told her so when he'd Skyped the night before.

One of the characteristics he admired most in his wife, even if it cost him an arm and leg, was her intuitive understanding of what she could do to hurt him most. This woman really "got" him, which only made her more attractive. After ditching the paps at the front gate, she'd driven straight to Tiffany's for some serious compensation shopping. Waving the heavy gold and diamond bracelet at him on screen last night, he had to smile and admire her taste, albeit through gritted teeth.

Even smarter, she'd worn the bracelet in public. She'd been photographed through the window of the most expensive restaurant in town, looking meaningfully at it as she showed it to her friends, knowing Tiffany's wouldn't take it back now. He would have to chalk that one up to New Zealand, but then it occurred to him – it could also serve as his baby gift to her. No cloud without a silver lining after all.

"Tim, good to see you back. You look good, considering," said Mike, walking towards him across the stones, hand outstretched. Jimmy was by his side and looked tired, the strain of the accident and the last few days of budget-shattering delay etched on his face.

"You too, Mike," said Tim, shaking his hand and surprising himself with how genuinely he meant it. "This time I promise I'll listen a little harder. Don't want any more delays, do we, Jimmy?"

The two men exchanged relieved glances. "We've finished the chopper scenes we could with a stand in, so I'm hoping we can wrap up today and tomorrow, Tim," said Jimmy. "Today Mike's going to take you over the route you'll need to follow. Then we'll do a quick run through, get the drones and the chase choppers into place and we should be good to go first thing in the morning. Any questions? No? Righto. Mike, I'll leave Tim in your capable hands. Pete the sound guy is going to get your mic sorted and then you can head off."

For the next twenty minutes, Mike explained everything to Tim – everything – and was gratified that the guy had dropped the know-it-all act and was finally listening. This time Tim was asking smart questions rather than making smart-arse comments. Mike showed him where the choppers would be coming from, and explained how he would be flying one of them and reporting straight into Tim's ear about the river conditions up ahead. He'd been here since dawn, mapping the exact channels Tim would take down the river, and had set up a system of marker sticks, stone cairns and tracks amongst the gravel, invisible from the air, to act as a back-up guide should anything go wrong.

"First, though, I'm going to take you up and show you the route from the air, and later you're going to drive it a couple of times so you can get used to the boat again."

"This is a Robbi or an R22," explained Mike over his headphones once they were in the air. "They were used to get wild deer out of the hills when the price of venison went through the roof. Very manoeuvrable, but also light and fast in tight spaces. Been in one before?"

"Not with both doors off," yelled Tim, trying not to look concerned.

Mike was a skilled pilot, judging by the way he was tossing the machine sideways towards the hills before swooping down to follow the ribbons of grey river below. Tim hung on tightly as the R22 broached a ridge, riding the updraft for a few seconds as the land disappeared from under them, lurching down towards the tussock–pocked snow falling away precipitously underneath. A few seconds later, a lichen–infested rocky ridge came from nowhere to meet them, too close, too visible, but was soon left behind.

Reaching the start point, Mike slowed and put the machine down on a flat expanse of gravel bordered on both sides by dark bush–clad hills. Around them towered snow–covered peaks, and ribbons of white water tumbled down sheer cliffs, fed by lakes high above. The regular *whump whump* of the roto blade echoed back at them. Sitting in the cockpit, Mike pointed out the small pile of stones he had made that indicated where the boat would be tethered, and showed Tim his marks. Tim studied each one, committing it to memory. When he gave the thumbs up, the chopper rose again and they headed back to location headquarters nearer the Lake.

When they were back on solid ground, Jimmy met them at the coffee truck. Hot food was waiting on a table in the shelter of another truck. They collected their meals and found a seat in the warmth of the sun, ready to go through everything again.

"The R22 carrying the bad guys will rise straight up from behind the ridge Mike showed you, and then hover for a moment. You'll hear a couple of shots fired from one of the guy's rifles – you react, run as fast as you can to the boat. We're laying the charges today, ready for tomorrow so they'll be going off around you. Follow the path between the stone marks and you'll be fine.

"The chopper will drop the load of deer carcasses hanging underneath it. They'll be as bloody as hell and should land behind you – you get to the boat and fire it up. The chopper will rear back after losing the carcass weight, and then it's all on. Their focus is you, and that's your cue. I've got three drone cameras on each side of you, just above your eye–line, plus one above you, so all you need to do is drive the boat the way Mike shows you today, looking back when you can.

"Follow Mike's route exactly, and listen to him. He's good, and he knows this river. After we've done the big shots, I'll need to shoot the close–ups and then you're done, mate. The weather's supposed to be great but it's going to be an early start – we'll need every bit of daylight."

Tim had finished his meal and sat with his head down, fiddling with the brim of his cap.

"I'm sorry if this is like teaching a man of your experience to suck the proverbial," said Jimmy. "What you're doing tomorrow is going to look amazing, but only because it's bloody dangerous, so we all need to be on the same page. Questions, comments, suggestions?"

Tim appreciated the amount of extra planning that had gone on while he'd been away. Casual as these Kiwis came across, they were professionals. They actually had it nailed. "Nahh, good to go, Jimmy. Respect, mate. Isn't that what you Kiwis say when they see a job well done?"

Jimmy smiled.

"OK. Mike's going to take you down the river a couple more times. We don't want another accident, so take things slowly until you feel confident. And Tim, guys take weeks to get the hang of driving this river, so take as much time as you need."

"I'm good. Always done my own stunts so I can't stop now."

Jimmy's phone rang and he walked away to take the call.

"You need to remember two things," said Mike when they were in the boat again.

Tim bridled inwardly – he couldn't help it. He wasn't used to being told what to do and had almost had his fill. But remembering he'd promised to listen, he breathed deeply and resigned himself to the impending lecture.

Tim and Mike spent the rest of the day rehearsing the route Tim would take tomorrow, slowly at first, gradually increasing speed as Tim's confidence driving the jet returned. There were worse ways to spend a day, Tim reflected, than speeding down a glacier-fed river in the sun.

The boat was fast and responsive once Tim properly got the hang of it. It was thrilling to bank steeply round corners in impossibly shallow channels, then to put the throttle down and skim along the surface. He'd been a speed freak his whole life, and his unadulterated joy in the jet was infectious. As Tim relaxed, his relationship with Mike gradually morphed into something positive. By late afternoon the banter was genuine and they made plans to have a drink together after filming wrapped.

Jimmy made a couple of drone practice runs beside them. Looking at the playbacks at the end of the day, Tim had to admit it was going to be one hell of an action sequence. He could relax and enjoy making another fantastic movie.

Mike volunteered to chopper Tim back to the Lodge at the end of the day. Skimming the machine low and fast – and definitely illegally – just above the surface of the Lake, Mike halted under the brow of the promontory on which the Lodge sat before rising from nowhere directly in front of the windows of the main building, surprising the other guests – a manoeuvre that appealed immensely to both men's immature senses of humour.

In the cockpit, the pair high–fived the success of their mission before Tim jumped out, ducking under the blades, to run inside, adrenalin discharged and happy for the first time in the weeks.

CHAPTER THIRTY-ONE

Elka returned to Maggie's in the early afternoon, unable to find fault with the way Kate was managing her restaurant. Just knowing the place was in capable hands meant she could relax. Kate was doing a marvellous job. Bookings were up, the staff liked her, the suppliers were on time and the catering for the film crew was going smoothly.

Damn it, she thought. *It would have been nice to find a few mistakes. Maybe I'm not needed after all. I've worked ten years with only the occasional day off, and because of what? Pride? A delusion that I'm indispensable and that the customers won't come if I'm not there to cook for them?*

That's all it was. A delusion.

Do I need them more than they need me? Maybe that's it, and I've been too caught up, too busy to see it.

Or maybe it's just that Kate's very good at her job, just like me. Maybe it's that we cook with the same love, the same respect, and that's what makes Elka's the best restaurant in New Zealand, three years running.

Last year's Auckland usurper didn't count, she reasoned. The judges had felt guilty, giving her the award four years in a row. *We need to give the others a chance,* one of them had whispered afterwards.

She remembered nodding sympathetically, knowing she'd win it again this year. *But first I have to get better. Thank goodness I can relax, knowing Kate is doing as well as can be expected in the circumstances. Yes, she's good, but now I think about it the chocolate mousse looked a little flabby, and I would have sent the butterfish back. It wasn't as fresh as I would have liked, but I suppose it will do.*

Elka had been surprised at how tired she was after the surgery. It had taken more out of her than she'd expected, and she'd spent the days at Maggie's doing nothing but sleep. Today was the first day she'd felt able to get dressed and make the short trip to the restaurant, and it had knocked her more than she'd thought possible.

She made herself a cup of green tea and, taking advantage of the quiet house, walked upstairs one step at a time and lay down on her bed. The magazine she started reading slid to the floor and she started snoring quietly.

Her phone rang. It was Sally Robertson, the surgeon from Dunedin.

"Hello, Doctor ... Yes, I can talk. I'm sorry I didn't wait to see you before I left. I wanted to thank you again and tell you how safe I felt with you. The next time you're in Queenstown, please come to the restaurant, as my guest."

"You have the results? ... Fantastic ... I understand. I feel so well ... Are you sure? There's no mistake? ... Thank you, that's the news I was waiting for ... Yes, I will see Dr Goodman in a couple of days. And when do you say I will need to come back to see you again? Just to make sure I understand. Ten days?

"Sorry, someone else is calling me and I have to go. I can't make an appointment now, but I promise I'll call back ... I know that, and as I said, I'm feeling fine. I've already been back to work. You did a great job. Goodbye."

Elka curled up on the bed, pulled the quilt up over her head, shut her eyes and fell into a deep sleep.

CHAPTER THIRTY-TWO

—————

"Nick, please, please, please. There's no one else. I know you have your deliveries, but someone else can do them, can't they? Bill's sick and there's no one else I can trust to know what to do."

Nick leaned against the door as Kate packed tomorrow's supplies for the film crew into large, air-tight plastic containers, ready to be loaded into the truck early the next morning.

"The containers are numbered and the numbers are recorded against content on the inventory, so you'll know exactly what you have and where to find it."

"I haven't said I'll do it yet," said Nick, knowing he had little choice.

It had been like this since they were children. Kate told him what to do, and he, no matter how reluctantly and at times inadvisably (according to their mother), eventually did as he was told.

He could hear the exhaustion and desperation in her voice. The containers piling up in front of him were testimony to a huge amount of organisation and planning. He relented, but only because he knew there would be ninety crew starving the next day if he didn't. Nothing resembled a crazed mob more than a film crew without access to good coffee and food between takes. And the food better be good, because this was one of the few perks of the job left, now production budgets were so tight and producers were looking to screw every last cent of value from every dollar spent. One complaint about the food or service, and Kate and Nick knew that would signal a quick and dirty end to any future catering work. He didn't want to be the one Elka came looking for, should that happen.

"Got it," he said, when Kate had finished explaining the system to him. "Looks good. You've done well – even better than Elka could have done. I'm impressed."

"Thanks, baby brother, but what would you know? You've never been interested in food, other than the quantity."

"I'll have you know," he said drawing himself up to tower over her, "while you were away poncing about in London with Eric, I was here working with Elka every holidays and some weekends. And this is, in fact, my fourth film job."

Kate smiled smugly. "I knew that. Brian told me. Why else do you think I asked you to help? Little brother, you have brains, but more importantly you have initiative, a rare quality in this world!"

"You're less than two years older than me. I don't think you get to be the grown-up patting me on the head just yet, Kate. But I will take a hug." And before Kate could duck to the side, Nick wrapped his older but shorter sister in his arms.

Kate struggled pointlessly until Nick released her.

"Interesting," he said, his head cocked to one side.

Kate turned away and made a show of counting out the containers and marking them off on the inventory. That might have worked if she hadn't already done it.

"Kate, you're blushing. I've only ever seen you blush once in your life and that was after that date when Mum caught you sneaking in at four in the morning." Nick looked into his sister's face. "Anything you want to tell me? I promise I won't tell."

"Nothing you need to know," she said firmly. "And if you ever do need to know anything, I will tell you."

"Nothing to do with that guy with the Brit accent who keeps ringing when you're at work, is it?"

Kate looked surprised. "What guy?"

"The one who phoned yesterday, and the day before, and the day before that. I left messages and his number under the coffee for you. He wants you to call him. Sounded desperate the last time I spoke to him."

Nick examined Kate. For someone so used to being in control, she looked decidedly off balance and very unhappy.

"You did get those messages I left for you, didn't you? I figured as the acknowledged coffee addict in the family you couldn't miss any messages if I left them there."

Kate shook her head.

"Is that bastard hassling you?"

"No, he's a friend, if it's who I think it is. Look, next time he calls, tell him I've gone away – gone travelling – would you? He wants me to go back and work in the UK. He's nice, but that life is over. I want to be here now, with you, Mum and Elka. I don't want to be dragged back to that life, it's too surreal. Do your best and fob him off, and whatever you do, don't tell Mum!"

"OK. But I'm here if you need me. Is this everything?" Nick indicated the containers stacked against one wall of the walk-in fridge.

"Yip, and thanks," said Kate, squeezing his arm. "You'll need to be up the Lake, all set up and ready to serve breakfast before dawn, so early start. I'm going to be here till late tonight, so try not to make a noise when you leave."

Nick called in to see Lizzie on his way home. Visiting daily meant he now knew her reasonably well, and had started to think of her more as a friend than a customer. He enjoyed going to see her as long as the windows were open. She was smart, straight and wickedly funny at times, and his mother's visit had somehow triggered a change in her. She seemed less prickly; lighter in her approach to everyone who visited.

"Of course, I don't mind if you can't come tomorrow," she said when he told her he had to take the food truck on location in the morning. "As long as you promise to come and tell me all the gossip when you get back. I want to hear all about Tim James and his doings," she said, unconsciously licking her lips. "I want to know if he looks as good in real life as he does on screen. I will be expecting details, Nick, details. Oh, and tell your Mum I'm waiting. She'll understand."

That night, no one slept particularly well in the Potter house. Maggie had to go out just after midnight to attend to a not-unexpected death at a nearby rest home, and by the time she had everything organised in the mortuary, it was just after two a.m.

Kate had come in after work and gone straight to her room, where she checked her messages online, deleting most without opening them. She'd eaten at the restaurant and lay on her bed listening to music, trying not to think about anything in particular. Although she was exhausted from the day's work, her mind wouldn't stop working enough to allow sleep to come. She heard her mother's return before she finally dropped off, only to be woken by her brother's alarm in the next bedroom at four a.m.

Elka was feeling a little better after a supper of soup and ciabatta, but wasn't in the mood to chat and went to her room to pack. She had told Nick and Maggie she was going home the next afternoon, and thanked them for looking after her. Lying in the dark, she made a mental list of everything she had to do to get organised for the coming months at the restaurant and the summer season, before finally swallowing some more painkillers and half a sleeping tablet, knowing there would be no rest otherwise.

Of the four occupants in the house, only Nick slept as soon as his head hit his pillow. When the alarm woke him at four a.m. he was surprised to find the upstairs bathroom door locked. Lately, Kate always seemed to be in the loo when he needed to go, and tonight was no exception. Typical. When it seemed she was never going to come out, he used the bathroom downstairs before tiptoeing quietly out of the house into the thin night air. The bathroom light was still on when he looked back.

CHAPTER THIRTY-THREE

The coffee machine sent its pungent aroma to overwhelm the delicate smell of the surrounding beech forest, still damp with the night's dew. The first of the semi-prepared food was almost ready by the time the fleet of vehicles had disgorged their bleary eyed passengers. There was a queue for coffee before the last few had disembarked.

A member of the film crew had been assigned to help Nick, and soon breakfast was ready for the ravenous and focused team, who waited impatiently to be fed so they could get on with their day's work. By their second coffees, everyone was up to speed with the jobs they had to do, well aware there was no room for expensive mistakes on what they all prayed would be the last day on location. Jimmy had made it very clear at yesterday's final briefing that they had enough money for one day's filming, and one day only. "But hey," he'd said at the end of his pep talk, "no pressure."

People moved to their respective tasks with a contained sense of urgency as they waited for the sun to rise. They'd been frustrated by the delay caused by the accident, not least because they hadn't been paid for the days spent lolling about in overcrowded motels – and the resulting atmosphere hadn't escaped Tim and his team.

Eager to make amends, Tim was already in costume when he arrived, and was having his make-up applied when Jimmy opened the door of his little caravan, stepping in without waiting to be asked.

"Come in, Jimmy," said Tim, trying to make a point which seemed to completely bypass his director. He could feel Jimmy's stress, and respected it, but he didn't need it. He knew that if Jimmy wasn't stressed then the crew wouldn't give everything to their work, but it was stress that had to be directed at everyone else, and not at Tim or Mike. They needed a zone of tranquillity around them in order to concentrate fully on the day ahead. They were the men literally putting their lives on the line for the sake of entertainment.

"Can I get you anything?" he asked, calmly. "I can send Gwen to get you breakfast?"

"No time." Jimmy sat nervously chewing nicotine gum.

Mike knocked on the door and climbed in, also not waiting to be asked. Tim sighed.

In the relative peace of Tim's caravan, which was basic to the point of rustic in comparison to his trailers back home, the three men again went over the plans for the day. The sound man joined them and fitted Tim and Mike with their ear pieces. It seemed very straightforward, and Tim wished Jimmy would get on with it. He'd always been a quick learner, and was confident he'd mastered the art of driving the jet well enough to get from the top of the valley to the lake as if he'd been doing it his whole life, and still be in time for an early lunch. But Jimmy wasn't taking any risks, and only when he was finally convinced Tim and Mike knew what they were doing did he go on up to the start positions.

Mike and Tim were silent on their quick flight up to the head of the river. Mike landed briefly to let Tim out, and to allow the crew to attach the deer carcasses, then he took off again, disappearing over the ridge behind the gravel beach.

Jimmy had followed them up in the other machine, which set down out of view.

The boat was fuelled and ready. One of the crew was taking it for quiet runs up and down the river, before bringing it back and tying it to the log.

An expectant tension hung around the crew as Jimmy waited for the cinematographer to give the all clear for filming to begin. Tim's make-up artist made the final touches and adjusted his sunglasses, while the charges in the gravel were checked and, finally, Jimmy called, "Action!"

Mike's chopper, heavily laden with the dead weight of three adult deer swinging slowly on a wire beneath, rose up from behind the ridge. The stuntman, Bill, leaned out from the passenger seat and aimed his rifle at Tim, who from a standing start began running towards the boat, dodging the charges popping in the sand beside him. The deer carcasses landed on the beach with a series of sickening thumps, and the chopper reared back and up, but then zoomed down to tree height, and from there the firing started in earnest. Tim ducked into a running crouch, zig zagging his way to the boat, and leapt in.

"Cut!" yelled Jimmy. "Bloody good, everyone," he said, before checking the cameramen were happy. "That's fine. Once more to be sure and while we have the sky."

They did the scene three more times before Jimmy was satisfied he'd got the best out of it and called a coffee break. The morning was warming up by the time the next scene was ready to go, and Tim was starting to sweat in the merino layers the costume department had provided.

"I don't think you met Bill, your shooter, did you Tim?" asked Mike. "Don't worry, he does very well considering he's not wearing his glasses. I think he can see the difference between live and dummy ammo when he's loading up. Anyway, you'll soon find out."

Tim laughed, as was expected. They were standing around waiting for the next scene, drinking coffee, sharing stories and a few bad jokes to pass the time until Jimmy was ready.

Tim's PA came up and asked for a private word. The dance clip had had over six–and-a-half million views on YouTube, and the likes now outnumbered the dislikes. She'd done a survey of the comments, and it seemed most viewers thought Tim had been dancing that way on purpose.

This was the best news he'd had all week, especially since the coverage was completely free of charge, thanks to his companions in

Auckland. He'd have to watch it when this was over, so he could replicate the moves for the talk shows when he got home.

Happy, Tim went back to sit with the boys, and Mike pulled out a pack of tatty cards to deal a game of five hundred on the stones in front of the log.

The morning dragged on. Nick produced a round of French pastries to general acclaim, but was worried he might not have brought enough coffee. The machine had been working overtime and it was only ten a.m.

Finally, Jimmy signalled they were ready to start the next scene, which had to segue into the one they'd just filmed.

Jimmy called "Action". Tim ran down the beach again, leapt over the side of the boat into the driver's seat, and started the engine. The twin impellors roared into life and the exhausts sputtered at the back. He reversed into the current and then, turning hard, put the throttle down. The boat lifted, taking off at full speed for the next hundred metres until Jimmy called "Cut" into Tim's earpiece.

They did another take to be sure they'd got it, and so as not to lose the light decided to move straight on to the next scene rather than break for lunch.

"This time," said Jimmy, "we'll film the long run up the river. Go as fast as you can, Tim, but remember to listen to Mike's instructions. By all means do a few fancy turns if you think you can, but do not under any circumstances disobey Mike or try anything we haven't rehearsed. Clear?"

Tim looked Jimmy in the eye. "Clear!"

Thirty minutes later, Tim was slouched comfortably behind the steering wheel in the boat, idling midstream, waiting for Mike's voice in his ear. Jimmy had the drones in position and Mike and Bill were doubling round and about to start their swoop towards the fleeing jetboat.

"GO, Tim – action!" roared Jimmy's voice in his ear.

Five-hundred metres behind him, the R22 zoomed out from behind the ridge, straight down the river towards Tim, who by now had the boat at full speed, the bow lifted, the hull planing as if it were dancing on a cloud.

"Left," said Mike, and Tim banked the boat around the bend ahead to the left, slowing just a little before using the width of the channel to weave from side to side, nearly touching each riverbank in the process.

"Less weaving, mate," called Mike in his ear. "Bloody shallow in those parts: *left left left*."

Bill was leaning out of the cockpit beside him, rifle at his shoulder, hair whipping around his glasses. Below them and out to the side, the drones buzzed in formation, their cameras trained on the boat.

Just in time, Tim took the narrower but deeper channel to his left. The river was starting to open up as a series of narrow routes over the gravel bed coalesced across the widening valley floor, like a plait unravelling. The R22 gained on him, but he sped ahead and again went too close to the bank on one side, hitting shallow water and skidding across the sand and gravel below. The boat wobbled perilously, but he kept his foot flat to the floor and amazingly it found grip again in the next channel and stabilised.

"Bloody hell, Tim, cut it out!" yelled Mike. "We've got enough to worry about up here."

Bill, leaning out the side of the chopper and balanced precariously on one of the struts, was taking aim and letting off shots which landed in puffs of river sand and water around Tim.

"Right, left, left, straight ahead in the main channel for the next half kilometre, Tim, just drive bloody fast. NOTHING else."

Tim heard Mike, but the thrill of the chase was too much. His heart was racing, the wind was in his hair, he knew he looked fantastic standing over the steering wheel of this wonderful craft, light pressure on the steering wheel all that was needed to slide into bends and power out. He screamed into the air, knowing the drones would get his whoops of triumph against this amazing backdrop of mountains and bush. In his mind's eye he could see the selected cuts of this sequence playing on chat shows for the next year, and who knows, a nomination for Best Supporting Actor might be in the offing. He looked back at the chopper, cursing for dramatic effect, completely forgetting to take the next left turn as Mike screamed the instruction into his ear.

Beneath the boat there was suddenly only a sliver of water a couple of metres wide, between heaped gravel banks. All thoughts of Hollywood disappeared in a trice as he reacted in a split second, levelling the boat in the shallows before booting it straight ahead, hearing the hull scrape across the gravel. The boat bounced a few times and he gripped the steering wheel hard, but didn't stop reacting as the boat took off into the air before dumping down into a fast, full-flowing grey-green current of deep water. He banked the boat to the left, flicking a spray of white water up to the helicopter behind him, fist raised, punching the air, yelling in triumph. He pulled the trim back, feeling the bow rise up; the boat lifted even higher in the water. Tim James felt young and strong – like the King of the Whole Goddamned World!

"Listen to me you yankee bastard," came Mike's relieved voice in his ear. "You're one of hell of a natural, but you do that again and I'll deck you, movie star or not."

"Right, Boss," yelled Tim, punching the air above him again, certain the drones had caught the whole thing.

Mike could only admire the actor's guts and outright skill. Not many experienced jetboat drivers could do what Tim James had just done.

Up ahead the river formed two wide channels, and the rest of the way to the Lake looked uncomplicated.

"Stay in the right-hand channel, boot it, Tim, and you should be fine."

In Tim's other ear, Jimmy spoke to Mike, telling him to take the 'copter low and alongside the boat so Bill could get off some rounds at the runaway Tim. One of the drones moved in to capture the shot.

Mike increased speed, swooping down towards the river, but was puzzled to see the windscreen in front of him suddenly and inexplicably obscured by a spray of his own vomit. Chewed French pastries and black coffee slid slowly down the inside of the curved plastic. In slow motion, Mike turned to look at Bill, but vomited again, this time right past Bill and out the open side of the copter. Mike tried to speak, but nothing happened when he attempted to move his mouth.

Bill dropped his gun, and reached over Mike's slumped body. Trying with all his might, he attempted to wrestle the controls out of Mike's hands, but the machine, the increased speed and the low swoop conspired against anything he could do to stop the R22's slow spin, straight towards the boat hurtling along directly beneath them.

Tim looked up and, locking eyes with the terrified Bill, saw Mike slumped across the control panel. He instinctively braked, burying the bow of the boat, at the same time turning it hard right to get away from the helicopter's line of fall and the lethal blades beating a death knell towards him. That's when he felt the hull hit the gravel bank too fast, and it rose up beneath him, blocking the sun.

Jimmy saw the rifle hit the stones, shattering on impact, and then watched with horror the slow-motion accident taking place before his eyes. One of the drones was caught in the blades and disintegrated, before the tip of the second blade hit the ground, buried instantly to a stop in the soft sand. The other blade arrested in a twisting mess before snapping off into the river, to be found two days later, five kilometres away washed up on the lake shore. The tail rotor kept turning chirpily, until it too smashed at full speed into the ground, shattering into thousands of pieces. The cabin of the chopper separated from the body and slumped sideways into the river, where it bobbed in the absolute silence that followed.

The crew were already on their way when the first blade hit the sand bank, driving vehicles at full speed through the water and hurtling across the gravel banks. The continuity man got there first, leaping out of the cab and jumping straight into the river beside the helicopter. Ducking into the freezing water he tried in vain to haul the unconscious Bill out of his safety harness, but all he could do against the current was hold the man's head out of the water until others arrived. It took four men working together to release Bill from the tangled wreckage and drag him to the side of the river, where others arrived with warm clothing and first aid equipment.

More men worked on freeing Mike. He, at least, was out of the water, and so it was easier to extract him from his seatbelt once they'd figured out the angle of the cockpit, while helpers in the river stabilised the cabin against the churning current.

Nick was in the second 4WD to arrive on scene. Seeing that the men in the helicopter had been rescued, he looked downriver to where the upturned hull of the boat had been flung and pushed hard up against a bank. Fording the river in the 4WD, he reached the boat, leapt out of his vehicle and banged on the top of the hull, hoping to hear a response. There was no reply – only the sounds of the rescue upstream and more vehicles arriving. He heard Jimmy yell at everyone to get downstream to scan for Tim.

Nick shrugged off his jacket, pulled off his shoes and plunged into the freezing water, now a dark muddy brown. Working his way around the side of the hull, he took a deep breath and dived under, trying hard to keep his grip against the current tugging him insistently towards the lake. With one final push he ducked down and pushed himself off the side. A few strong kicks and he came up into an air pocket under the boat. It was pitch black, so he had to feel his way around. The spongy back of one of the front seats hung down into the water, and he knew he was at the front.

Just then the boat shifted forward, scraping the gravel bottom, every rivet in the hull groaning with the unaccustomed position. Nick was knocked off balance under the water, which rushed into his mouth. He kicked off the bottom, spitting and sputtering once he found air again.

A piece of clothing wrapped itself around his legs. Pulling it up, he guessed it was Tim's jacket. He could hear people yelling above, and he yelled back, telling them to stay where they were and to hold the boat steady. There was only room and air enough for one, and the air was running out.

Then he felt it. A hand, cold and listless, floating in the water beside him. Grabbing it, he followed it up the arm to the shoulder and the rest of the man, floating head down in the current. He pulled, but nothing happened. Tim was trapped upside down – his foot probably caught behind the steering wheel.

Feeling his way to Tim's legs, Nick realised the culprit wasn't the steering wheel, but the throttle lever. He reached Tim's boot, untied the laces and tugged as hard as he could. His foot came free and Tim slithered into his arms. Supporting his head, Nick clutched him against his body and squeezed his chest with all his might, over and over again. Tim's head lolled forwards, and Nick grabbed his hair with his mouth and pulled his head back. It was the only way he could think of to straighten Tim's airway.

"Hold the boat still!" he screamed to the people above. "I've got him. He's not good." He took another mouthful of hair and pulled, silencing the rebellion from his tongue. The water was cold and relentless as it tugged against the boat, pulling it downriver. He could feel the temperature in his body dropping, draining the feeling from his limbs, but still he hugged Tim against him, squeezing his chest, mentally counting out the beat from *Staying Alive* with each compression, his CPR training from school playing back in his head. If he hadn't been able to hear people shouting above and around him, he would have given up. The cold was rapidly draining energy from his body, but knowing help was here kept him going.

He heard hands on the hull, feet in the gravel around the boat, and then a count. *One. Two. Three.* He shut his eyes against the sudden daylight. The boat was up and carried away and dropped unceremoniously on the bank. People splashed towards them, prised Tim out of his arms and carried him to the bank, where a blanket was thrown over him and someone carried on the chest compressions. One of the sound techs started mouth to mouth. Three of the crew walked-carried Nick out of the water where he collapsed, spitting hair and water from his mouth. Blankets and people crowded him, rubbing his arms and legs in silence, fear etched on their faces.

Nick was shivering violently. He was alive, but was Tim?

After a few minutes Nick sat up, but couldn't stop the shivering. He pulled the blanket tight over his head and body. He didn't feel one of the grips rubbing his back, while another pulled off his socks and jeans and rubbed his legs. He couldn't hear his own teeth chattering loudly in his head. It was if he was behind a darkened window from where he could only survey the devastation scattered across this idyllic landscape. Like his mother, he was used to death – but dying was different. He could feel death stealing towards them, swirling around the scene playing out on the gravel bank in the middle of the river. He opened his mouth to warn them, but no sound came. A hand appeared in front of him, holding a cup of hot sugared tea. He took it, but was shaking so much the hot liquid slopped onto the blanket, which he registered was red.

The minutes stretched. Word came to them ... Bill was going to make it. No one said anything about Mike, and no one stopped working on Tim, even though there had been no response. For all intents and purposes, the star was dead. Nick shut his eyes and slumped into the blanket.

A low murmur followed by a triumphant yell split the air. Tim James had coughed. He was rolled onto his side, and Nick, alert now, watched as brackish river water streamed from his nose and mouth. Just for a moment, Tim opened his eyes. Someone reported a neck pulse. He was alive – just.

"Keep still, Tim," said one of the crew. "Help's coming. You're gonna make it buddy." Tim lapsed back into unconsciousness, but now he was breathing on his own, his colour still awful but improving.

The thud-thud of a helicopter coming up the lake was the best sound Nick had heard all day. Tucking his head into the blanket against the whirlwind of dust as it landed, he heard footsteps running towards him. A paramedic in a high vis vest gave him a quick once over, left some instructions and then ran over to join Ben Goodman, who was working on Tim. Another team was working on Bill. Within ten minutes, Tim and Bill had been stabilised and loaded into the machine. The second–best sound Nick heard that day was the thud-thud of the helicopter flying down the lake, ferrying the two injured men to hospital.

CHAPTER THIRTY-FOUR

"It's about time you showed up, mate," said Lizzie a few days later, when Nick appeared in her doorway with her order.

"Yeah," he mumbled. "Been a bit busy."

"Busy? I hear you're a hero in this town. Tim James would have drowned if you hadn't been there. I've never had a genuine hero deliver my food before. The nurses told me what you did. Now pull up that chair and tell me everything – and I mean everything."

Nick was getting tired of being called a hero when he couldn't remember much of what had actually happened. Flashes of memory played back in front of him at the oddest times. For no obvious reason, he would suddenly be flooded with chilling memories of darkness, cold and the sensation that he was being held down by something or someone. His lack of memory was frustrating not only for him, but also for the police and the insurance assessors, but they reassured him his lapses were not uncommon and he should take his time.

Strangers had seen his photo on the front page of newspapers in New Zealand and around the world, and were curious to find out more. They would stop him on the street to tell him how brave he'd been, before asking what they really wanted to know. What was it like in the river, holding Tim James's head out of the water, not knowing if the boat was going to break free and drown them both?

Such questions didn't help his state of mind, so he stayed home for a few days, hoping interest would wane and he'd be left in peace. When he did go out he took to ducking into doorways each time someone approached him asking, "Aren't you that guy who ...?"

"I came here to get away from the questions, Lizzie, not to answer more. It's over. I want to get back to normal and talk about other people again. How about you tell me what it was like winning that world championship only to lose everything?"

The distress in his voice triggered something inside Lizzie. Her own memories replayed in her mind's eye, as they had every day since the accident. She sighed and sat back.

"I was seventeen. After winning, I only had a short break before I had to start training again. I had a new coach. One of my sponsors found him and insisted I use him. Enzio. He was very good looking and very strict, except when we were off the field. Then he wasn't strict at all. I was young and pretty, if I do say so myself. Next time you come, I'll show you my photos and medal if you like. They're here somewhere. Anyway, hindsight is a wonderful thing. I was also silly, and I let it all go to my head. He let me try all sorts of things I shouldn't have, which is why my father came to get me. He was worried, and I was so mean to him, Nick. He was the one who really cared about me and had my best interests at heart, not Enzio, but I didn't find that out till after the accident. You have to remember how different it was then. No internet, no mobile phones, no phone cameras and the press obeyed rules. Your life was your own and not something other people could sell without your permission."

"Tell me about it," said Nick.

"Most of the sports journalists were at the same parties. They couldn't expose me, because they were just as bad as I was.

"It changed after the accident. People love bad news, especially when it happens to someone else. I had been New Zealand's golden girl before. Afterwards I felt as if people were hoping for the worst, to teach me a lesson for rising so high. It's the most horrible feeling and I didn't understand it. One of the journalists had bribed a nurse at the hospital. She told him I would never walk again, and certainly never ski again. Imagine seeing your life written out for you on the front page over breakfast, and so ... look at me. I could have done it better. I know that now. Maybe it's not too late? What do you think?"

Nick reached over and took her hand, and she let him. He smiled at her and she smiled back.

"I hear both Bill and Tim will be OK," said Lizzie. "People are saying that if Ben Goodman hadn't got there so quickly, and if he hadn't been really good at that sort of work, things would be different and all your efforts under the boat would have been wasted."

Nick shrugged. "The guys who gave him CPR for so long and who didn't give up helped too. They were amazing." He thought for a moment. "Life's funny, isn't it Lizzie? One minute humming along and then ..."

Lizzie laughed. They sat together in companionable silence for a few minutes, neither in a hurry to break the peace.

Nick was the first to emerge from his thoughts. He looked Lizzie up and down. "Lizzie Martin, I think you've lost weight."

"Might have, but that's my business, not yours," she said defensively.

Nick smiled. Life was getting back to normal when Lizzie went on the attack. "Keep it up, you look fabulous!" he teased as he got up to leave.

"It's none of your business you nosy hero," she yelled.

Nick reached up, catching the empty coke bottle thrown at his head with surprising accuracy, but when he shook it, he noticed only water in the bottom.

"Aha!" he said, waggling the bottle at Lizzie. "I was right. Stop wasting your money on the real thing and drink water, Lizzie – it's free!" he called as he stepped onto the stairs, shutting the door just in time to avoid being hit by the next bottle. This one, he could tell by the thump on the door, was full. "I'll cancel your coke order," he yelled. "Tomorrow you can show me your medal."

Nick caught his foot on the lifted tread on the second step and nearly fell, saving himself just in time.

CHAPTER THIRTY-FIVE

"Are you sure you can do this, Elka?" asked Maggie. "There's no rush."

"I need to get out of the house and get some exercise or I'll go mad. Come with me round the block a couple of times. I'm sure I can manage that, but I don't want to go alone, just in case."

It was seven o'clock in the morning, and Maggie had driven over to Elka's house so they could resume their morning walks. Elka met her at the gate already dressed in the brightly coloured clothes she loved, and Maggie didn't have the heart not to go with her. They walked slowly together for the first few hundred metres before Elka seemed to find her stride and the pace picked up. *Thank God*, thought Maggie selfishly.

"So, have you heard from Dunedin? Do you need to go back? With all the fuss from up the lake your problems have taken a back seat," said Maggie.

"Sally – that's my surgeon, remember? – she rang me while I was still at your place. Everything is sorted out. I'm supposed to go back to see one more doctor and then that's it. I don't understand why he can't talk to me on the phone, but there you go. Doctors! God knows what I would have done without Kate. The restaurant is humming along so well without me, I almost feel redundant in my own business. And you too, of course, you've been great."

"It's good news then?" said Maggie, looking carefully at Elka for her reaction.

"Yes. Couldn't be better. I knew it would be," said Elka definitely.

"Nothing to tell me then," said Maggie, still uneasy.

"Nope. Done and cleaned."

"Dusted."

"Sorry?"

"We say done and dusted, not done and cleaned."

"Of course, that's what I meant."

Maggie had a feeling Elka was not being completely honest with her, but she knew Elka could be stubborn. She was a private woman who brooked no interference in her life, not even from Maggie. She would have to wait for Elka to tell her whatever needed to be said in her own time, because without resorting to truth drugs or physical torture, if Elka didn't want to tell her something, Maggie couldn't force her.

"How's Nick?" asked Elka. They were walking on a track that skirted the lake and took them around a headland amongst tall trees creaking in the soft breeze. The smell of pine needles, warm in the spring sunshine, was delicious, and Elka stopped to take a deep breath. "He was quiet the last time I saw him. Pre-occupied. Kate tells me he's starting to come out of his shell, now the press have stopped hounding him."

"He'll be fine. Takes a bit to process, though. It's Mike's family I feel sorry for. Susie took his body up north when the coroner was finished, for the tangi on his home marae. Their son came back from Australia to be with his family, but they're struggling."

"Does anyone know what caused the accident yet?" asked Elka.

"Nothing official. The investigation will take months, but there's been talk Mike might have had a brain haemorrhage. He's such a good pilot, only something like that could explain it."

Maggie noticed that Elka had gone very pale and had slowed right down. "Are you all right?"

"Fine. But let's stop for a minute – I need to catch my breath. And then, I think, my fit friend, I'd better go home. Don't look so worried, I think I've done well on my first morning out. Nothing a hot shower and some more painkillers won't fix. And before you say anything, I do not need any help."

"I didn't say a word," said Maggie. "As long as you're sure. I need to get home anyway, because I'm suddenly busy. The flu is starting to take its toll at the rest homes and I'm full up."

Maggie saw Elka to her door, relieved to see some of the colour returning to her face. "What time would you like me to pick you up tonight?

"Tonight?" queried Elka.

"Estelle's drinks," Maggie reminded her. "Tonight. But we don't have to go. I'm quite happy with pizza and *Coronation Street*."

"I suppose if I sleep now it'll be OK." She paused. "No, we are going. What do we wear?"

"Smart casual, it said on the invitation."

"How about I lend you a dress? Something with colour, just for me. Since Kate mentioned you only ever wear black, I've been thinking of seeing you in colour, and I like the idea."

Maggie looked hurt. "*Et tu*, Elka. Really? I'll think about it. But I don't need a hand me down. Contrary to what Kate's been telling everyone, I do own non-black clothes.

A chill wind blew off the lake and up the street, making both women shiver. "Inside and hot shower, now. I'll be here at five-thirty. No need for us to be the first there, and we don't have to stay too long. Not on your first night out."

When Maggie arrived home she couldn't miss the red stiletto designer shoes sitting on the bench with a note: *These will fit you Mum – wear them tonight. Make Mr Choo proud.*

Maggie thought about this less–than–subtle hint from her daughter. On the one hand it was lovely to be in her daughter's thoughts, but on the other, she didn't like being treated like a child. But thirdly ... she smiled gleefully. Jimmy Choo! *Sex and the City!* What red–blooded woman under the age of seventy would say no to the chance to wear such beautiful shoes?

Maggie kicked off her sensible walking shoes and had just slipped the first shoe on when the phone rang. Hobbling over to the bench to answer it, she noticed straight away how comfortable the shoe was, and how absolutely gorgeous it looked on her foot. Holding her foot up in front of her, twisting it this way and that, she wasn't paying proper attention to the caller.

"No, this isn't Kate. This is her mother, Maggie ... No, Kate's at work. I can give you her work number if you like ... No, she won't be home until much later tonight. What did you say your name was again? ... Eric. Eric? *The* Eric? I've heard about you. You worked my poor daughter to exhaustion and then you don't sponsor her to stay in the UK. Why don't you stay away? She doesn't want anything to do with you ... You're coming to Queenstown? ... You're already on your way? Is Kate expecting you, because I'm not sure ... She *is* expecting you. Well, OK then. Look, call me when you get here and we can go from there. Kate is really busy today and tonight there's a function ..."

Maggie gave him her number and hung up. She hobbled back to the counter and put on the other shoe, then paraded up and down the living room, holding her baggy track pants up over her knees and out of the way. The shoes looked fabulous, and it suddenly occurred to her she had the perfect dress to go with them, still with the Dunedin label attached and stuffed in a bag in the back corner of her wardrobe.

CHAPTER THIRTY-SIX

There was something holding him in place. It was a feeling, connecting him to the present; a feeling of restraint keeping him from going somewhere serene, a place where he knew he would feel at peace. Sensations poured around him. All he could see was light. He could taste it, too, and with the taste came with a wonderful perfume that brushed him lightly as it swirled around him. Warm presences wrapped around in an all-forgiving wisdom, layered with time. Voices came and went, some kind, some he knew and preferred to forget, but now was the counting time – when he faced his past and it was absorbed. For a moment he saw Mike ahead of him, silhouetted against the brightness, getting smaller and smaller until he was taken up and into the light.

The feeling pulled at him, insisting he turn away. He could see Nick in his red blanket on the riverbank, ashen faced, watching. He remembered the river gurgling past him and the splashing of people bringing help. The feeling was all powerful and he couldn't escape it. He searched the light, but didn't find what he was looking for and turned back. As he did so he knew everything would be as it was supposed to be.

Tim James woke from his dream with a jolt. This wonderfully serene dream, which had haunted his sleep for the past week, was gone, but the feeling stayed – he was the most content he had ever been. He looked past the end of his hospital bed, past the flowers choking floor and shelf space, and past the open door to the sterile hospital corridor. Something had woken him, and there she was.

Standing on the polished linoleum in her sensible waitressing shoes stood the woman he'd thought he would never be happy to see again – alive. His mother. Sylvia James.

Tim had no time to prepare himself before Sylvia flung herself across his bed, clutching him to her, stroking his hair, telling him how much she loved him and how everything would be all right – just as he remembered she had soothed him when he was a little boy. He remembered how fiercely she had loved him then, back when they were very poor and it had just been the two of them.

"Yes, Mom," he said. "Everything will be all right. Trust me, I know."

They held each other for what seemed an eternity before his mother finally levered herself off the bed to sit on the chair, still clutching his hand, her eyes examining every part of him, carefully checking that nothing was missing.

"You look awful," she said, when she found her voice.

"And you look old," he replied.

"Believe me, you don't look so young any more either, sonny boy."

"Good to see you, Mom. Paid your own ticket to get here, I hope."

"Nahh, your lovely wife – who I have only just met, I might add, not having been invited to your wedding and all – she sent your jet to get me. Lovely flight – had the plane all to myself. I hope you weren't saving the wine for anyone special. The poor man had to open five bottles before I found one I liked, and by then I was too tired to drink it. The bed on the plane is fabulous. Your bed – I mean the guest bed – looked a little lumpy and so I told the attendant, as your mother I would sleep in your bed. He didn't look happy, but hey, we're family. And Tim, I am loving the suite at the hotel. It is so good to meet Jenny. At least she understands the importance of family. And that boy of yours – so smart for his age and handsome, sheesh, he looks nothing like you when you were a baby, which is a good thing, I promise you. You were a very ugly baby."

Tim smiled. Was it good to have her here? Meh. He'd changed since nearly drowning, but his mother would always be same. She was the one person in the world who treated him with no respect, ever, expecting him to spend his money on her in front of her friends as some sort of vindication of herself and her life. He used to hate it, but now he realised, after what he'd been through, none of it mattered. He was alive. It was good. He'd looked down the barrel of the alternative and wasn't frightened. That was good too. Knowing.

At night, when he was waiting for the pain medication to start working, he would get flashbacks to the helicopter falling out of the sky towards him, the blades chopping the air, closer and closer. He could feel again the boat rising up underneath him, turning mid-air and burying him in the gravel, his foot stuck behind the throttle holding him face down in the water, unable to breathe, the river invading his nose and mouth, his arms flailing in pointless protest, until nothing.

He shivered and his mother stopped talking. He frowned at her.

"Don't look at me that way," she said. "I'm your mother, I'm allowed to worry about you even if you don't want me too. You're too caught up in being the big star to spend time with your mother. Too Mr Fancy Pants to remember me. I remember those pants, Mr Big Star, and how many times I had to change them when you were a baby."

His mother paused for breath and Tim, long used to the speeches she called a conversation, seized his opportunity. "I love you, Mom. I really do. I'm sorry I said all those things about you. I'm sorry I didn't invite you to meet Jenny or to our wedding. I promise I'll be a better son from now on. It's just ..." he paused, "you've always been such a pain in the ass."

Sylvia fumbled deep in her handbag for a tissue, head down, refusing to look up and let Tim see her face.

"And I love you too," she said, between sniffs. "There's no mother who could be prouder of her son. But dammit, Tim, you hurt me."

"No more, I promise."

"Good, because even before you said those lovely things, Jenny has asked me to move in. You have a nanny flat to spare, something about the night nanny storming off in a huff a few weeks back. I'm not going to let you push me out of your life again. I'm going to be a grandma to your boy. Did you see that mark on his neck – the same one you have? What a way to make peace. You almost dying. Twenty–four hours I was in labour without drugs, I'm telling you. Next time you want to talk, no boat accidents – just pick up the phone, I'll be downstairs."

Tim lay back on his pillows and shut his eyes.

Sylvia was still speaking. "And in future, no rivers! No boats! No more stunts. You're not a young man, that hair dye doesn't fool me. No countries where they drive on the wrong side of the road! Is that too much for a mother to ask? I don't think so. Do you?"

"No, Mom. You're right," he said, adding, "but only for today," under his breath. "Tomorrow you'll be wrong again and we can get back to normal."

"Are these people looking after you? I mean, properly? How civilised is this place? Have they spoken to the real doctors back home about you?"

"They're fine, Mom. It's all good. Couldn't have had better treatment. It was a Kiwi doctor who saved me, remember? Now, are *you* being looked after?" he asked, and then slapped his head. "Of course you are, I forgot. The suite, the private jet."

Thankfully, Jenny, carrying Isaac in his car seat, walked in to stop the reunion of mother and son from deteriorating further. She unhooked the baby and lay him down on the bed beside Tim. Isaac was a good–natured child and threw a big gummy smile at his father, melting the hearts of the three adults who each made silly noises in response.

As the baby gurgled and sucked his fingers, kicking little legs erratically, for no reason other than that they were free and he could, Jenny asked what the doctors had said on their morning ward round.

"My leg's doing fine, and so are my lungs. I need to take antibiotics for a while longer and I'll be on crutches for the next month. By then I'll be allowed to fly. Best of all, they're letting me out tomorrow. I checked with the specialist in LA and he said the same. One of the guys here sent over the x–rays and MRI, and they've had a few Skype consults. Everyone agrees the bone is healing well – and Mom, my head is normal.”

“Fabbo,” said Jenny. Tim and Sylvia winced, united in their distaste.

Jenny took no notice and continued, “Matt has booked the Lodge for all of us for a month. You can recuperate there in peace and quiet. No interviews, no scripts to read, and no meetings. Peace and quiet!”

Tim looked apoplectic. “The Lodge? For a whole month? For everyone? Goddamn it, Jenny, how much will that cost? And you sent the jet for Mom ... I mean, where does it end? I’m not made of money, even though the two of you seem to think otherwise. And on that subject, the bracelet you bought goes back. I won’t be able to work for a while and we need to economise, especially now.”

“Insurance,” said Jenny, playing with Isaac’s feet, much to the boy’s delight.

Tim stopped at the sound of the magic word. A beatific smile descended on his face as he sank back into his pillows.

“Insurance,” he said, making it sound the sexiest word in the entire English language. “Well, that’s all right.” He reached over and playfully tickled Isaac’s chubby little tummy, hoping for another big smile.

Jenny winked at Sylvia, who winked back.

After his domestic entourage had left to go shopping – because Sylvia, of course, needed new clothes – Tim’s nurse came in.

“I couldn’t help overhearing your mother,” she said. “I didn’t realise she was from New York. And is she Jewish?”

“She’s not,” said Tim, glumly. “She’s from Texas and she’s Episcopalian, has been all her life. That’s like your Presbyterian. She started out a Woody Allen fan, and then she started channelling Estelle Constanza – George’s mother in *Seinfeld*,” he explained. “She was talking like a Jewish mother before I left home. It made her feel more maternal when it was just the two of us, and I played along. I’m surprised she didn’t bring chicken soup.”

"She did. She made me promise to give it to you for lunch, as a surprise."

"I hate chicken soup and she knows it. Tip it out," he said in a stage whisper. "But tell her I loved it and want more." He chuckled. "Let's see who gets the real surprise."

CHAPTER THIRTY-SEVEN

The party was in full swing when Maggie and Elka arrived. Champagne had been flowing generously for an hour, and they were greeted enthusiastically at the door by Estelle. She was in her element as the flamboyant and generous host to clients and friends alike. Waiters were making the rounds of the invited, proffering hors d'oeuvres on silver trays and refilling glasses.

Everyone had dressed for the occasion. Maggie was relieved she'd ditched the black in favour of the red and gold silk tunic dress she'd purchased in Dunedin. It fitted like a glove, and Kate's stilettoes complimented it perfectly and made her look sophisticated, something she hadn't felt in years. She had to resist the urge to twirl every time someone commented on how fabulous she looked.

She was surprised at how many people she knew, and how pleased they were to see her, so it was twenty minutes before, glass in hand, she was able to squeeze her way through the crowd to speak to Kate about the phone call. As she reached the kitchen door, she caught sight of Ben, looking impossibly handsome, being kissed warmly on both cheeks by Estelle. Ducking behind one of the columns near the ladies loo, Maggie drained her champagne in one go. The twirling feeling came to a sudden halt, as shame and embarrassment washed over her. Why, why, why had she come, when she knew he would be here?

Elka sidled up to her. "What are you doing?"

"Trying to avoid a certain doctor," hissed Maggie, as a waiter thoughtfully refilled her glass.

"You've got to face him sometime. I don't know exactly what happened, Maggie, but was it really so bad you have to hide?"

"It wasn't me. I didn't do anything."

"Well then. You look fabulous. Time to act it. Now head up, shoulders back. My god you're tall in those shoes. Behave. He's on his way over. Smile, Maggie. Pretend he's a puppy."

"A what?"

"You know what I mean. Just smile, then. Let me talk."

"How are you, Elka?" inquired Ben.

"Better and better each day, Ben. I'll be back at work next week."

Ben looked surprised, but quickly turned to Maggie, who was now assiduously examining the bottom of her glass, which was already empty again. "And you, Maggie? You're well? I haven't seen you since Dunedin."

Maggie could hardly not reply, especially when Ben seemed to be making an effort to be civil. Her heart thumping in her chest, she looked up into brown eyes twinkling in amusement at her discomfort. What was so damned funny?

A waiter reached over and refilled her glass.

Before she could say anything meaningful, they were joined by Estelle, who entwined her arm in Ben's, standing as close as was physically possible to him without standing on his shoes.

"Doesn't everyone look wonderful?" she gushed. "Maggie, it's so nice to see you off duty and out of black – such a surprise, don't you agree, Ben?"

"I've always suspected there was colour lurking somewhere," he said, laughing, "but you're right Estelle, she looks beautiful. That dress is such a departure from what you usually wear, the person who helped you buy it must have an eye for what suits you."

Maggie cursed inwardly and took another sip of the delicious bubbly, completely at a loss for words.

Elka answered for her. "That's the dress Kate brought you from London, isn't it Maggie?"

"Kate has excellent taste. She gets it from me, but this dress, I bought it in Dunedin."

Estelle was growing bored at not being the centre of attention at her own party, and draped herself even more intimately over Ben, forcing him to look at her. "Ben, darling, the whole town has been talking about how you saved Tim James's life. Aren't we lucky to have him, ladies?" Almost as an afterthought she looked at Maggie and said, "And you must be so proud of Nick. I should have invited him. Call him and tell him to drop by. There are lots of people who'd like to meet him. His bravery, combined with the skill of this fantastic doctor have put Queenstown on the map. The Mayor was telling me the servers at the Lakes District council were overloaded as soon as news of the accident got out. Of course, we are also very sad to have lost Mike," she added.

Estelle beckoned them closer. "Real estate is going through the roof," she whispered, loudly enough for everyone else in the room to hear, and then more quietly, "You bought the Lake Hayes house at the right time, Ben. Well done. Now, if any of you hear of anyone wanting to sell, remember me, won't you? I must mingle." And with that she swept off to talk to a well-dressed couple on the other side of the room.

Maggie, Elka and Ben smiled at each other awkwardly, wondering who was going to be the first to break the silence.

It was Maggie. "You got that house for a good price, didn't you Ben? I suppose you were able to take advantage of a terrible situation. The competition was hardly in a position to object, was it?"

Ben's face froze. He looked uncomprehendingly at Maggie, first with hurt and then with vague contempt, before excusing himself politely and moving away to talk to another guest.

"Can you explain?" asked Elka.

"I can and I will," said Maggie, slurring her words just a little. "Lucy and Mark – you remember, the man who died on the chairlift and his lover – were going to buy that house. They'd put in an offer which they expected would be accepted. But when Mark died, it of course fell through and Ben swooped in for the kill, so to speak." She finished with a triumphant nod at Elka.

"No!" said Elka, "I don't care about the house. I want you to tell me why you were just so hideously rude to a man who obviously likes, or should I now say *liked*, you. A lot. It's none of your business what he paid for the house, or who he bought it from, and to bring it up in public is strange, Maggie. It's not like you, and the fact that you are already half drunk is no excuse. One day you can tell me what really happened in Dunedin, but right now I would rather we didn't speak."

Maggie was speechless. She felt as though Elka had stripped her bare and found her wanting as a human being. Hot tears pricked her eyes. Never in all the years they had been friends had Elka spoken to her like that.

Ducking her head, she escaped to the loo and locked herself in one of the stalls, trying to understand why she'd said what she said. It's the principle, she thought. He thinks money and charm can get him everything he wants. It's how he got the house when Lucy was so vulnerable. I'm the only one who knows the true story. They wouldn't think he was such a hero if they knew what he'd done.

She staggered upright and unlocked the door, then did a quick check in the mirror, deciding what she would do – after all, no one really cared what she looked like. Smoothing her dress down she picked up her glass and set out in search of Elka to make things right between them. At the door she hesitated. This was the reason she didn't go to parties. She couldn't trust herself to behave. Nothing good ever came of them. She wished she could just snap her fingers and instantly be transported back to her cosy living room and *Coronation Street*, but she needed to see Elka first.

Maggie slunk back to the party in her red Jimmy Choos. The noise in the restaurant had increased markedly in her absence as the champagne continued to flow, and the waiters seemed busier than ever. Maggie's glass was quickly refilled as she stood alone, searching for a familiar and friendly face who might provide some form of social asylum.

Estelle's voice floated in beside her. "I wanted to get you on your own

Maggie. How's Elka? I mean, really? She looks all right – thin, perhaps – but did the surgery go well?"

Relieved to have her mind taken off her own misery, Maggie replied, "I think she's all right. She doesn't say much but she's making plans for summer, so that's positive."

"Excellent. She's done a lot for this town, hasn't she? Without her restaurant providing some more sophisticated dining, I would have gone nuts. I mean, all those young people plummeting off bridges and down mountains is great, but they don't spend a lot of money on anything else, do they?"

"I guess not."

"And," said Estelle, confiding in Maggie in a way she'd never done before, "I hear Tim James is coming back to recuperate at the Lodge after he leaves hospital. Evidently he believes Dr Goodman is the only one who can look after him properly. He can't fly for a month. Tim James, not Ben. He's bringing his wife and son and the whole entourage with him. Tim James, not Ben. That would be silly, he doesn't have a son. Ben, not Tim James."

A waiter refilled their glasses before they could wave him away. Maggie wobbled a bit. It was hard to balance in the heels.

"Nick won't talk about it," said Maggie. "He wants to forget it happened and get on with his life."

Estelle nodded solemnly. "Quite right. My father was a fighter pilot. Didn't talk about it – the real heroes never do. Let's drink to heroes, Maggie."

They both drank.

"Estelle, now that we're friends," said Maggie, "tell me about the sale of the Lake Hayes house. I haven't heard a thing from Jilly's estate, so I assume there were no complications."

"It sold the night before that man, Mark Holmes, died on the chairlift, which was very sad, wasn't it? Ben made the more generous offer, way above any price I thought the place would get, and it was accepted. Of course, I rang Mark and Lucy to ask them if they wanted to go higher, but neither of them could manage it. They asked for time, but Jilly's husband – ex-husband, I mean – said no. He was happy with Ben's price and my efficiency. I'll get more business from him, you mark my words. Anyway, I couldn't get a hold of Mark and Lucy because they were skiing. I had to tell her afterwards. You know, after he ... you know. I hate that word, death. I don't know how you do it, Maggie. Such a depressing job." Estelle looked up from her glass. "You don't look so good, Maggie."

It had taken a few moments for the facts to sort themselves out in Maggie's head, and when they finally fell into place she felt foolish – incredibly stupid, even. Why couldn't she have kept her big mouth shut?

She threw back the contents of her glass and searched for the waiter to bring her another. She hadn't eaten all day, and was having increasing difficulty balancing on both finely crafted stilettos, which suddenly seemed to have a will of their own, each choosing to go in different directions.

She'd made wrong assumptions about a man she was only just getting to know. Not only that, she had practically accused him of unethical behaviour, based on no evidence whatsoever.

Oh God, what had she done? She felt sick to her stomach.

Estelle saw her struggling, and eased her into a nearby chair before asking the waiter to bring some water.

Ben Goodman came over to offer his help, realising something wasn't right. This was the last straw for Maggie. How could he be so nice to her after her rudeness to him earlier?

"I'm fine," she said quietly, wishing Estelle would stop fussing and Ben would go away. "Altitude sickness from the shoes Kate lent me. Enjoy the party and let me sit here quietly for a few minutes. I'm fine."

Then, "I'm sorry," she blurted out. "I'm sorry I said those things to you about Lucy and the house. I was wrong and I'm sorry. I was so wrong and I'm so sorry."

Ben looked surprised at this turn in the conversation, but shrugged his shoulders. "It's OK, Maggie. One apology is enough, I assure you. We all make mistakes. After all, I shouldn't have ..." But he stopped.

"Shouldn't have what?" asked Maggie, wanting him to continue, but the noise of the party had suddenly dropped, and heads were turning towards the door. Maggie pushed herself to standing, trying to see what was happening.

Nick was standing at the entrance with a tall dark man who Maggie thought she recognised. Estelle's guests made way for the two men, parting and then re-grouping to whisper as the pair walked determinedly towards the kitchen.

"Isn't that Eric Mansfield?"

"I think so. But what's he doing here?"

Estelle could barely contain her excitement, no doubt thrilled that one of the world's most famous celebrity TV chefs was walking through the guests at HER party. Eric Mansfield owned restaurants in New York and London, had made countless television shows and sold millions of recipe books. His face was synonymous with the best of modern cuisine, and he was here, live, in Queenstown, at Estelle's party. She dug around inside her handbag, looking for her phone.

"You must be Elka," they heard the man say as he reached the kitchen. "You're a good cook. You taught Kate well."

The guests made futile attempts to pretend they weren't listening. Even the waiters had stopped pouring drinks.

"You're correct. I am Elka and you must be Eric. Kate has told me all about you. I've heard you can cook too."

Maggie's ears pricked up. Kate had told Elka about Eric. She'd said nothing to her. *I'm her mother*, she thought, and stepped forward, still wobbly on her high heels. Eric was the man she'd spoken to on the phone. She took another step towards the kitchen, unaware that Estelle was behind her, moving closer to take a photo.

Unaccustomed to the combined effects of stilettos and too many glasses of wine, Maggie staggered, caught a heel in the thick carpet, and pitched headfirst into Ben's outstretched arms.

Ben took his time making sure Maggie was capable of standing upright, before only partially releasing her.

"Kate. Come out here. Please," said Eric, loudly enough for everyone to hear and for them to finally stop all pretence of minding their own business. They turned their attention to Kate, who was standing behind the serving hatch.

Kate turned slowly to look at him. She took off her cook's apron, smoothed down her jacket and walked into the restaurant. The room fell silent. Even Estelle, who'd dropped her phone when Maggie had fallen, stopped muttering.

"Kate, you're pregnant," said Eric and Maggie in shocked unison, breaking the spell.

And Kate, standing before them in her chef's clothes, her baby bump obvious to all, nodded defiantly whilst staring straight into Eric's eyes.

A man coughed. There was a flurry of thank–yous and people looking for their coats. Car keys rattled in pockets and the door opened and shut behind departing guests. Waiters started clearing away glasses and picking up discarded food and serviettes.
Estelle could not have been more delighted. No one would ever forget this party.

CHAPTER THIRTY-EIGHT

"Elka, why didn't she tell *me*? Why couldn't she talk *to me* about what happened in London?" Maggie burst into a flood of fresh tears, reaching past Elka for another tissue before loudly blowing her nose.

"Ben, is that tea ready?" called Elka, looking at the pile of soggy tissues on her otherwise pristine glass coffee table.

"Coming."

"Kate was going to tell you soon – very soon. She wanted time to make her own decisions and to think about her choices without your advice. Maggie, you know she loves you. I blame the champagne for this. Right, Ben?" she asked, looking meaningfully at him as he put down a tray of mugs on the table.

"Definitely the champagne," he said slurring his words for effect. "I always blame the champagne, especially that French muck your restaurant serves, Elka. Makes people pregnant without their mothers finding out."

"Very funny," said both women, helping themselves to tea, Elka looking askance at the carton of milk Ben had plonked on the tray.

"I think you have to accept Kate is all grown up, and wants to take responsibility for her own decisions," said Ben, sitting down opposite her.

Maggie looked up sharply. "So you knew too. Everyone in Queenstown but me knew my only daughter was pregnant." Another wail broke the silence.

"Maggie, stop it!" ordered Elka. "You're feeling sorry for yourself. This is not about you. This is about Kate and what she wants. Stop the weeping and wailing, get a good night's sleep and talk to her when *she's* ready. Not you. Your daughter is a hard worker and very talented. She knows what she's doing. Trust her or you will drive her away."

It was the second time that evening Elka had been brutally honest with Maggie; the second time Maggie felt as if she'd been slapped by her best friend. The alcohol was wearing off, and little hammers were starting to bang behind her eyes. Now was not the time to say anything. She needed sleep. She needed aspirin and she needed to talk to Kate. How dare she keep this from me?

Ben stood up. "Come on, Maggie, I'll drop you home. Nick took your car when he saw your fall from grace, which you'll be relieved to know wasn't seen by everyone. A word of warning – don't party with Estelle, she is way more used to the demon drink than you. That way disaster lies, especially in red Jimmy Choos! And Maggie, It's time you accepted you can't control the world and everyone in it."

Another slap. Why now? she thought. Why do they feel so free to tell me what's wrong with me tonight?

She got up, picked up her shoes and padded meekly down the hall to the front door. She knew that if she turned around she'd see Elka and Ben sharing a look; a look she wasn't ready to see.

Outside The Stables, Ben got out of the car and opened the door for her. On the doorstep he said, "I don't think I could do it."

"Do what?"

"Be a parent. Watching everything friends and patients go through for their children, it seems awfully hard."

Maggie looked up at him, grateful it was dark and he couldn't see her bleary eyes. "Thank you," she said wearily, trying to ignore the hammering in her head. "And I'm sorry I was rude to you again. You have been very kind when you didn't have to be." She hesitated. "I would like to be friends, if that's all right with you?"

"If that's all you want, and think it's best, then I suppose I have to accept your offer. Let's just be friends." He bent down and gave her a friendly peck on her forehead before leaving.

Maggie let herself into the house and tiptoed upstairs. Kate was fast asleep when she peeped into her room, and Nick was snoring away.

As she switched off her bedside lamp, Maggie replayed the doorstep conversation in her mind. *Maybe he thought I was going to invite him in? He did lock his car.* She remembered the beep and the lights flashing in the dark.

You're drunk, Maggie. Of course he didn't. As if you'd ever make that mistake again.

She sighed. It was good to know they could be friends – normal friends, as she was with Elka. Lying there with her head spinning unpleasantly and feeling very sick, she was suddenly sure friendship with Ben was the best option – the *only* option. Anything else had caused embarrassment to them both. After all, she'd survived this long without love, "whatever love might be," as Prince Charles had famously said on his engagement. Did she even know what it was? And love wasn't the be all and end all, was it? Life is bigger than love, she thought. Well, that sort of love, anyway. And yet it wasn't friendship she dreamed about later that night when she finally drifted off to sleep.

CHAPTER THIRTY-NINE

"I don't understand you, Kate. And I don't understand this silly behaviour of yours, ignoring my calls, my emails, making me come twelve thousand miles to make sense of your behaviour. It's peak season and yet here I am. I think you owe me an explanation, don't you? Why did you leave without a word?"

The kitchen staff had made a hasty exit when it became obvious Eric and Kate needed privacy. The pair were standing in the half light of the cleaned and empty kitchen, surfaces gleaming and everything put away.

"I did tell you, Eric. I told you over and over again. I couldn't stay because my visa had run out. You were the only person who could have changed that. And I didn't stay because you're married! I love you but I can't have you. Simple! It's better for me to be with people who return my love twenty–four hours a day, seven days a week, year in and year out, not with someone who can sneak away for an hour once or twice a week. I deserve better. So does our child. Stay with your wife – it's the right thing to do. But you have to leave me alone. I can look after myself, but I can't do it in London."

"Kate, I understand you had to go, and I do remember you saying something – I think. But sneaking away without saying goodbye, without a saying anything, after all we had. And a baby. *My* baby."

"Keep your voice down, Eric. This isn't your kitchen, this is my kitchen. This is where I work, and I don't want you shouting my business to every person within cooee."

Kate was angrier than she'd ever been in her life. The feelings she'd been bottling up since her return erupted. "How dare you come here and tell me it's your baby. You gave away any rights to me, my life and my body when you made it perfectly clear you would never leave

Sandra, your *business partner*," she said, lacing the last two words with heavy sarcasm.

"And Toby," said Eric, with equal sarcasm. "Don't forget my twelve-year–old son and my duty to him. Of course I can't leave my family and everything I've worked so hard for, Kate. You said you understood."

"I do understand. It's only a pity you didn't tell me about Toby before we slept together the first time, or the second or the third. It took a while for you to be honest with me, and when you were, I took it. I sucked it up. I walked. Now you goddamned do the same. Get the hell out of my restaurant and my life. I don't need you and I don't want you. Coming here was the worst thing you could have done to your family and to me. Goodness knows where you keep your brains."

There was a discreet cough, and Kate turned to see Nick in the doorway.

"How long have you been there?" she asked.

"Long enough," said Nick quietly. He took a step towards Eric. "My sister would prefer that you left. And to make things easy for you, I have your bags in my car. I'm happy to drive you to a hotel. It would be better for everyone if you gave Kate, and us, her family, some space before you leave for good."

Eric reluctantly relented. He bid Kate a formal and insincere goodnight and walked past them both. Nick followed, telling Kate he'd be back in a few minutes to take her home.

CHAPTER FORTY

Maggie woke the next morning with a piercing pain behind her eyes and a foul dry taste in her mouth. Lifting her head off the pillow, she immediately wished she hadn't, as a wave of abject discomfort surged all the way from her stomach to a spot inside her poor tortured brain, where it hammered on her skull trying desperately to get out.

There was a timid knock at her door and Kate walked in, bearing a tray with a large glass of sparkling iced water, a strip of paracetamol tablets, a huge plate of eggs, bacon and baked beans cooked just the way Maggie liked them, a pot of strong tea and two mugs.

"Sit up, Mum. I've brought you Kate Potter's famous hangover cure and an apology."

Maggie opened one eye. The light was severe so she closed it again. The smell of Kate's breakfast was both tempting and sick making.

Kate popped two tablets out of the foil and put them in her mother's hand. Maggie had no option but to sit up and take them.

"Now we can talk," said Kate.

"They take a few minutes to work, don't they?" asked Maggie pathetically. "I am never going to drink again in my whole life. God, I feel awful."

Kate walked over to the window, flung the curtains back with unnecessary gusto, and opened the window, inviting in the fresh air and sunshine of spring. Maggie flinched as the sunlight precision-lasered its way into the spot behind her eyes, a sensation rather like ice picks flung with force into jelly.

Kate seemed completely oblivious to her mother's distress.

"It's not that I didn't mean to tell you, but I was feeling really grotty when I came home. I could only sleep and vomit, usually at the same time. I had no idea what was wrong with me until I saw Ben, then I needed time to think. I was about to tell you when you hijacked me to look after the restaurant. I was working long hours, we were never home at the same time and there was no opportunity to sit down and explain."

She hurried on. "I couldn't leave a note saying, by the way I'm pregnant, the father lives in London and is married to someone else."

Kate poured the tea and handed a mug to Maggie. "Actually, a note might have been better than the scene in the restaurant last night. That should keep the gossips occupied for a few days."

Maggie sipped her tea. "It's not just the Queenstown gossips who'll be riveted," she said. "Eric is one of the best-known celebrity chefs in the world. It wouldn't surprise me if there weren't photos, or – oh my god – a clip of last night's performance already on the internet."

Kate put the tray down on the bed and took her phone out of her pocket. She tapped the screen and gasped. "It's in the *Telegraph*! It's all over the *Daily Mail* and *Stuff* – it's the lead article, Mum. Look!" she wailed. They sat in stunned silence, neither wanting to say out loud what they suspected would happen next.

Maggie was just reaching across to feel Kate's tummy when the phone beside her bed rang, followed by her cell phone. Kate's cell phone also rang, and downstairs someone was knocking insistently on the front door. Below the open bedroom window, someone was calling Kate's name and asking her to come out.

Maggie and Kate shut off the phones one by one, and Maggie got up to close the curtains and window. Thank goodness the paracetamol were kicking in and she could walk with both eyes open at the same time.

"I have to get to work, Mum," pleaded Kate. "Elka can't do it, she isn't well enough yet. What am I going to do?"

Maggie took a deep breath. "If you truly have to go to work, then I will get you to work. Get dressed and I'll drive you. You're going to have to duck down in the back seat. Once you're there you should be safe.

I'm sure Brian and the others will keep the press at bay. Be happy their expense accounts don't run to the price of your meals."

"I didn't mean the photographers, Mum," said Kate tearfully. "I meant, I'm pregnant. I'm due in a few months. I have no home, no money, no partner – what am I going to do?"

"You're going to have a baby, Kate. Women do it all the time. We'll cope, just as we always have. And this is your home. Together we've got more than enough money, and you may not have a partner but you have us. It's so exciting. Has it moved yet? Please tell me you don't know the sex. The surprise is half the fun. It's going to be more than fine, Kate. It's going to be great."

Maggie saw the look of fear on Kate's face. "Please don't worry. We'll look after you and the baby until you're ready to stand on your own two feet again. Now, as Betty would say, shoulders back and walk tall."

Maggie pulled on pants and a jersey. "Go and get changed and we'll work out how to get you past the people downstairs. Honestly, the press must think Queenstown is the mother lode, the goose that lays the golden egg of gossip. First Tim James and now Eric Mansfield. Such a pity Betty isn't here – she would have loved all this fuss. She'd have been in her element."

"And Eric? What should I do about him?" asked Kate, keen to delay facing the world and the judgement waiting for her on the front step.

Maggie paused on her way to the bathroom. "He's a busy man who's dropped everything, including his wife and son, and flown halfway round the world to see you – before he knew you were pregnant. He must have feelings for you, Kate. You can't just turn your back on him and expect him to walk away. You need to talk to him properly. Imagine how his poor wife is feeling. The papers in the UK will have rammed this news down her throat by now and she's having to face it alone, knowing he's here with you. It's a bit late, but you need to consider her feelings."

Kate dropped her head, unable to look her mother in the eye. "I did think about her, Mum, but not the way I should have. I messed up big time, didn't I? I thought if I left and came home, it would all go away and she wouldn't be hurt – truly I did. Eric would carry on as normal and no one need ever know. I didn't ask him to come." she finished lamely. She sighed and left to get ready for work.

Sneaking a look at the bump in Kate's dressing gown, Maggie couldn't understand how she'd missed it before.

CHAPTER FORTY-ONE

It took a week for the story to die down and the press to lose interest in Kate and Eric. Photography in the restaurant was banned, and most customers respected this. The staff took huge delight in publicly shaming anyone they saw sneaking a shot, and, as Maggie predicted, menu prices were too high for the paparazzi to sit and spy from the tables.

The James women, on the other hand, were a godsend. They were well dressed, and Jenny was not only beautiful but also happy to be photographed. She often wandered the town with Sylvia, shopping and chatting to locals in the cafés, always accompanied by Isaac, his face all but obscured in his pushchair by the large floppy hats his grandmother plonked on his head.

Left to get on with her life, Kate continued to work as hard as always, and her staff rallied round and made sure no one got in her way or made silly comments. She was a popular chef, not only because of her skill, but also because she was calm in an industry renowned for panic and angry outbursts in hot close environments, where pressure was a constant, only dissipating when the last order had left the kitchen.

The staff's loyalty to Kate was important, as Elka still hadn't returned to work. This had created an unspoken uncertainty in the workplace which, in combination with the avalanche of bookings following Eric's arrival and the revelations of Kate's pregnancy, meant everyone had to be on their toes and functioning at their best. Several restaurant critics had come in incognito, their highly favourable reviews the only evidence of their visits.

Elka stayed in regular contact by phone, and as time passed and she was feeling better, popped in more often. She declared herself delighted with the way things were being managed, and seemed in no hurry to come back to work – she was enjoying her first real holiday in years.

"I don't have to be anywhere, and I'm so proud of what you and Brian are doing. I don't need to rush back yet. Time enough for that later," she said, nodding meaningfully at Kate's expanding waistline.

The only fly in the ointment had been Eric's insistence on eating at the restaurant every day, both lunch and dinner. He sat at the same table in the far corner, and during the course of the week had ordered every dish on the menu, sampling, tasting and writing notes. If it had been any other chef, Kate would have kicked him out, but part of her was keen to get his opinion. Usually he would nod, taste and nod again, before polishing off the whole dish.

The staff, busy with the full restaurant, got used to him. Seeing him finish a plate was immensely gratifying, and Kate gave herself a metaphorical pat on the back each time for the implied approval. When it seemed he didn't like something, she was in despair, and would torture herself trying to figure out what was wrong and what she could do to make the dish better.

Kate and Eric didn't speak that week, but each was keenly aware of the other as the media spewed forth speculation and vitriol about their affair. The local papers tried to be restrained in their coverage of the deeply wounded wife, but they couldn't avoid the subject altogether. Kate and Eric were too absorbed in their shared passion for food to take much notice of what was being said about them. Neither of them particularly cared. What was done was done, but there was always another more exciting way to cook lamb.

When the local vintners found out how Eric was spending his time, they delivered bottles of their best wine to the sommelier, in the hope that he'd persuade Eric to try them. Occasionally the great chef would raise a quizzical eyebrow, request the contact details of the vineyard and place an order.

At the end of the week, a note arrived in the kitchen: Kate: Tomorrow afternoon, 1.30 – my table. E.

Kate had anticipated this, but was still anxious when the time came for their meeting. Her palms sweating and heart racing, she couldn't tell whether she felt more anxious about his review of her cooking, or what he would say about their relationship. But it was no doubt time to hear what he had to say about both. In all honesty, the time away from him meant she cared more about his opinion in regards to her cooking than anything else – almost. She admired Eric's ability and talent hugely, and heartbreakingly there was also a part of her which still adored him. But only a small part.

CHAPTER FORTY-TWO

Waiting at the usual spot early the next morning, stamping her feet to keep them warm in the grey dawn, Elka was looking and feeling better than she had in weeks. So much so it took Maggie a few minutes to settle into the fast pace Elka set as they walked down to the track around the lake.

"You've had the all clear?" asked Maggie, trying to slow her breathing to match her strides.

"Thankfully I never have to go back. The appointments and tests are over. I have my life back," replied Elka triumphantly.

"So what's next?"

"I want to enjoy life," replied Elka as she slowed down. "Having this time away from the restaurant has made me realise how hard I've worked. Years and years without a break. Now I sleep well and I wake up at a reasonable time, because I don't have to worry about getting to the markets, or the menu, or bookings or the accountant or tax. You're a businesswoman. I don't have to tell you what it's like and the relentless grind of it. I recommend you take a leaf from my book, Maggie. Take some time out to enjoy everything you've worked for and do it soon, because you never know what's going to happen."

Maggie stopped and looked out past the Frankton Arm inlet of the lake to the great lump of land forming Mt Earnslaw. A breeze had blown up from the south, making the water choppy, with white caps sprinkled over the grey–blue. She shivered, and without turning around said, "A few weeks ago, what you're saying would have made sense. But now there's a baby to think about. Kate will have to take time off. No income. So I guess I don't have a choice about stopping yet. I don't mind, I really don't. It's just that I didn't think I'd be a grandmother this young."

When Elka didn't reply, Maggie turned and saw her friend was a good way ahead and hadn't heard her. She ran to catch up.

"It's such bliss to enjoy my home, Maggie," said Elka. "All the things I'd put on hold until some mythical time when I'd be able to do them properly. This scare has taught me that the present is all there is. And while I have Kate, I can reassess what I'm going to do. I know I'll have to go back when she has the baby. But for how long? That's the question. And in what capacity? That's the other question. Did you know the restaurant is booked solid for two months because of her cooking and the rave reviews she's been getting? I don't have to be there. I'm not indispensable."

"You are to me," said Maggie. "As a friend, not a cook. I know Kate's good, Elka. It's this mess with Eric and the baby, who'll be here soon – that's the nightmare. Eric's been at the restaurant every day for the past week, eating Kate's food and writing notes. He hasn't said a thing to her about what he's going to do. Thank goodness the novelty's worn off and the photographers have left them alone. Poor Tim James and his lot are their victims again. I heard one photographer developed hypothermia after lying in the tussock all night on a ridge above the Lodge, waiting to get a shot of Tim on crutches."

They rounded a promontory and started into another bay, the houses to the left mostly empty, waiting for their owners to return in summer. A few willow trees were covered in the first green buds of spring, and camellias in full flower coloured the lakeside gardens. The path was wider now and they walked side by side.

"Women didn't own businesses when we started," said Elka. "Well, not many. Betty helped us get over that, didn't she? If it hadn't been for her I would've gone back to Germany, worked in an office and bought a cat – hell, maybe two cats. She made me believe I could do anything I wanted, and if it didn't work, then so what. Do the next thing. I miss her."

"So do I. Especially since I found out about Kate."

"When does Jim get back?"

"I don't think he's coming back. He went to Brisbane to get some sun, and he wants to stay. He's learning to play golf, if you please. Betty would turn in her grave. You know how much she hated golf, especially in a man. Susan told me he can't bear to come home, knowing Betty won't be there."

"Maybe it is better to be single. Then you don't have the pain of loss. Can't say I ever met a man I valued more than freedom. Could have been cowardice on my part, but I don't think so. You helped, being generous with your children. Having them in my life mopped up my excess hormones. Some people need the family thing more than others, and I guess I didn't. Having this time to myself means I can finally say that and mean it. I recommend you have an operation too, Maggie. It makes you slow down."

"Too chicken," said Maggie. "I think Estelle has the right idea, going off to those women–only health camps where you can sit and contemplate your naval for days at a time and no scar. Her method is better than yours. Hey, we should go together, next year, when your peace has worn off under the hurly-burly pressures of being a restaurateur again."

"I'm hoping I will feel this way till the end of my days, Maggie."

"You might have slowed down, but I haven't. Come on," she said. "We'd better hurry. I have a service and burial at two."

"I'm going to try a few hours at the restaurant this evening, helping Kate. How the tables have turned – the young have so much energy. I know I don't want to be young again. Having to relearn those hard lessons of life would be too much."

"Anyone listening to us would think we were in our seventies instead of our thirties."

"Forties."

"You Germans have to be so precise."

"No point in running away from time. It runs faster than you ever can."

"I don't think I could handle the drama of my youth. I feel great now. But looking young wouldn't be so bad. I'd like to look my best at this age, when I feel my best," said Maggie. "The whole age on the outside and feeling fantastic on the inside is a cruel trick. Looks are wasted on the young, not youth! But we look young enough, don't we? Well, I do, when I'm not wearing my glasses. Come on, pick it up, there are people waiting to be fed and buried."

CHAPTER FORTY-THREE

Eric leaned casually back against the wall, half-listening to the physiotherapist firmly over-rule the vehement objections of her patient. Sweat beading on Tim's famous face, coupled with pain etched deeply around his eyes did the man no favours, he noted idly.

He remembered when he had first met Tim, an aspiring actor starring in his first West End production while Eric was a lowly sous chef at that god-awful chop-house in Soho. They'd been going out with the same actress, and when they confronted her and she told them both to piss off, they had drowned their sorrows together and been best friends ever since – in that alpha male competitive sort of way. Eric took some satisfaction in seeing Tim looking his age, and could tell Tim hated that he was there to see it.

He pretended to focus on the text conversation he was having with his son in London.

U r a TOTAL bstd. Mum cries all day. Still! R u coming home? Or not?

I'm back next week. Hold tight. Be all right I promise.

?????? FFS I don't think so

Luv u. Tell Mum to take my calls. Can explain.

"I'll see you again tomorrow morning, Mr James," said the well-toned young woman, her dark hair tied high into a ponytail that swung saucily with each step she took towards the door.

Eric looked up, temporarily diverted from his son's misery.

"Remember, it's your upper body strength you need to build up, so you can use the crutches without causing any damage. Do another twenty minutes of the reps I showed you and then you can relax."

"Sandra still blanking you?" asked Tim, when the door had swung shut behind her. "Funny thing about wives – they just don't get the whole 'sex with another woman who is pregnant with your child on the front pages of all the papers' thing. No sense of humour."

"Tell me about it," said Eric. "It's not like I was ever going to leave her and run away to New Zealand. She knows I wouldn't live here, so why is she giving me so much grief?"

Tim looked at his friend through the pulleys and steel wires of the machine he was using. "You're serious, aren't you Eric?" he said. "You really don't get the whole humiliation and betrayal thing. Imagine if the shoe was on the other foot."

Eric looked puzzled.

"Imagine if it was Sandra who had the lover and travelled halfway around the world to be with him, not discreetly but in full view of the media. What I don't understand is, why did you come when you had no intention of staying? Kate had given you a free pass on a platter."

"I wasn't to know your exploits would have stacked the place with media with nothing to do while they wait for you to recover. Tim, old friend, we're both men of the world. We know Kate is not the first or the last. And my fans and the press love it when I'm naughty. OK, maybe not the baby," he said. "How was I to know the silly girl would get herself pregnant?"

Tim was doing some pull downs and so had his back turned to Eric.

"I didn't come all this way for love, Tim. I came because Kate is one of the few chefs, male or female, who I consider my equal – or rather, she will be one day. I wanted her to come back to work for me. That's why I came. I was planning to teach her, but more importantly I wanted her right where I can watch her. The last thing I want is for her to work for the competition, and the boys in London were starting to make their moves. Now the silly girl has gone and done the best thing possible to ruin a magnificent career – pregnancy. Women!"

Tim stopped doing his reps and towelled off his neck and head. "So the baby's nothing to you. And Kate is only important because she can cook. And Sandra?"

"Before you get too preachy, Tim, I suggested Kate comes back to the UK with me. I told her – have the baby, your mother can look after it. Sandra will understand. It's business. Kate comes back to cook. Her career is saved. And Sandra can watch her every move."

"I bet she said yes," said Tim, unable to keep the contempt out of his voice.

"Amazingly, no. She said no, I mean. I could make her famous and rich in a couple of years. Of course, I told her we couldn't be lovers, but she always knew we were just a kitchen thing. She knew I was married to Sandra."

"Would you get me my water, Eric?" said Tim. "My throat feels as though I've just been sick."

Eric passed Tim the bottle. "We have restaurants and businesses on both sides of the Atlantic. Sandra and I work well together. She'll calm down and this will all be forgotten. I've told Kate I can help with money for the baby, but the silly girl said no again. I can look you in the eye and tell you honestly, I have done everything a decent man can do, Tim. My conscience is clear."

Tim drank the water slowly.

Eric blithely launched into a discussion about the arrangements for the dinner he was to cook for Tim and his guests in a few days' time.

"Let's concentrate on the important things in life," he said. "Your dinner on Saturday is the only reason for me to stay. I want to support you in your time of need, after all, what are friends for? I've told the chef here at the Lodge, that Kate and I will take over the kitchen in the morning to prepare. He can stay and help if he chooses, and in fact it would be good to have an extra pair of hands I can trust. He seemed grateful."

"This is the menu which, as you requested, uses only New Zealand ingredients and wine. It's been a struggle, my friend, but Kate has helped. Sadly that only reminds me of how much I'm going to miss her, but it's not your fault. I promise not to let my sadness affect the occasion."

Tim edged back on the bench towards the wheelchair. He had to twist awkwardly to reach it, nearly losing his balance as he did so. Straining, he hooked it with his left hand and pulled it towards him. He made sure the brakes were on before lifting himself awkwardly across to the seat, his leg in full-length plaster unsupported and heavy, poking straight out in front of him until he could get the support adjusted.

Eric walked past him to look at the view of the lake below. "It's beautiful here. So peaceful."

Tim, pale from the pain after his workout, was quiet. He wheeled himself over to join Eric at the window. "There'll be twelve for dinner, Eric. Ben Goodman; my surgeon and his wife; Jenny and Sylvia; Mike's widow and her son; Matt; Maggie and her son Nick, and Elka. Bill is still in hospital, poor guy, but Jimmy, my director will make up the twelve."

"Thirteen – there will be thirteen including yourself, Tim," said Eric.

"Thirteen? I'm not superstitious but I think my physio should come too and make it up to fourteen. I'll ask her tomorrow. Matt's given you the budget. Stick to it, Eric – just don't tell Jenny I said that. She hates it when she thinks I'm being mean with my money. Matt's also organising a photographer, so try and look dignified. We'll send out the menu you and Kate have created with the photos."

"No need to mention Kate," said Eric quickly. "My public is only interested in what the master does – not the apprentice. Besides, it would hurt Sandra."

Their business finished, Eric held the gym door open for Tim and watched as he propelled himself awkwardly down the walkway towards his cottage, glad it wasn't him in the wheelchair. Although the undivided attention of the young physiotherapist every day would be a bonus.

Tim wasn't the only one struggling with a disability that afternoon in

Queenstown. Lizzie had slid herself to the edge of the sofa, clutching her drooping skirt to her ever-diminishing girth and tucking it into the waistband. She used both hands to put her weight onto the walker and pull-push herself up. Taking one tottering step after another, she swung her damaged leg in front of her with each painful step. She was breathless and sweaty by the time she reached the door. Determined, she leaned heavily against it to get her breath back, then set off again. This was the fifth of the ten room circuits she had decided to finish that afternoon. Walking was much harder than she remembered.

She could feel her heart thumping hard and fast deep inside her chest, and wondered if she might die there and then, while she was still too big to fit through the door. She'd noticed since stopping the coke that she had to pull her skirt tighter around her waist or it would fall round her knees when she stood up. Nick hadn't said anything more about her weight loss, but she noticed the pizzas he brought were thinner, and skimpy on the cheese and meat. The other orders he'd brought were all half sizes, but she'd let it go until this morning, when he'd had the temerity to drop off only three vegetarian pizzas garnished with *raw* vegetables. This had been too much, and she'd rung the restaurant and complained to that poor knocked-up sister of his, Kate.

Just one more lap to go and she'd allow herself rest and sleep. In the last week she'd slept more deeply than she had in the past ten years, and miraculously had stayed asleep for several hours. She was getting fit enough to die, and thin enough to fit in the casket Maggie had let her know had arrived, she thought blackly.

CHAPTER FORTY-FOUR

Maggie, Elka and Nick climbed out of the limousine at the front door of the Lodge. Nick, the first out, was feeling awkward and uncomfortable in the shirt and tie his mother had insisted he wear. He undid his top button and loosened the tie, shrugging his shoulders as if to shake off the invisible shackles of his mother's old-fashioned standards.

Maggie was wearing her usual black, but the dress was anything but dowdy as it flattered the slim body beneath and highlighted her hair worn loose on her shoulders. She'd thought it best not to repeat the mistake of the Jimmy Choos and had chosen heeled black boots, which gave height, but more importantly, stability. Her gold necklace and simple pearl and gold earrings complemented her overall appearance, making her look both elegant and beautiful.

Elka was wearing a flowing robe of many colours, a dress she hadn't been able to wear for years but now could, making the most of her slimmer figure, post surgery.

Dressed up and being treated like celebrities, it was impossible not to be excited about the evening ahead. When Kate had talked to them earlier, she'd been unable to contain her enthusiasm for the menu. She'd worked day and night to create a very special dinner, every dish approved by Eric.

A waiter with a tray of chilled champagne bubbling in elegant flutes met them at the door. Near the entrance hall fireplace, flanked by his mother and his wife in formal evening dress, sat Tim James. His dinner suit was loose on him, revealing the physical toll the last few weeks had taken.

Maggie's party was the first to arrive, and with champagne glasses in hand, Matt took them over and introduced each in turn to their host and his family, before leaving to welcome the next arrivals.

As soon as he heard Nick's name Tim beckoned him closer before reaching up and grabbing the boy, hugging him tightly and whispering a heartfelt thank you. Jenny and Sylvia followed suit. It was the first time the two men had met since the accident. Tim said he had no memory of being under the boat, but that he'd been told how Nick had saved his life at great risk to himself.

Maggie and Elka stepped back, making way for others to be introduced. The room was lavishly decorated with huge arrangements of orchids, roses and peonies, lit by candles everywhere. In the middle of the hall, the table for fourteen was set with thick white linen, gleaming silverware and a glittering array of crystal. At each setting, marked with beautifully written place names, sat a small eggshell–blue box.

When Ben arrived, Maggie had to turn away to admire the darkening view. He looked overwhelmingly, mouth-wateringly handsome in a tailored dinner suit. His appearance wasn't lost on Elka, or on any of the other women in the room. Elka and Maggie exchanged looks over the rims of their champagne flutes, eyebrows raised, barely able to stop smiling let alone retain any semblance of dignity. Nick, catching sight of their schoolgirl silliness, grimaced.

When all the guests had arrived, Matt discreetly called for their attention, and Jenny pushed Tim forward in his wheelchair. The room hushed and he raised his glass. "I've asked you here tonight to thank each one of you. Thank you for my life. Without you I wouldn't be alive to be a husband to my wife, a son to mother and a father to my son. And the world would also have lost its greatest movie star!" He took a long drink, during which there was an embarrassed pause. Matt looked desperately at Sylvia.

"Has George Clooney been in an accident too?" she asked, loudly. There was polite laughter, and everyone relaxed.

"Thank you, Sylvia," said Tim. "Seriously, I owe you all my life and as a token of gratitude I have a small gift for you, which you'll find in the box beside your place name. Please take your seats and I'll ask Matt to let the kitchen know we're ready."

Maggie was seated between Nick and Ben, but wasn't too worried about what to say to Ben, as he'd no doubt be distracted by the beautiful Jenny who was seated on his other side. She was dressed in a floor–length white designer dress complemented by the largest gold and diamond bracelet and matching earrings Maggie had ever seen. Maggie noted Jenny's looks weren't lost on the good doctor, and was relieved she'd have Nick to talk to.

Mike's widow, Susie, was seated between Sylvia and Matt, who'd been charged with helping her through the evening. Mike's son, Haami, still grieving for his father, was next to Nick. They had known each other at school and there was much to catch up on. Maggie recognised Kate's thoughtfulness in the seating plan.

Encouraged by Jenny and Sylvia, the guests opened the little boxes beside their plates. The women had each been given an exquisite pair of enamel and gold earrings from Tiffany's, and the men received cufflinks, also in enamel and gold.

Jenny broke the silence. "I hope you like your gifts. I chose them, and had them flown down. I adore pieces from Tiffany's, as you can tell," she said, waving her wrist with its heavy bracelet.

Tim turned pale green at the sight of the bracelet he had been planning to tell Jenny to return. Mentally he totted up how many significant occasions this gift could possibly cover, adding their upcoming anniversary, to the birth of Isaac and contrition for Auckland. He also made a mental note to himself to cancel the account at Tiffany's at the earliest opportunity, but when he looked at his mother he realised it was too late. She was wearing earrings, and a necklace and a bracelet, all from Tiffany's. He wondered when the tiara would be brought out.

Taking a long, deep draught of champagne to steady his

bank–balance phobia, he raised his glass and announced, "Tonight we have a special dinner for you, prepared from the finest ingredients to be found in Aotearoa/New Zealand and matched with your finest wines. This dinner has been created for you by Eric Mansfield, a three-star Michelin chef, author of best–selling books and the owner of Eric's in London and New York – a man I have known for many years."

Nick saw Maggie's and Elka's eyes meet. No mention of Kate. He squirmed in his chair at the omission of his sister's name. He knew how hard Kate had been working, and the amount of preparation she'd done for tonight's dinner.

"But first we will take a minute's silence to remember Mike. Haami and Susie," continued Tim. "I only came to know Mike the week before our terrible accident, but I was, and I can say this sincerely, looking forward to getting to know him better. I share only a small part of your grief, but I can share a large part of the celebration of the man you loved. He was a fine pilot, a good man and I'm deeply sorry for your loss. We all are, so I ask you to stand and observe a minute's silence for Mike, or Mikaere, as he was known to his family."

During the silence, Matt and Sylvia supported Susie between them. As the others sat down again, Susie remained standing, proudly looking around the table.

"Mikaere spoke about you, Tim," she said. "He spoke of you as a friend, a man from another world who he'd not liked at first. No, really," she said, looking at the genuine surprise on Tim's face. "He thought you were a bit stuck up, and that's the polite version."

"Appreciated, Susie," said Sylvia.

People looked down at their glasses, not wanting to catch the other guests' eyes for fear of their smiles being caught by their host.

Susie continued. "That morning when he left for work, he told me how he'd got to know you better. He said what a strong man you were, and how day after day you bore the load of everyone's expectations for the film. He told me he liked you, and deep inside, underneath the

Hollywood stuff, you were real. Being 'real' is the highest compliment Mikaere paid to anyone, isn't it, Haami? So thank you, Mr James – Tim – for being a friend to my man and for making his last day on earth 'real'. And thank you for tonight. He's with us as we celebrate your recovery and life. The best thing we can do to remember my Mikaere is to eat, drink and enjoy each other's company."

Susie sat down to a round of soft applause, and on cue the doors from the kitchen swung open and a stream of six waiters brought out the first dish. Two wine waiters whisked away the champagne flutes, and another two waiters filled glasses with a crisp New Zealand sauvignon blanc.

Course after exquisite course followed: venison; racks of wild rabbit baked with central Otago wild thyme; fresh goats' cheese drizzled with manuka honey flown in from the Bay of Plenty; dark paua meat from Fiordland; fresh crayfish from Kaikoura; salmon from the Southern Alps served with fennel and chives; marbled Angus fillet steaks from Hawke's Bay served with the soft round flavours of a Martinborough pinot noir. Fruit sorbets, perfect crème brûlée, baked fruit possets contrasting with homemade pomegranate ice cream set with golden kiwifruit candies. Boutique cheeses made from sheep and buffalo milk, served with freshly baked crackers and bread and accompanied by a cold dessert Riesling, followed by liqueurs, coffee, hand-made chocolates and petit fours.

Kate's talent, skill, imagination and execution was obvious in every course, every dish. She'd barely slept for two days as she did the preparations, driven by her need to prove to Eric that she was the better chef and always would be, even if she was confined for the time being to a resort town at the bottom of the world. Having the dinner to focus on had helped her cope when he'd told her he was leaving. In her head she knew he could do nothing else, but the way he'd told her made her finally understand and accept that he had never cared for her. She was just another notch on his belt, another kitchen romance, and she cursed herself for her naivety. She had barely listened when he'd offered her work at any of his restaurants, regardless of his wife's objections, but only if she left her baby with her mother – not *our* baby, *her* baby. Stupefied by the dawning realisation of her own foolishness, believing his lies when he'd wanted to be her lover, she closed off a large part of her heart. She had done this to herself. Her romantic belief in the honesty of her love had brought her to this place, with this man who had stolen her integrity as well as her recipes, heartbreakingly and with her total complicity. Kate felt the door close in her soul and she knew what she had to do. She cooked.

The dinner was over and the waiters were serving final coffees, port and liqueurs.

Matt had arranged for photographs to be taken of everyone together, and individually with Tim and his family, the smiles genuine and broad.

"We need a photograph with the chef," said Tim. "We should drink a toast to him and the wonderful meal. He outdid himself this evening. The food tonight was even better than at our wedding, Jenny, wasn't it?"

Reluctantly, Jenny turned her attention away from Ben. "Sorry, Tim, I didn't hear you."

"I said Eric outdid himself and the food was even better than at our wedding." Tim held out his hand for her to come to him, away from the handsome doctor.

"I think you're right. Tonight was fabulous," agreed Jenny, moving to his side.

"I wouldn't know," said Sylvia. "I wasn't invited to my son's wedding. Go figure."

Susie patted her hand comfortingly.

"Matt, bring out some Krug," called Tim.

The waiters reappeared with fresh glasses and several bottles, just before Eric made his grand entrance in his spotless kitchen whites.

Tim raised his glass. "To Eric. My friend and the best chef in the world."

The photographer took photos of the two men shaking hands while raising their glasses to each other.

"What about Kate?" asked Nick. "Doesn't she deserve to be here too?"

"It's not usual for the sous chef to be included," said Eric, before turning his back and talking quietly to Tim.

"It was Kate who created the recipes, and it was Kate who prepared and cooked them. She deserves to be acknowledged," Nick said again, loudly enough for everyone to hear.

The other guests stopped talking, turning first to look at Nick, and then to Eric to see what would happen next.

Matt looked for guidance to Tim, who gestured to him not to interfere.

Eric shifted uncomfortably and looked to Tim for support. Tim shrugged. Eric huffed, but realising he was fighting a losing battle, walked to the door and called for Kate and Pete, the chef at the Lodge to come out. They arrived looking dishevelled and tired, their kitchen whites stained with splashes of food and their hair plastered to their foreheads with sweat.

Eric handed them each a glass of champagne and quickly asked everyone to toast his assistants.

"Speech, Kate", said Nick.

"Do be quiet," said Kate. She looked uncomfortable in the spotlight, and she tried to usher Pete back through the door with her to anonymity.

"No, wait a minute," said Pete. "I agree with Nick. I think everyone should know. It was you who created the menu, Kate. You who scoured the country for the ingredients and supervised the quality, you who did most of the prep work, with help from me. It was you who discussed the wine with the sommelier and you who cajoled the rare bottles from the vineyards. You created and cooked this meal. And this three–Michelin–star–chef Eric bloody Mansfield just sat on his British backside and has done nothing except take all the credit."

"So, ladies and gentlemen, I realise you aren't here tonight to discuss the work etiquette of those who have cooked for you, and I sincerely apologise for the intrusion, but I do think if credit is to be given, it should be to the person who deserves it – Kate Potter."

The locals raised their glasses and cheered. Sylvia, who had had too much to drink, cheered the loudest, before the waiter refilled her proffered glass.

And then, as captured by the photographer in a remarkable series of still shots which would be sold to newspapers all over the world, Eric Mansfield angrily launched himself across the room, arms outstretched, teeth exposed in a fierce grimace, eyes fixed firmly on his target – the throat of Pete, the honest chef at The Lodge, Queenstown, New Zealand.

In the background of the photos, which would form an award–winning photo essay on the subject of human emotions, Tim James could be seen in his wheelchair laughing uproariously, looking genuinely happier than he had in years. Jenny, her hand resting lovingly on his shoulder, was clearly enjoying the moment with her husband, while Sylvia was draining the last of the champagne from her upended glass.

It was this photo which reassured the studios Tim James would soon be well enough to return to acting full time, and which meant he was sent a pile of scripts that would keep him booked for the next three years.

As Eric landed spread-eagled on the floor, in the space left vacant by the nimble Pete, who had side–stepped neatly out of the way, Ben Goodman leapt onto him and pinned his hands behind his back, telling him this was enough and he should behave. "There are ladies present, old chap."

The photo of the handsome doctor in his immaculate dinner suit sitting astride the world–famous chef, exhorting him to behave, appeared on CNN News with the caption "First, Catch your Chef!"

CHAPTER FORTY-FIVE

Eric left town quietly the next morning, before the locals and the last remaining members of the press had woken up. Hidden behind dark Ray-Bans, and shrouded in a fedora and large black coat, he scurried up the steps of the jet kindly lent to him by Jenny James, who only informed her husband of his generosity after the plane had left New Zealand airspace.

A week later it was Tim and his entourage who made a quiet exit from the country when he was finally allowed to fly, but not before Susie and Haami took them to Mike's marae. Tim wanted to pay his respects to the man he had just been getting to know. This visit wasn't made public, despite Matt's recommendations.

Winter seemed to stretch long into spring, with a late September snowfall crushing fruit blossoms and daffodils alike. The snow was welcomed by the ski field operators, but not by farmers on the surrounding stations, especially those with early lambs.

Flu did the rounds again of the town's rest homes, keeping Maggie busy as she arranged funerals attended by the vaccinated who would live to see another summer.

Nick continued his deliveries and helped out in the restaurant when needed. Lizzie, his favourite customer, was fading away before his eyes. Unfortunately her mood hadn't improved, and woe betide him if he forgot any of the three pizzas she now consumed each day, accompanied by salad and fresh fruit.

Lizzie continued her circuits of the living room, bumping her walking frame into walls and the few pieces of furniture, cursing aloud if she knocked her twisted right foot. Ben Goodman visited most weeks, impressed with her progress

Kate was blooming with the excitement of her work in the busy restaurant. Her burgeoning stomach was increasingly in the way in the narrow kitchen areas, but as pregnancies go, hers was uneventful. She was gaining a normal amount of weight, felt energised by the life growing inside her, and had none of the sickness or swelling other women complained of.

No one at the restaurant had heard a word from Eric since his ignominious return to the Northern Hemisphere and the long–suffering Sandra. His television work had dried up as his cooking programmes were cancelled by the major networks, following the social media campaign from the #MeToo movement.

Sylvia and Jenny had become firm friends in their crusade for the welfare of husband and sons. As promised, Sylvia moved into the vacant night–nanny's flat and became a daily presence in the life of her son and grandson. She also converted to Judaism, something she had been meaning to do for twenty years.

When his leg was fully healed, Tim accepted a role that took him to Ireland. Sylvia stayed with Isaac, and Jenny, reluctant to let her impulsive husband out of her sight, went with him. Their marriage and their family thrived.

Jimmy, exhausted and stressed by his dealings with insurers and the police, nevertheless had no time for a break. With the insistent urgings of his producers ringing in his ears on a daily basis, he moved to Wellington to work on post–production, aiming for a tentative release date for the yet to be renamed film, in the New Year. Tim's physiotherapist, Anna, went with him.

Elka luxuriated in her slow convalescence, and a month after the dinner at the Lodge had still not returned to work full time. She and Maggie were walking each morning, perhaps not as far or as fast as they had walked in the past, but there was always so much to discuss that the slower speed suited them both. Maggie thought her friend looked happier than she'd ever seen her, and often commented to others how relaxed Elka was now that she wasn't trying to do everything herself.

Ben commissioned an interior designer from Christchurch to completely redecorate the house at Lake Hayes. Estelle called in unannounced several times in the early evening, bearing a bottle of good red on the pretence that she had a buyer for the house, just in case he was thinking of moving on. The first time this happened he made the mistake of opening the wine, but he soon learned Estelle was not a one–glass guest and didn't repeat the hospitality the next time she happened by.

Ben and Maggie saw each other now and then, in town or when someone had passed away. They had developed a casual easiness in their relationship, with no more awkward misunderstandings to blight their growing friendship. Elka, Nick and Kate watched them with amusement, often making less than subtle references to one about how good looking the other was, just to watch them feign disinterest. The three matchmakers weren't above arranging coincidental meetings. Maggie was surprised at how often she would find Ben in front of her at the supermarket checkout, Kate having told her she urgently needed something. Ben in his turn was starting to notice how often Maggie dropped into the restaurant to see Kate, just after he had sat down to a quiet meal alone.

Maggie mentioned the coincidences to all three conspirators, but there was no glimmer of response so she couldn't take her suspicions further. Even Lizzie had been primed by Nick to arrange her meetings with Maggie for a time when she knew Ben would be at her flat. It was a great source of entertainment for Lizzie, watching the two of them as they exchanged polite greetings and carefully side-stepped their way around the top of the stairs to avoid physical contact.

Unfortunately, the conspirators were rewarded with nothing more than polite small talk between their remarkably suited victims, who remained frustratingly and puzzlingly immune to developing a deeper relationship. Eventually they grew tired of matchmaking and got on with their own lives.

One morning, when Maggie had returned from her walk and was still in trainers and track pants, there was a brisk knock at the door. A young woman in a business suit, coat and high heels, her hair pulled back into a tight bun, stood expectantly on the doorstep. It took a few moments for Maggie to identify her as the grown-up version of the laughing teenager featured in the photos on Jilly's bedroom wall. A gloved hand was thrust towards her and the young woman introduced herself as Sarah, Jilly's daughter, and politely but firmly requested five minutes of Maggie's time.

Maggie had no choice but to invite her in, and when Sarah had taken up position in front of the empty fireplace, offered her coffee. She was only a few years older than Kate, and while she was evidently used to the deference of others, Maggie detected vulnerability beneath her steely exterior.

Without waiting for the coffee, Sarah proceeded to tell Maggie she understood from her father's PA that she'd been entrusted with the disposal of the Lakes Hayes house and contents after her mother's death. Sarah had also been told Maggie had arranged the funeral and had seen to her mother's burial.

Maggie nodded, and waited.

Sarah then started on a list of questions, such as how her mother had died, who'd found her, and where she was buried. Without waiting for replies she explained she didn't have long, because she was booked on the afternoon flight back to Auckland to connect with a flight to New York.

Maggie waited purposely before replying, "Perhaps you'd like to have that coffee. And take your coat off. These are difficult questions for a daughter to ask about her mother. I promise to answer them and I won't hold you up, but you have rather caught me and I need a coffee, even if you don't."

She walked into the kitchen. Sarah followed, and they stood waiting for the pot to boil. Sarah tapped her foot.

"You must have a busy life, and I would imagine a very demanding job," said Maggie, trying to make conversation. "It would have been awful for you being so far away and unable to do anything by the time you found out about your mother. Your father's PA told me you were skiing. In South America. No way to contact you in time."

Sarah stopped tapping and looked at Maggie properly for the first time. She seemed to relax when she understood she wasn't being judged, and that Maggie's concern was genuine. "Argentina. I was skiing in Argentina. The coffee smells good, doesn't it."

Maggie poured two mugs and motioned for Sarah to sit at the kitchen table.

"How did she die?" Sarah asked again.

"She died of a heart attack. Her cleaning lady found her," said Maggie, seeing no need to burden this young woman's memory with visions of empty bottles, the last drunken binge and Jilly's poor dead body not being found for days.

"And now? Where is she now?"

"I can take you to her grave after we've finished our coffee. I'm pleased you're here, because I need instructions about your mother's headstone, and I didn't know who to ask."

Sarah looked at Maggie and smiled weakly. "I feel bad, you know. Not coming to the funeral. You must think I'm the worst daughter. I am, I guess."

"What I think doesn't matter. It's what you think, and more importantly feel, that's important."

"I'm not sure what I feel, but I know I'd like to see where she is."

"I'm very happy to take you. It's good you've come, truly."

In the car on the way to the cemetery, they passed several shops in front of which cheerful bunches of spring flowers were arrayed in colourful displays. Initially Maggie slowed the car, anticipating Sarah would want her to stop so she could buy something to put on her mother's grave, but no such request was made and they arrived at the cemetery empty handed.

The mound of earth marking Jilly's grave had been flattened by the winter weather. A small white cross with a brass plaque engraved with her name was the only marker.

"As you can see," said Maggie, pointing at the cross, "this isn't going to last long. I've been waiting for instructions about the headstone, but despite my calls, no one has told me what to do." It was as if, with the sale of the house, Jilly had all but ceased to exist until now.

It was a cold day and a biting southerly wind was coming off the lake straight onto the graves, making for a gloomy, coat–hugging atmosphere. Maggie looked at Sarah's shoes doubtfully. They were suited to the pavements of big cities, not to boggy lawns around the graves. After several steps Sarah gave up walking on tiptoes and ploughed on, water staining the fine Italian leather. Maggie was still in her walking clothes, and soon froze in the damp chill of the cemetery, dark under the pine trees on the side of the hill.

Sarah's business–like demeanour dissolved as she contemplated the dark rectangle of mud marking her mother's grave. Maggie, standing beside her, passed her a tissue and moved a few steps away to give the girl space. Sarah had come prepared to deal with the finality of her mother's leaving on her own terms – much as, Maggie suspected, she had had to deal with most things in her life.

The wind stirred up the trees on the hill behind them, branches creaking in resistance. This cemetery was not a silent place, sited as it was on a busy tourist thoroughfare that had sprung up around it over time. Cars and buses formed a constant procession to the entrance to the gondolas, which whisked sightseers up to a magnificent view of the lake and mountains, and a popular café and restaurant. A parachute swung giddily to ground in a nearby park, its screaming, thrill–soaked passenger wrapped securely in the arms of the instructor. Nearby, a family playing mini golf could be heard arguing over the accuracy of the younger brother's score card.

"I heard you organised a minister to say a few words," said Sarah. "That was good of you. She believed in God so would've liked that. There was no one was there, was there? No one she knew, I mean."

"A few people," said Maggie. "Her cleaning lady, the minister, the doctor and I think Estelle the estate agent was there as well."

Sarah walked awkwardly around the edge of the dirt in her ruined wet shoes, heels sinking into the turf, apparently oblivious to her surroundings.

"At one time, Jilly – Mum – would have had a huge funeral. She had so many friends then. When I was growing up she was the life and soul of Auckland. Everyone loved her. She was so much fun. The house was always full of people laughing and enjoying themselves. I remember seeing Dad come home, exhausted, only to find Mum and her friends out by the pool having yet another party. He was OK with it for a while. He liked that side of her. But he would still go off to his study and work, and that used to drive her nuts.

"She trained me to pour the drinks as soon as I was old enough to hold a bottle. When you're a kid you don't realise, do you? But she was happy, which meant I was happy too."

"Things changed, when I got to high school, didn't they, Mum? It was just you and me then. Dad worked too hard, you said, and was never home, and everyone else stopped coming. I had my own friends. You never liked being alone. So you made Dad buy the land at Lake Hayes and for a while everything was all right again. You had architects and builders to be your friends. I heard Dad talking to you, begging you to come home, but you wouldn't."

"I bored her, she told me later, and Dad bored her too. We'd stopped her living the life she'd really wanted. Taken her potential, she said. By then I was old enough to know it was the wine talking, and not her. Of course when the house was finished, and the workmen went away, she got worse. No one wanted anything to do with her. She used to rave at me on the phone about how much she loved me and why wasn't I with her. In the end, I stopped taking her calls because I knew she was always drunk and she never remembered talking to me anyway. Sometimes she'd call ten times in a row, by hitting redial. You know the rest. I bet you thought we were awful, Dad and me, not coming to the funeral."

Maggie shivered and hugged her jacket tightly around her, hands thrust deep in her pockets.

"I don't think that, now I know what it was like for you," she said. "And it's not my business, but I do understand and I'm sorry. She was sick. She didn't mean to be that way to you."

"That's what I keep telling myself."

"Look at you," said Maggie. "Your shoes are ruined and your feet must be blocks of ice. Do you need more time, or do you want to come back to the car and warm up?"

"No. I'm done," Sarah said, looking up to the mountain framed in the distance by the craggy cliffs to the north. "She would have liked the view."

"I forgot to say," said Maggie. "I found a photo of you in her bedroom. I put it in her casket to keep her company."

Tears welled up in Sarah's eyes and she turned away. She didn't look back as she walked to the car.

Seated in the warmth, out of the wind, Maggie waited. When she thought Sarah was ready she took an envelope out of her handbag. "I'm not sure whether you would like these, and please don't feel you have to look at them. I took photographs of your mother, when she was–"

"Dead," said Sarah.

"Yes."

Sarah didn't hesitate. She flicked through them for a few seconds before putting them in her own handbag.

"I don't know how you can do this," she said, looking out over the rows of graves. "Isn't it difficult?"

"I was brought up with the dead, so no, I don't find it difficult." Maggie paused. "I used to hate it when I was your age. Now, though, I like cemeteries. Maybe it's the peace. No one can stay angry when they visit the dead. It's pointless."

"There are so many stories under these stones, all with the same ending and all reminding us that this is our ending too."

Sarah eased off her sodden shoes and wriggled her toes in the warmth of the heater. She was starting to look better, more like the professional woman she had become.

Maggie couldn't help herself. "Your mother loved you, and she would have been so proud of you, Sarah."

"Do you think so?" asked Sarah, the hope of a little girl shining in her eyes.

"She was surrounded by photos of you when she died. Does that answer your question?"

Sarah nodded then sighed. She was spent. It wasn't time to leave just yet, so Maggie filled in the silence. "A cemetery is where history is buried. Over there in the best spot are the gold miners. There, that's where the Chinese miners are buried. The names on the stones mean nothing to us, which is very sad, knowing they were so far from home when they died. Over there are the merchants, the farmers and their wives, the story of each person carved in stone for all to read. How long this one lived, where they died, who loved them or not, who their children were – the really important things in a life. Some of the older stones are just beautiful, works of art or sometimes beautiful slabs of the local rock. Each memorial chosen by the people left behind, who want to remember." Maggie stopped. "Sorry to go on."

"No, it's good. You're lucky to be doing work that means something. I don't suppose you could do me two last favours? I need to get new shoes ..." she looked down at the mud–soaked pumps lying beside her feet, "and I need lunch. So, a shoe shop and a good restaurant in that order would be a huge help. I hear there's a new chef at Elka's who's supposed to be very talented. I can order a taxi to take me to the airport from there."

Maggie drove the short blocks into town, double parking in the narrow street near her favourite shoe shop.

"You've been wonderful," said Sarah. "I *was* listening, and I will email you about Jilly's stone. I'll give you my card, just in case I get caught up when I get back and forget."

Maggie watched the young woman squelch down the pavement, head held high, in search of shoes.

CHAPTER FORTY-SIX

Lizzie was walking well. Only around her flat, but it was progress. She was still big, but not as big as she had been at the beginning of winter. It wouldn't be long, the nurse told her, before the scales registered an actual weight rather than just hitting the maximum recordable before stopping, defeated.

And to her surprise, the more she moved each day, the more the pain in her foot retreated, little by little, slowly but surely improving. Now she could look out of her window onto the life in the street below, focusing on something outside herself, outside this room. She still played computer games at all hours of the day and night, but now she had a new interest, spending a lot of her day sitting behind the tattered curtains, watching people, curious about how they lived. Occasionally someone would look up, unsure if they'd caught a shadow of a face in the window, and she would pull quickly back, then watch them shake their head before passing by.

Hunger still gripped her when she'd had a bad day, or when cold seeped into the metal screws in her ankle and gnawed into the misshapen bone, whittling back her resistance. But instead of gorging the terrible ache away, she would move, walk, hobble, stamp – anything but submit to the immobility of her victimhood. Sure enough the pain would recede, never leaving entirely, always lurking annoyingly in the background, waiting for her resolve to weaken, tiring and draining, but manageable. Just.

Under the guidance of her nurse and Ben, Lizzie had restricted herself to three meals a day, no longer prepared by Ronald, or the Colonel, or even by Elka, but by Jenny Craig. And she was surprised at how much she enjoyed food eaten at regular times, rather than all–day grazing.

Today was a sore day, and she was using her walker again. She figured any movement was better than no movement, and so allowed herself the extra support.

"Small steps. No need to rush, Lizzie," she wheezed.

Taking a deep breath she heaved the walker round and started on another circuit of the living area and kitchen. Stopping to peer down into the street below, she was constantly amazed by the changes that had taken place during her exile on the sofa. When she'd first moved into her flat, the street had been quiet, made up of plain windowed concrete block offices accommodating the lesser local accounting firms, real estate and letting agencies.

Now the buildings were made of cedar tiles with slate roofs, and cobbled pavements heralded the changing nature of the area's businesses. Ski shops, jade and jewellery emporiums, boutiques and a smart industrial–themed café lined the street opposite, attracting more and different people.

Reaching through the tatty curtains, she opened the window. Shutting her eyes and taking a deep breath, she filled her lungs with fresh air warmed with sunshine. Sounds from the street were no longer muffled, the clarity resonating with her new mood. She watched Nick's scooter buzz up the street and park at the bottom of the steps just under her window.

"I see you, Lizzie," called Nick as he unhooked her carton of prepared Jenny Craig meals.

Caught out, she recoiled, letting the curtain swing back in front of her. *Idiot*, she thought. *What if someone snapped you with their phone, what then?*

Her good mood was gone by the time Nick had thumped his way up the stairs and flung open the door, surprised to see her standing, back to the window.

"I never get over how tall you are, Lizzie," he said, opening the carton and loading the meals into her fridge.

"Tall genes," she said, shortly. "I used to be taller, but life happened."

"It's only one leg that's the problem, isn't it? You're a bit like Long John Silver. Maybe a parrot?"

Lizzie looked at the epitome of healthy youth in front of her, not sure whether to hit him, yell at him, throw him out or just ignore him. What the hell did he know about pain and suffering? She reached over and picked up an orange, hurling it at his departing back. Nick ducked and it flew over his head before smashing into pulp on the street below.

"Next time, I won't miss," she yelled through the slammed door.

"Nice to see you too," came the laughing reply.

Lizzie looked at the mirror at the back of the room. A woman smiled back at her.

CHAPTER FORTY-SEVEN

Maggie went into the quiet restaurant hoping for a moment alone with Kate. She was on her way to the Bide-a-Wee Rest Home to collect Mr Paget, an ex-teacher who had taught many of the town's residents at primary school. Mr Paget had been renowned for impressing the importance of neatness and manners on his pupils. He had died quietly in bed at the age of ninety-two, without a fuss, as consistent in death as he had been in life.

Elka was sitting at a corner table with a man Maggie recognised as a local lawyer. She looked up guiltily.

"Thank you, Arthur," she said, shuffling the papers spread out in front of them into a messy pile. "Call me when you're ready."

Arthur shoved the documents into a folder, which he tucked firmly under his arm, then left, nodding to Maggie on his way out.

"Hi," Maggie said, deciding to ignore what was obviously none of her business. "Is Kate here?"

"She's in the kitchen. I was meaning to tell you – I'm sorry, but I can't do our walk tomorrow. I'm so busy getting everything organised in the restaurant, I need the morning to myself." And as if to prove how busy she was, her mobile phone and the restaurant phone rang at the same time, clamouring for her attention.

"No problem," mouthed Maggie as Elka answered the restaurant phone. "I'll call you later."

She walked through to find her daughter and the other staff eating soup at the kitchen table before the lunch crowd arrived. Kate was now very obviously in the last stages of a healthy pregnancy. She sat on her chair, legs wide apart, her tummy bumping up against the table. Her rosy hue highlighted the sparkle in her eyes. Working was doing her no harm whatsoever, in fact she was positively thriving on the stimulation, and on the support of the team.

"Mum, come and have some soup – leek and potato. And Marco's made the most delicious bread."

One of the kitchen hands who'd finished gave up his seat to Maggie relishing the opportunity to have a quick cigarette outside while Kate was occupied. The others soon made their excuses, leaving mother and daughter to talk.

Maggie helped herself to a bowl of steaming soup and sat down. "Don't worry, I'll be quick," she said, between hurried mouthfuls. "I have to collect Mr Paget, and then I have a burial at two. I wanted to know when you were planning to stop work."

"Another two weeks, I'm thinking," replied Kate. "The baby isn't due for another month. Marco's going to take over the kitchen until after the birth. Elka tells me they can share the workload while I'm off. Don't worry, it's all organised – truly."

Maggie had no choice but to accept Kate's assurances. Her daughter looked healthy, and she knew the midwife at the medical centre was checking her regularly.

She finished her soup and looked over to see if there was any more, but was interrupted by the staff filing noisily back into the warm kitchen, wreathed in the smell of fresh cigarette smoke as they got ready to go to work. Kate took Maggie's empty bowl over to the dishwasher as someone called "Chef!" in a loud voice. The first orders were coming in.

"We'll talk soon. Thanks for the soup."

On her way out, Maggie blew a kiss to Elka, who was filling in for Brian as maître d'. She looked relaxed and totally in her element as she welcomed a table of four well-dressed American tourists. Maggie glimpsed Ben sitting in a corner, head down, reading his phone messages, but he didn't see her. Her heart always beat a little faster when he was around. She still hadn't figured out if it was because she was excited, or embarrassed. What she did know was that it wasn't getting any better, despite their so–called friendship.

CHAPTER FORTY-EIGHT

Two days later, Elka hadn't arrived at their meeting point by the normal time. It was unusual – her penchant for punctuality was well known. She deplored lateness, rarely giving anyone a second chance if she was kept waiting. Maggie stood alone on the corner, feeling a little silly as delivery trucks rumbled past on their way to supermarkets. Between the trucks were occasional carloads of skiers, hoping to get up the mountain before the snow turned to slush in the spring sunshine.

After ten minutes, Maggie decided to jog up the hill to Elka's cottage. She was curious, but also conscious of how busy Elka had been lately. That was probably why she hadn't appeared. Maggie remembered the cancelled walk from the day before, but was sure Elka hadn't said anything about missing today as well. Maybe she hadn't listened properly, or maybe Kate was supposed to have passed on a message and forgot.

Stopping outside the cottage, she peered over the fence to see if Elka was home. The front door was slightly ajar, so she opened the gate and walked down the gravel path, hoping the noise of her feet on the stones would elicit a response. At the door she could hear the voice of a breakfast TV host interviewing a visiting musician. She must be home. The door swung inwards, so she called out, fully expecting to hear Elka's voice shout an apology followed quickly by an offer of coffee.

Maggie took off her shoes, leaving them by the door, and padded down the hall to the back of the house, where two years ago Elka had knocked out walls to create her dream kitchen and living area, from which two sets of French doors opened onto a sun–drenched courtyard filled with lavender and standard bay trees.

The room was empty. She found the remote and turned off the TV. The sound of the kitchen clock, ticking away seconds, filled the silence.

Maggie looked around at the gleaming appliances lined up on the dark granite bench. The fridge started humming quietly in the corner, almost but not completely drowning out the clock. The living room, with its white linen sofas and red brocade cushions, was neater than she'd ever seen it. Persian rugs on the polished floors had been recently vacuumed and straightened. Fresh spring flowers arranged en masse in a huge crystal vase dominated a marble side table. Elka took enormous pride in the home she'd created from scratch, and this morning it looked perfect. There was no trace of dust or dirt anywhere. Even the windows were polished to transparency. It was if some cleaning wonderwoman had been in, attacked every surface then disappeared after arranging the flowers.

Something was missing, and for a few moments Maggie couldn't put her finger on it. She took a deep breath and realised ... there was no smell of cooking, something she automatically associated with Elka's home. The only aroma came from the flowers.

"Elka?" called Maggie again.

The clock ticked. The fridge hummed.

Maggie walked back down the hall, opening each door in turn. The bathroom, the guest bedroom, and Elka's small study were all as spick and span as the rest of the house, and all were empty.

When Maggie reached the door to Elka's bedroom, she hesitated, overtaken by dread at what she would find when she opened the door. Slowly turning the handle, she inched it open and looked inside.

Elka was lying face down in her bed under a mess of bedclothes, the pillow stained green, her hair in disarray, matted with fluid. On the bedside table a row of empty containers sat beside a glass, a dried yellow crust on the bottom.

The rest of the room was perfect. Wardrobe doors were shut, the curtains were open. The fountain Elka had discovered in an Arrowtown junkyard and restored to its former glory, was trickling water in the formal garden outside the window. More flowers were arranged in bowls on every surface in the room, the perfume unable to mask the bitter smell coming from the bed.

"Oh, Elka. How could you?"

Maggie walked over to the bed and, despite knowing it was hopeless, felt for a pulse. There was none. Elka, eyes shut, lips blue, was cold to her touch.

Maggie climbed onto the bed beside her friend and curled against her back, one arm over her body, and lay there. The fridge clicked off, the ticking of the clock filling the house with noise until slowly, the sounds of the fountain crept into the bedroom.

"What am I supposed to do now, Elka?" she asked quietly. "We were going to grow old together." She reached up and stroked Elka's hair, over and over again.

"The baby – you'll miss the baby," she murmured. "We were looking forward to it, you and me. Oh God, Elka, how am I going to tell Kate and Nick? We all love you, we always have. You know that, don't you? You did know that."

Maggie raised herself on one elbow and examined Elka's face for a reaction. Nothing. She pushed her, hard. Harder than she meant to, and Elka flopped over, green slime dribbling from her slack mouth onto the sheet. Gagging, Maggie turned away and sat on the edge of the bed. It was then that she started to cry. She didn't cry quietly; she wailed, she roared, she screamed her rage and stamped her loss, and finally she flung herself on the floor and sobbed in the perfect room in the beautiful house.

Later, repulsed by the smell of stale whisky from the glass on the bedside-table, she sat up and wiped her face. She took out her phone, dialled III, and waited.

When Ben arrived just after the police and ambulance, Maggie was sitting on the window seat in Elka's bedroom, looking out at the sunshine sparkling in the waters of the fountain. People walked in and out of the room, but she didn't pay attention. To them this was just another job: a middle-aged woman commits suicide. She heard them muttering to each other that it looked like suicide. The coroner would need to be involved, a post-mortem arranged and the funeral director called, except Maggie was already here.

She heard Ben say quietly to the constable that perhaps another firm should be involved, because Elka had been her best friend. At that she stood up. "I'll do it. I'll look after her. She would have wanted me to."

Ben looked at her intently, then shrugged and told the constable it would be all right.

"Suicide, Doc?" the constable asked, his back turned to Maggie.

"Probably, but can't be sure."

The constable sighed.

"I'm not sure what half these bottles had in them, sorry," said Ben. "The labels are in German so I'll need to get them translated. The coroner's office can decide if they need a chemical analysis."

"Right, I'll go back to the station and make the calls. Have you seen a note?"

Sitting on the dressing table beside the door was a small stack of envelopes, numbered and named in large florid handwriting. Maggie was surprised Elka hadn't drawn a huge arrow on the mirror directing everyone's attention to them.

A paramedic picked up the first envelope and handed it to Ben, who took the letter out of the envelope and unfolded it, before sliding it into a ziplock bag passed to him by the constable.

"It's addressed to you," Ben said, holding it out to Maggie.

Dear Maggie, she read to herself.

I had to do this. I need the death that I want, not the one nature was going to give me. I want to go now, while I can. I needed you to find me, not a stranger. I'm sorry, but I wasn't sure how I'd look when it was all over.

I know you are hurting but it will pass. Don't judge me Maggie, and don't be sad or angry. Understand instead. I couldn't tell you what I was going to do for so many reasons.

The operation wasn't a success. The cancer has spread from my ovaries to almost every part of my body, and I had maybe a few months left

I didn't choose the indignity of this horrid disease. Despite my German backbone, I'm not good with pain and I did this – selfishly – because it is best. For me.

Trust I am happy. I am happy. I have lived a wonderful life. I am grateful. You and Kate and Nick have been part of that. There's no one in Germany. My parents were the only people I cared about, and they died.

Forgive me, be happy for me, and when you are ready, follow my instructions in the letters. I have taken care of everything.

Envelope 2 is the suicide note for the police.

When I see Betty, I'll tell her all the news, and we will watch you from wherever we are.

My Last Advice. Open your eyes to what is right in front of you. Grab life with both hands and live it. You can do it only if you leave your fear behind.

All my love forever,

Your friend

Elka.

"Envelope 2. That's the suicide note," she said.

The constable picked it up with obvious relief. "Once you tell me what's in those bottles, Doc, I'll let the coroner know."

The paramedics left after expressing their condolences to Maggie, and the policeman excused himself, going outside to wait for the photographer. They heard the snick of the front gate closing.

"Tea?" said Ben.

Maggie nodded and they walked down to the kitchen.

"There's fresh milk in here," said Ben, looking in the fridge.

"But she took her tea and coffee black," said Maggie.

"I know," said Ben. "She must have been planning this for a long time. I bet if we looked, we'd find a list."

"I bet we wouldn't. The last item on the list would be to destroy the list." She paused. "Did you know?"

"That she was going to kill herself? No. But I knew about the cancer. I was waiting for her to tell you. I begged her to talk to you, but she'd stopped listening to me. She refused to discuss it after her final trip to Dunedin. She wouldn't let me tell a soul, and she rejected every offer of help. Why do you think I had so many meals at the restaurant? It was the only way I could talk to her and see how she was."

He handed her a mug of tea, and she huddled against one end of the huge sofa, cradling it her hands, unable to look up, unable to drink the tea. Ben sat beside her, took the mug and put it on the coffee table. He opened his arms to her and she leaned forward into the comfort of his chest. His warmth and strength soothed her, but not for long. Anger and bewilderment reached inside, gripping and twisting her heart. Struggling, she broke free.

"I could have looked after her. She knew that, but still she killed herself. How could she do that? How could she leave me, how could she not trust me? Did I mean nothing to her? Did we all mean nothing?"

Questions tumbled from her, rage with Elka curdling her voice before she remembered. "Oh God. Nick, Kate. I have to tell them before someone else does." She patted her pockets for her phone, but she'd left it in the bedroom. She looked at Ben, suddenly lost. He took his phone out and gave it to her. She looked at it as if she didn't know what it was. "Ben?"

He had no answer to the questions in that one contorted utterance of his name. Tears sprang into his eyes. "I'm sorry, Maggie. I'm so sorry."

For the second time, Maggie found herself in his arms. This time they were both crying – for their sadness, the pain of Elka's leaving, of being left, the grief and the fear of the unknown. And Maggie cried because next door, Elka waited, and she didn't know if she could bear it.

The phone beside the sofa rang. Ben let her go and she reached over and picked it up.

"Kate? Yes, it's true. Where are you? Is Nick with you? ... He isn't? Where is he?"

"Tell her I'll come and get her," said Ben. "You try and find Nick."

"Did you hear that, Kate? Ben is coming to get you."

CHAPTER FORTY-NINE

Nick heard the low murmur of the district nurse's voice as he climbed the stairs to Lizzie's flat. It was another beautiful morning; the sun was shining and the last of the snow had melted on all but the highest peaks across the lake. Leaves peeped bright baby green out of buds on bare branches, bringing fresh colour to the town, lifting it out of the drab grey of winter. With the warmth, people wearing T-shirts, their pale skin bared to the sun, had come back to the outdoor cafés and onto the streets. There was a new buzz in the town.

Helen – by now Nick knew the nurse's name – had been speaking quietly, but as he stepped into the doorway at the top of the stairs he heard her say "suicide". Lizzie gasped. "Not Elka."

"Not Elka what?" he asked breezily, unpacking the boxes of food onto the bench.

Neither woman said anything. Helen hurriedly packed away her equipment into her case and looked at her watch, before muttering something to Lizzie and making a beeline for the door.

"Goodbye, Helen," Nick called out pointedly after her.

"What's this about Elka?" he asked, going over to Lizzie.

She didn't look up. "Sit down, Nick." There was kindness in her voice.

"OK, now I'm really worried," he said. "What is it?"

"Your mother went to Elka's house this morning. She's ... I'm so sorry, Nick, but Elka's dead. Helen shouldn't have said anything, and I'm sorry this is how you found out, but she told me it was suicide."
Lizzie watched Nick turn pale and the light drain from eyes. He looked at her, as if waiting for her to say it was a mistake, that it wasn't true. She watched the hope in his eyes retreat as the silence between them grew.

"Mum. Kate," he said. "They need me." He patted his pocket for the key to his scooter then stood up, eyes blurred with tears, stumbling to the door and down the stairs.

"Be careful, Nick," called Lizzie. But she knew he hadn't heard her. She heard his scooter roar into life and then disappear down the street, as happy chatter from the people in the cafés below rose up and occupied her flat.

Pulling the walker towards her with practised ease, she went over to the window. The breeze floating the curtains around her was soft and inviting, as were the sights and smells of the new café, opened a week ago. She took a deep breath and savoured the aroma of freshly roasted coffee, smiling at a sudden memory of a café in France where she used to go for breakfast before training. Downstairs the patrons chatted companionably, or just sat alone, content to watch the world go by. Others read the paper or fiddled with their phones while white-aproned waiters bustled to and fro, balancing food and glasses on shoulder-high trays.

The world was going on without her.

She flashed back to the devastation on Nick's face. Maggie, Kate – what would they do? She turned back to look at the room where she had spent the past ten years of her life. She saw the filthy sofa, its base beaten by her weight, sagging on the food-stained floor. She saw the huge TV, the games console, the spotless kitchen, the overflowing rubbish bags, and the medical supplies stacked in a haphazard pile beside the extra-wide commode in the corner.

Lizzie stared down at her twisted right foot, and then, for the first time since her accident, looked carefully at her healthy left foot, watching as her toes wriggled on command. It was as if her left foot had been away for years and had just returned. Sure, the toenails were long and it was a bit grubby, but it looked so good, so new, and it wasn't painful. She leaned back against the wall beside the window and lifted it up for closer inspection. She watched as she rotated the foot at the ankle, and marvelled as it went all the way around. She pointed her toes. Where had this foot been?

Lizzie pushed herself away from the wall and planted her left foot firmly and painlessly on the floor, taking all her weight on the leg rather than on the walking frame. She stepped onto her right foot, and pain shot up her leg. But it wasn't as bad. It was bearable, even. Limping and leaning on the kitchen bench, she aimed herself at the open door. At the threshold she stopped, as much to catch her breath as anything else. When she felt ready she stepped outside. Gripping the stair rail, she stopped again, savouring the fresh air against her skin as she stood and surveyed the scene below.

A waiter looked up, surprised to see an enormous woman at the top of the stairs, squinting, clearly unaccustomed to the sunlight. He watched as she awkwardly manoeuvred in the small space, feeling for support as she hobbled forwards. He saw her step and trip as she caught her toe on the stair. He watched her grab uselessly at the broken rail as she tumbled first forwards, then backwards, over and over, down the stairs. He heard the sickening sound of bones breaking as she fell, and dropping his tray on the nearest table, ran to help. He saw her land in a huge mound on the concrete at the bottom of the rickety steps, just below a wall of painted-out graffiti, her legs at crazy angles underneath her.

Others from the café followed him. They put jackets over her, desperate to help in any way they could. Someone supported her neck with his sweatshirt.

The woman opened her eyes and looked at the handsome face of a local jetboat driver asking if she was OK, and telling her to stay still because the ambulance was on its way.

A woman asked if anyone knew who she was, but no one did, so the woman climbed over her and went upstairs to her flat, looking for some sort of identification she could give to the paramedics when they arrived. "Lizzie Martin," she called down to the crowd below. "She's called Lizzie Martin."

"Got it," said the waiter, who was phoning 111 again to ask where the ambulance was. It seemed ages since he'd called.
Lizzie could tell from the undisguised looks of horror and revulsion that things weren't good. *Funny*, she thought, *I feel fine. I'm not sore and it's so nice to be outside again.* She smiled and squeezed the hand of the jetboat driver.

And then the world went black.

CHAPTER FIFTY

"I understand, but I don't," said Kate. "That doesn't make sense, I know that. But I am so angry with her. Why couldn't she trust us? Why did she die alone, instead of with us? "

Kate picked up the box sitting on her knee and shook it. The rattle of ashes and bone knocking against the wood reverberated in the car.

"You bloody should have said something, Elka. We loved you. But you didn't love us."

"That's not true, Kate – take it back," said Maggie. "She *did* love us. We know she did. But I agree with you, it's hard. I think I understand why she did it, but that doesn't make it better and it hurts. It really hurts."

They lapsed into silence. It was getting dark outside, and starting to rain as Maggie negotiated the hearse around tight bends on the narrow road between Dunedin and Queenstown. Nick and Ben were following behind in Ben's car.

In one of the letters, Elka had requested – demanded – that Maggie be the one to drive her body to Dunedin for the post-mortem and cremation. Kate, Nick and Ben wouldn't let her go alone, and they also wanted to be with Elka. The funeral procession on the way there became a convoy on the way home.

Small towns had shut down for the night, the slivers of light escaping drawn curtains the only evidence that there were people in the tight little houses bunched together on either side of the road, before the cars were once more in the darkness of the countryside.

In the days since Elka's death, the Potters had talked themselves hoarse, going over and over the last months to see what clues they had missed, trying to understand where they had let Elka down and what they could have done to stop her lonely death, asking each other how they could have helped. Always they came to the same conclusion: she wouldn't have let them do anything. Partly because she had made her decision and partly because of her pride, but more out of her love for them.

Kate blamed herself for being so caught up in the restaurant and all the publicity around Eric and the baby. She said repeatedly she should have suspected something wasn't right, when Elka kept handing her more and more responsibility, all the while teaching her how the business worked behind the scenes.

Kate's guilt knew no bounds when she then found out Elka had not only left her the majority share in the restaurant (with the rest left jointly to Brian and Nick), but had also left her the house. *Kate, you need a home for you and your baby, have mine,* she'd written. Kate had wept bitterly when she read this, unable to bear the thought of living in the home she'd watched Elka put her heart and soul into renovating. She'd had her first cooking lessons there, and the house and Elka had been her refuge when she was a teenager and needed space from Maggie and Nick. Kate had been angry, too, at the thought that Elka wouldn't be there to see her baby or to be part of this new child's life, as Elka had been such a part of her own.

Her emotions swung between anger and guilt as she remembered seeing Elka, pale and tired at the end of the day, obviously in pain, and how she had thought this was part of her recovery. *I didn't ask, did I? I just assumed. How selfish must I be?*

Kate struggled with her thoughts to the point of exhaustion. When the crematorium assistant had brought out Elka's ashes, she had been the one to claim the box and hadn't let it go, nursing it protectively on her lap in the car, as if in some way she could finally give comfort. *But it's too late, isn't it, Elka? I'm too late.*

Maggie had listened to the confusion, anger and loss coming from Kate and Nick. Numb, listening was all she could do. She was furious. She felt utterly useless, and betrayed. At other, more rational moments, when she was alone and re-read Elka's letter, Maggie could perhaps find a glimmer of understanding and respect, but it didn't last. Her anger and impotence would overwhelm her again, and she couldn't yet bring herself to forgive the pain Elka had caused them all.

The days together in Dunedin had been tense and slow, as they had waited for the officials to sign off the documents so Elka could be cremated and brought home according to her wishes.

Wishes! thought Maggie. More like bloody orders.

She looked over at the box resting on Kate's knee. A rectangular shadow in the darkness, its contents all that remained of a person, of a whole body. Something she, if anyone, should be used to. She wondered how and when they would be able to carry out Elka's last wish – that her ashes be scattered on the lake, in the spot where they used to go for picnics when the children were young.

Elka had been most specific about the place she wanted her ashes cast before the wind, because in future, when Kate, Nick and Maggie brought the new baby for picnics on hot summer days, she wanted to be there in the trees and bushes, with them, enjoying the fun.

Outside the car, the rain had grown heavier, and Maggie switched the windscreen wipers to full speed, slowing down to cope with the decreased visibility. In her rear–view mirror she saw Ben's headlights recede as he slowed to increase his following distance behind her. The road twisted around the craggy hills, the drop to the treacherous Clutha river on one side, invisible in the darkness.

"Phone Nick and tell them we're going to stop at the next café," said Maggie.

The café was just about to close when they pulled up outside. The owner had tidied away all but the last of the food, but reading their mood and feeling sorry for them, he fired up the coffee machine and offered to warm some pies in the microwave.

The coffee was hot and the pies plain but filling. As they had in

Dunedin, they ate in silence. Kate barely touched a morsel, and her leftover pie was quickly seized, smothered in tomato sauce and wolfed down by the ever–hungry Nick.

Maggie only had coffee. She'd hardly eaten since she'd found Elka in the house, cold and dead. She wasn't hungry. Food only reminded of her of Elka.

"Nick, you drive Kate in my car for a bit," said Ben. "I'll go with Maggie and give her a break from driving."

They were back outside, and the café owner had already turned off the lights. Nick agreed so quickly, that Maggie detected a prearranged plan. She was too tired to argue. Hunched under coats held high over their heads, they scurried quickly out into the rain to the cars to resume their journey home.

Maggie, rarely the passenger in her own hearse, sank back gratefully into the seat. Ben didn't try to attempt conversation, and the silence and the steadiness of his driving in this awful weather, was reassuring enough for her to let her eyes close. She slept.

In the car behind, Nick was enjoying playing with the controls and fiddling with the sound system, much to Kate's annoyance.

"Keep your eyes on the road, why don't you?" she snapped.

Nick ignored her, but had already found the music he wanted to listen to.

Kate felt horrid – about everything, but mostly about the way she was treating the people closest to her; about how mean she was being. Maybe that was why Elka hadn't confided in her. Maybe she *was* horrid.

She felt the baby kick up under her ribs, and then a leg slowly and luxuriously arc across her belly, testing the limits of her uterus and setting off one of the mini contractions the midwife had told her about – Braxton Hicks or some such name. In the past few days these had been getting stronger, to the point of stopping her in her tracks while she waited for the pain to pass. She moved to get comfortable, twisting in her seat to face Nick.

"Sorry," she said. "I should be nicer. Even to you."

Nick shrugged, not taking his eyes off the road and the car ahead.

"How was Lizzie?"

"Great," said Nick. "Falling down those stairs was best thing that's happened to her in years."

"You're joking. Nick – she has no legs now. Well, no legs below the knees. I thought she'd be a complete mess. I would be."

"Yeah, *we* would be, Kate, but for her, the accident has made things better. She believes she'll be up and about really soon. At first she'll be on crutches, and then once her scars heal over and she gets her prostheses, she's really positive she'll walk again."

"And she'll do that, do you think? Walk again."

"Walk? She's talking about skiing! When the guys from the limb centre found out who she was, they got very excited about getting her a set of carbon fibre legs so she can ski. They've been showing her all their brochures and YouTube clips of other double amputees skiing and even competing. She's so fired up about it all she challenged me and Ben to a race next winter. That's what I mean about this being the best thing that's happened to her. She's stuck there while everyone runs after her and she's lapping it up. I think the unhappy Lizzie was left at the bottom of those bloody steps, and the old Lizzie Martin's back. Watch out, world."

Kate felt another tightness creeping up and over her stomach, but this was stronger than the last. Unconsciously she took a deep breath and blew it slowly out through her lips as the pain – because that's what it was this time – receded.

Nick had turned up the music and was absorbed in Florence Welch. Kate was pleased he was able to enjoy something. Neither of them saw the sheep on the road until it was too late. Out of nowhere, a large unshorn woolly white behemoth with two startled eyes loomed large in their headlights. On one side of the road was a sheer cliff; on the other it was pitch black. Nick yanked the wheel round hard, at the same time planting his foot flat on the brakes, sending the powerful car into a slide across the other lane, before it spun round backwards through the fence and into the dark.

An hour after they left the café, Maggie woke instantly, alert to the quiet sound of concern in Ben's voice. Outside the wind and rain had got worse, lashing the heavy hearse from all sides, visibility now cut to just a few feet in front of the car

Ben pulled over to the grass verge beside the road.

"I can't see Kate and Nick's lights behind us," he said. "I've been watching; I slowed right down so they could catch us up, but I can't see them. I'm going back."

He turned the car around. "You keep an eye out your side and I'll look this side. Try phoning, texting – anything – and keep doing it because the signal isn't good here."

Maggie's heart raced as her mind was strangled with thoughts no mother ever wants to have about her children. Panic threatened, but she forced herself to remember all the times there had been innocent explanations for lateness and even absence. She made herself hear the patronising tone in Nick's and Kate's voices, telling her she worried too much, that they were grown–up now and able to look after themselves. She brought up their numbers, hitting redial again and again.

"No service." She tried to keep her voice steady and casual. It was taking all her strength to stay in control.

Ben said nothing as they searched the road ahead for any sign of the car.

Every few seconds, Maggie dialled their numbers again, in the hope they would hit a patch with a signal.

"How long ago did you see their lights?" she asked.

"About twenty minutes before we stopped and turned back."

Another agonising thirty minutes passed in worried silence, then they saw it at exactly the same time – a weak beam of light pointing through the rain at a crazy angle, into nothing.

CHAPTER FIFTY-ONE

Without leaving the road, Ben stopped as close as possible to the light below them. He put the windows down and turned off the engine. They listened, but heard nothing apart from the sound of the storm, the rain beating down remorselessly on the roof while the wind tugged and rocked the heavy 4WD.

Maggie peered out towards the light shining weakly a few hundred metres below them, hoping to see some sign of life, but there was nothing: no shadows, no movement. Ben manoeuvred the vehicle so it was perpendicular to the road and directly facing the beam of light, the headlights on high beam and the hazard lights flashing. Maggie took a sharp intake of breath as she saw the flattened fence hanging uselessly from a gatepost to her left, and tyre tracks disappearing into the distance.

Ben edged the car forward over the flattened fence into what was thankfully a paddock sloping down towards a line of willows on a riverbank, their frenzied branches whipped in every direction by the gale sweeping down the narrow valley.

As they drove closer, they could make out the back of Ben's car, splattered with globs of mud, its back wheels buried deep in the paddock. Nick had clearly been trying to reverse the car, but they could see why his efforts had been unsuccessful. The front wheels of the Audi were wedged up and over an old log. The car was well and truly stuck.

Ben stopped well away from any dangerous ground. Maggie struggled to get out to her children, but Ben held her back. "Put this on first," he ordered, pushing a jacket at her. "You won't be any use to anyone if you get hypothermia."

How can he be so sensible? But he was right, and she was grateful for the jacket as soon as she got out of the car. The night was freezing, and within seconds the cold rain had plastered her hair to her head, almost blinding her with its ferocity. Huddled over in the shelter of the car, her back to the wind, she zipped up the jacket, thankful to be wearing boots and trousers. Looking up she saw Ben beside her, tall and strong in the storm, forming a human windbreak, holding her steady in the mud.

He took her hand, called, "One, two, three!" and they ran over to the stranded car. He opened the passenger front door and almost pushed Maggie in, tumbling in after her and pulling the door shut.

"Mum, Ben. Thank God."

Nick was crouched low on the floor, wedged between the front and back seats, looking more stressed than Maggie had ever seen him – and that included after the helicopter accident. Kate was lying flat across the back seat, her legs bent up, knees just a little apart, her head propped on Nick's rolled-up down jacket, grimacing and holding her stomach.

After a few moments she relaxed, opened her eyes and smiled at them. "I think Storm might be a good name, don't you, Mum?" she said. "I think it would suit either a boy or a girl."

Her smile vanished quickly, replaced by another grimace of pain. Screwing her eyes up tightly, she took deep puffy breaths, all the while squeezing Nick's hand hard, and, judging by the look on Nick's face, painfully. They waited in silence until the contraction passed, Maggie and Ben exchanging worried looks.

Finally Nick was able to extricate his pulped hand from Kate's grip. Massaging it to restore the blood flow, he explained about the sheep, and the skid that had sent them careering off the road through the fence and into the paddock. He'd tried over and over again to get the car off the log, but the rain-soaked ground had made it impossible. It didn't help, he added, that Kate was being a typical girl and wouldn't get out and help between contractions. Kate was too tired to do more than give her brother an upright digital sign, prominent enough to be visible in the gloom.

Maggie was so relieved to see them both alive and unhurt, it took her a few minutes to register the predicament they were in. Kate, virtually helpless in labour, was wedged into the back seat of a car embedded in the middle of a paddock miles from anywhere, and judging by the frequency of her contractions, was going to have her baby at any minute.

"What are we going to do?" she asked Ben, only to see him disappearing out the door.

Another contraction gripped Kate's belly, this time stronger, and she reached out to her mother and grabbed her hand. Maggie could have wept with the pain, but had no choice other than to hold on and try and get Kate to focus on her breathing.

Nick smirked. "See, I told you."

"You'll keep," said Maggie and Kate.

Ben climbed back into the car with an emergency bag retrieved from the boot. "Nick, can you get over here so I can check Kate?"

Kate laughed at them as they eased past each other awkwardly. "Car Twister," she said, before another contraction took her body and she started huffing and puffing.

Ben put on a glove and waited for the pain to finish before asking Nick to look away. "Six centimetres," he said. "You're right in the middle of labour."

"No shit," said Kate.

"Where are we, do you think?" Ben asked.

Maggie looked at her watch. "We left the café about an hour and half ago, and then we doubled back for thirty minutes, but slowly, so I guess we're about an hour from Alexandra. And we have no cell coverage – I just tried again."

"I don't want to worry you," said Ben, "but we're going to have to move, and by we, I mean all of us, including you, Kate. When I was getting my bag just now I could hear the river. I'm worried it's burst its banks and the paddock's going to flood. I've never been a fan of water births."

The fear in Kate's voice was palpable. "Mum."

Maggie reached over and gave her an awkward hug. "You concentrate on the contractions, Kate. Leave everything else to us. Ben, can I see you outside for a minute? Nick, Kate needs your hand again."

Nick appealed to his mother not to make him do it again, but seeing the look on her face, submitted with a small whimper.

The rain was still pelting down, and once out of the car, Maggie too could hear the sound of the river close by. Ben flicked his torch towards the willows, but it was too dark to see anything definite. They'd have to trust their suspicions and move to higher ground before it was too late.

"Maggie, listen to me," said Ben. "As soon as this contraction is over, I want you to wrap Kate in the warmest clothes we have, and when she's ready, you and Nick walk her up to the hearse. We can't risk bringing it closer and getting bogged down too. I'll go and turn on the heating and get it set up. Nick can drive carefully back to the road and you and I will look after her in the back. Got it?"

Maggie, suddenly overwhelmed by the seriousness of the situation, couldn't find her voice.

"Got it?" repeated Ben more loudly, holding her by the shoulders, forcing her to look up at him. "Trust me, Maggie. It will be all right. I promise."

Maggie heard the certainty in his voice and said, "Got it."

Ben disappeared towards the hearse and Maggie went back to the Audi, retrieving one of the overnight bags from the boot.

Back in the car she took out jackets and jerseys, and she and Nick bundled poor Kate into them, between contractions. They helped her out of the car, and taking an arm each over their shoulders, half carried, half frogmarched her towards the hearse.

"Did you just pee?" asked Nick, as she pleaded with them to stop.

"Who knows and who cares?" yelled Kate, her voice whipped away by the wind.

Kate screamed with the next contraction, shrieking her pain into the wild night. "It's coming!"

"What?"

"Mum, it's coming. I have to push!"

Maggie and Nick all but carried Kate the last few metres, guided by the light in the back of the hearse, then lifted her into the warmth. Ben had the engine going and the heater on full blast; the contents of his medical kit were lined up along one side of the back of the car. He'd flattened the cardboard casket that had carried Elka to Dunedin, covering it with an old sleeping bag Maggie always kept in the vehicle in case of emergencies.

Taking one look at Kate, Ben said, "There's no time to get to Alexandra. Nick, give Maggie your shirt. Maggie, hold it in front of the heater and when I tell you, take the baby and wrap it up tightly. Cuddle it inside your jacket to keep it warm, but remember the cord so don't go too far. Kate, I need you to listen to me and do exactly what I say, when I say it. We're all going to have a baby."

And they did.

Alexander Benjamin Potter was born normally, at nine twenty–one on a dark and stormy night in early spring, in the back of his grandmother's hearse, in a paddock in central Otago. He weighed 7 lbs 13 ozs, and was full of fight and noise, much to everyone's relief and joy.

Mother and baby well.

Grandmother, uncle and doctor – stressed.

Elka – in a box on the front seat.

CHAPTER FIFTY-TWO

Beside the lake, a baby boy lay in his cot under a willow tree. Warmed by the sun, his toes clutched in his pudgy hands, he watched with fascination the myriad shadows and colours at play above him. Delight dimpled his fat little cheeks and excitement welled up inside him, spilling over into a throaty chuckle for his very first laugh.

Everyone heard it.

"He laughed."

"Yes, he did," said his proud uncle, swooping over to the cot and picking up Zandy, carrying him triumphantly to join the others beside the lake.

Plates, glasses, and the debris of a delicious lunch littered the table. Kate, content to let Nick cuddle his nephew, lounged back in her chair at peace.

Ben reached over to take Maggie's hand into his lap and lazily stroked the back of it, eyes closed behind dark glasses. A fly buzzed around his head before moving off to richer pickings on the table.

Maggie opened her eyes under the broad brim of her sunhat and looked over to her captured hand, and then at Ben. Lifting his glasses and opening one eye, he looked back at her, smiled, and shut it again, leaving her hand where he'd put it. They stayed this way for a while, enjoying the day.

"Are you ready to do it now?" Maggie asked, a little later.

"I suppose so," answered Kate. "It's the perfect day. She would think so too."

Maggie untangled her fingers from Ben's lap and fetched the box from where it sat in the middle of the table. "Does anyone want to say anything?" she asked, as they joined her at the side of the lake

Zandy cooed loudly and then burped in the silence.

"Does it for me," said Nick, cuddling the little boy tighter and playing with his fingers.

Maggie unscrewed the box to reveal lumpen grey ash with the odd solid piece mixed in. Over the last eight weeks they had each made their peace with Elka, and come to their personal understandings about her decision to leave them. Kate's anger had been left in a paddock near Alexandra. Nick was looking to his future but had delayed any major decisions for the time being. Maggie's anger had given way to acceptance. She had stopped thinking she was responsible for everything that happened, and that she needed to be in control of anything that would affect the people she cared about. It was an impossible task. She let it go.

A whisper of wind stirred the top coating of powder, lifting it up and out, into the air, curling above them. Maggie waded into the water and upended the box into the currents of summer air. They watched Elka fly off, away into the trees, the lake and the sky. What didn't fly off sank in lumps amongst the stones, disappearing from view. A little bit of her stuck in the bottom of the box, and Maggie had to bang it against a nearby branch to free it.

"Be gone, Elka. Back to the beginning with our love."

They dropped Nick at the restaurant on their way home. It was late afternoon, and to her mother's surprise, Kate had asked them to take her to Elka's house, saying she and Zandy had plans to spend the evening in their new home. Kate hadn't been able to bring herself to sleep there yet. Or move in properly, because although she was no longer angry with Elka, she wasn't ready to take over her home and thereby occupy her precious memories.

Walking up the gravel path, the roses smelling sweetly in the garden, she unlocked the front door. "We're home, baby boy," she said, stepping into the quiet house. But Zandy was fast asleep on her shoulder and didn't hear a word.

Ben walked Maggie to the front door of The Stables.

"Thank you for bringing me home," said Maggie. "Elka would have loved today."

Ben didn't say anything but looked at Maggie expectantly.

Maggie knew what his eyes were suggesting, and felt the familiar fear beat in her chest. It lasted only as long as it took for Ben to bend down and claim her lips with the gentlest, most exciting kiss she had ever had.

"Would you like to come in?"

"I'd thought you'd never ask, Maggie Potter."

About the Author

Rosy Fenwicke is a doctor, writer and mother of three adult children. She edited *In Practice: The Lives of New Zealand Women Doctors in the 21st Century* (Random House, 2004). In 2017 she released *Hot Flush*, the first novel in the Euphemia Sage series, to excellent reviews. She lives in Martinborough, New Zealand.

Also by Rosy Fenwicke
Hot Flush
In Practice: The Lives of New Zealand Women Doctors in the 21st
Century

Acknowledgements

Thank you to all those patient friends and family who have read through various versions of this book and made comments and helpful suggestions. In particular, Josie my daughter and Judy Sachdeva my old school friend who both gave valuable feedback. I am grateful to Keith Newell of Lychgate Funerals for taking the time to explain aspects of his industry to me. Any errors in fact are entirely my own. Thanks to Sue Copsey for her editing and Martin Taylor for his invaluable guidance to publication.